JEREMY AND HAMLET

Jeremy and Hamlet

A Chronicle of
Certain Incidents
In the Lives
Of a Boy,
A Dog, and a
Country Town

By
HUGH WALPOLE

CASSELL AND COMPANY, LIMITED
London, New York, Toronto and Melbourne

First published 1923

Printed in Great Britain.

To

MY FATHER AND MOTHER

FROM

THEIR DEVOTED FRIEND

THEIR SON

It is not growing like a tree
In bulk, doth make man better be;
Or standing long an oak, three hundred year,
To fall a log at last, dry, bald and sear;
    A lily of a day
    Is fairer far in May
Although it fall and die that night——
It was the plant and flower of light.
In small proportions we just beauties see,
And in short measures life may perfect be.

—Ben Jonson.

CONTENTS

JEREMY AND HAMLET

CHAPTER I

COME OUT OF THE KITCHEN . . .

THERE was a certain window between the
kitchen and the pantry that was Hamlet's
favourite. Thirty years ago—these chronicles
are of the year 1894—the basements of houses
in provincial English towns, even of large houses
owned by rich people, were dark, chill, odourful
caverns hissing with ill-burning gas and smelling
of ill-cooked cabbage. The basement of the
Coles' house in Polchester was as bad as any
other, but this little window between the kitchen
and the pantry was higher in the wall than the
other basement windows, almost on a level with
the iron railings beyond it, and offering a view
down over Orange Street and, obliquely, sharp
to the right and past the Polchester High School,
a glimpse of the Cathedral Towers themselves.

Inside the window was a shelf, and on this
shelf Hamlet would sit for hours, his peaked

beard interrogatively a-tilt, his leg sticking out from his square body as though it were a joint-leg and worked like the limb of a wooden toy, his eyes, sad and mysterious, staring into Life. . . .

It was not, of course, of Life that he was thinking; only very high-bred and in-bred dogs are conscious philosophers.

His ears were stretched for a sound of the movements of Mrs. Hounslow the cook, his nostrils distended for a whiff of the food that she was manipulating, but his eyes were fixed upon the passing show, the pageantry, the rough-and-tumble of the world, and every once and again the twitch of his Christmas-tree tail would show that something was occurring in this life beyond the window that could supervene, for a moment at any rate, over the lust of the stomach and the lure of the clattering pan.

He was an older dog than he had been on that snowy occasion of his first meeting with the Cole family—two years older in fact. Older and fatter. He had now a round belly. His hair hung as wildly as ever it had done around his eyes, but beneath the peaked and aristocratic beard there was a sad suspicion of a double chin.

He had sold his soul to the cook.

When we sell our souls we are ourselves, of course, in the main responsible. But others have often had more to do with our catastrophe than the world in general can know. Had Jeremy, his master, not gone to school, Hamlet's soul would yet have been his own; Jeremy gone, Hamlet's spiritual life was nobody's concern. He fell down, deep down, into the very heart of the basement, and nobody minded.

He himself did not mind; he was very glad. He loved the basement.

It had happened that during the last holidays Jeremy had gone into the country to stay with the parents of a school friend Hamlet had had therefore nearly nine months' freedom from his master's influence. Mr. and Mrs. Cole did not care for him very deeply. Helen hated him. Mary loved him but was so jealous of Jeremy's affection for him that she was not sorry to see him banished, and Barbara, only two and a half, had as yet very tenuous ideas on this subject.

Mrs. Hounslow, a very fat, sentimental woman, liked to have something or someone at her side to give her rich but transient emotions —emotions evoked by a passing band, the reading of an accident in the newspaper, or some account of an event in the Royal family. The kitchen-maid, a girl of no home and very tender years, longed for affection from somebody, but Mrs. Hounslow disliked all kitchen-maids on principle—therefore Hamlet received what the kitchen-maid needed, and that is the way of the world.

Did there run through Hamlet's brain earlier stories of an emotion purer than the lust for bones, of a devotion higher and more ardent than the attachment to a dripping saucepan?

Did he sometimes, as he sat reflectively beside the kitchen fire, see pictures of his master's small nose, of woods when, at his master's side, he sniffed for rabbits, of days when he raced along shining sands after a stone that he had no real intention of finding? Did he still feel his master's hand upon his head and that sudden twitch as that hand caught a tuft of hair and twisted it? . . .

No one can tell of what he was thinking as he sat on the shelf staring out of his window at old Miss Mulready, burdened with parcels, climbing Orange Street, at the lamplighter hurrying with his flame from post to post, of old Grinder's war-worn cab stumbling across the cobbles past the High School, the old horse faltering at every step, at the green evening sky slipping into dusk, the silver-pointed stars, the crooked roofs blackening into shadow, the lights of the town below the hill jumping like gold jack-in-the-boxes into the shadowy air.

No one could tell of what he was thinking.

II

He was aware that in the upper regions something was preparing. He was aware of this in general by a certain stir that there was, of agitated voices and hurrying footsteps and urgent cries; but he was aware more immediately because of the attentions of Mary, Jeremy's younger sister.

He had always hated Mary. Are dogs, in their preferences and avoidances, guided at all by physical beauty or ugliness? Was Helen of Troy adored by the dogs of that town and did Sappho command the worship of the hounds of Greece? We are told nothing of it and, on the other hand, we know that Lancelot Gobbo had a devoted dog and that Charon, who cannot have been a handsome fellow, was most faithfully dog-attended. I do not think that Hamlet minded poor Mary's plainness, her large spectacles, her sallow complexion, colourless hair and bony body. His dislike arose more probably from the certainty that she would always stroke him the wrong way, would poke her fingers into his defenceless eyes, would try to drag him on to her sharp, razor-edged knees and would talk to him in that meaningless sing-song especially invented by the sentimental of heart and slow of brain for the enchantment of babies and animals.

She was talking to him in just that fashion now. He had slipped upstairs, attracted by a smell in the dining-room. Watching for the moment when he would be undetected, he had crept round the dining-room door and had stood, his nose in air, surrounded by a sea of worn green carpet, sniffing. Suddenly he felt a hand on his collar and there followed that voice that of all others he most detested. "Why, here's Hamlet! Helen, here's Hamlet! . . . We can get him ready now, Helen; there's only two hours left anyway, and Jeremy will care much more about that than anything. I'd like to leave him downstairs, but Jeremy will be sure to ask where he is. Which colour shall I use for the ribbon, Helen? I've got blue and red and orange."

A pause. Then again:

"Which shall I use? Do say."

Then from a great distance:

"Oh, don't bother, Mary. Can't you see I'm busy?"

A heavy sigh. "Oh, well, you might. Never mind. I think the blue's best." All this time Hamlet was desperately wriggling, but the hand, with knuckles that pressed into the flesh and hurt, had firm hold.

"Oh, do keep still, Hamlet. Can't you see that your master's coming home and you've got to be made nice? Oh, bother! I've gone and cut the piece too short. . . . Helen, have you got another piece of blue? "

A pause. Then again: "Oh, Helen, you might say. I've cut the piece too short. Haven't you got another bit of blue? "

Then again from a long distance :

"Don't *bother*, Mary. Can't you *see* that I'm so busy? "

"Oh, very well, then." A terribly deep sigh that made Hamlet shiver with discomfort. "Come here, Hamlet. On to my lap, where I can tie it better. There, that's right. Oh, *do* keep your head still—and how fat you are now! "

Insult upon insult heaped. He raised his eyes to heaven, partly in indignation, partly because the entrancing smell could be caught more securely now from the elevation of Mary's lap! But the discomfort of that lap, the hard boniness, the sudden precipitate valley, the shortness of its surface so that one was for ever slipping two legs over, the moist warmth of the surrounding hand, the iron hardness of the fingers at the neck! He played his best game of wriggle, slipping, sliding, lying suddenly inert, jerking first with his paws, then with his hind legs, digging his head beneath his captor's arm as the flamingo did in " Alice."

Mary, as so often occurred, lost her patience. "Oh, do keep still, Hamlet! How tiresome you are, when I've got such a little time too! Don't you like to have a ribbon? And you'll have to be brushed too. Helen, where's the brush that we used to have for Hamlet?"

No answer.

"Oh, do keep still, you naughty dog!" She dug her knuckles into his eyes. "Oh, Helen, do say! Don't you know where it is?"

Then from a great distance: "Oh, don't bother, Mary. No, I don't know where it is. How stupid you are! Can't you see I'm busy?"

He wriggled, Mary slapped him. He turned and bit her. She dropped him.

"Oh, Helen, he's bit me!"

"It's bitten, not bit."

"No, it isn't; it's bit. . . . Perhaps he's mad or something, and I'll suddenly bark like a dog. I know they do. I read about it in 'Hopes and Fears.' You're a horrid dog and I don't care whether Jeremy sees you or not. Oh, Helen, you might help. It's four o'clock and Jeremy will be nearly here."

Hamlet was free, free of Mary, but not of the room. The door behind him was closed. He sat there thinking, the piece of blue ribbon hanging loosely round his neck. Something was stirring within him—something that was not an appetite nor a desire nor a rebellion. A memory. He shook his head to escape from his ribbon.

The memory came closer. From that too he would like to escape. He gazed at the door. Had he never smelt that alluring smell? . . .

He slipped beneath the dining-room table, and, lying flat, resting his head on his paws, stared resentfully in front of him. The memory came closer.

III

Two hours later he was sitting in a ridiculous position two steps from the bottom of the hall stairs—ridiculous because the stair was not broad enough for his figure, because the blue ribbon was now firmly tied and ended in a large blue bow, because Mary's hand was upon him, restraining him from his quite natural intention of disappearing.

They were grouped about the stair, Helen and Mary, Barbara and the nurse, Mr. and Mrs. Cole and Aunt Amy in the hall below. Helen, Mary and Barbara were wearing cocked hats made of coloured paper and carried silver tissue wands in their hands. Barbara was eating her tissue paper with great eagerness and a vivid, absorbed attention. Helen looked pretty and bored; Mary was in a state of the utmost nervousness, clutching Hamlet with one hand while in the other she held a toy trumpet and a crumpled piece of paper.

B

Everyone waited, staring at the door. Mr. Cole said:

"Five minutes late. I must go back to my sermon in a moment."

Aunt Amy said: "I hope nothing can have happened."

Mrs. Cole said tranquilly: "We should have heard if it had."

The front door bell rang; a maid appeared from nowhere and opened the door. From the dusk there emerged a small, heavily coated figure. Mr. and Mrs. Cole moved forward. There were embraces. Mr. Cole said: "Well, my boy." A husky voice was heard: "Oh, I say, mother, that old squeak of a cabman——"

The short, thick-set figure turned towards the staircase.

Instantly Mary blew on her trumpet. Barbara, suddenly disliking the tissue paper, began to cry. Hamlet barked.

Through the din the quavering voice of Mary could be heard reading the poem of welcome:

"Thee, returning to your home,
    Back from school and football too,
Coming to us all alone,
    Mary, Helen and Barbara welcome you.
Hail to thee, then, Jeremy dear,
Over you we shed a tear
Just because you are so dear.
    Welcome to your home."

There should then have followed a blast on the trumpet and three rousing cheers. Alas! the welcome was a complete and devastating failure.

Jeremy could be heard to say:

"Thanks awfully. . . . By Jove, I *am* hungry. How soon's tea, mother?"

Barbara's howls were now so terrible as to demand immediate attention from everyone. Hamlet had slipped from control and was barking at Aunt Amy, whom he delighted to annoy. Mrs. Cole said: "Now that's enough, children dear. I'm sure Jeremy's tired now." No one had heard Mary's verses; no one noticed the cocked hats; no one applauded the silver wands. The work of weeks was disregarded. No one thought of Mary at all. She crept away to her room at the top of the house, flung herself upon her bed and howled, biting the counterpane between her teeth.

But are not these home-comings always most disappointing affairs? For weeks Jeremy had been looking to this moment. On the frayed wallpaper just above his bed in the school dormitory he had made thick black marks with a pencil, every mark standing for a day. Hard and cynical during his school-day, a barbarian at war with barbarians, at nights, when the lights were out, when the dormitory story-teller's (unhappy Phipps minor) voice had died off into slumber, in those last few minutes before he too slept, he was sentimental, full of home-sick longings, painting to himself that very springing from the cab, his mother's kiss, Hamlet's bark, yes, and even the embraces of his sisters. On the morning of departure, after the excitement of farewells, the strange, almost romantic thrill of the empty schoolrooms, the race in the wagonette (*his* wagonette against the one with Cox major and Bates and Simpson) to the station, the cheeking of the station-master, the crowding into the railway carriage and leaning (five on top of you) out of the carriage window, the screams of " Bags I the corner," the ensuing fights with Cox major, after all this gradual approach to known country, the gathering-in as though with an eager hand of remembered places and stations and roads, the half-hour stop at Drymouth (leaving now almost all your companions behind you—only young Marlowe and Sniffs major remaining), the crossing over into Glebeshire, then the beat of the heart, the tightening of the throat, as Polchester gradually approached—all this, yes and more, much more, than this, to end in that disappointment! Everyone looking the same as before, the hall the same, the pictures the same, father and mother and Aunt Amy the same, Mary and Helen the same only stupider! What did they dress up and make fools of themselves like that for? Mary always did the wrong thing, and now most certainly she would be crying in her bedroom because he had not said enough to her. . . .

In one way there had been too much of a reception, in another not enough. It was silly of them to make that noise, but on the other hand there should have been more questions. How had he done in football? He had played half-back twice for the school. He had told them that in three different letters, and yet they had asked no questions. And there was Bates who had stolen jam out of a fellow's tuck box. One of his letters had been full of that exciting incident, and yet they had asked no questions. It was true that they had had but little time for questions, nevertheless his father, at once after kissing him, had murmured something about his sermon—as though an old sermon mattered!

Of course he did not think all this out. He only sat on his bed kicking his legs, looking at the well-remembered furniture of his room, vaguely discontented and unhappy. What fun it had been that morning, ragging Miss Taylor, laughing at the guard of the train, saying good-bye to old Mumpsey Thompson who recently spoke to him as though he were a man, asking him whether his parents had decided upon the public school to which, in two years' time, he would be going—Eton, Harrow, Winchester,

Craxton, Rugby, Crale and so on. Time to decide, time to decide!

One's public! The world widening and widening, growing ever more terribly exciting —and here Mary, sobbing in her room, and father with his sermons and the long evenings. At least no work—only a silly holiday task, a book called "The Talisman," or some rot. No work. His spirits revived a little. No work and lots of food, and Hamlet. . . .

Hamlet! He jumped off his bed. Why, he had never noticed the dog! He had forgotten. He rushed from the room.

When he was half-way down the stairs he caught the echo of a voice: "Tea, Jeremy. All ready in the schoolroom." But he did not pause. In the hall he saw the housemaid. "I say, where's Hamlet?" he cried.

"In the kitchen, I expect, Master Jeremy," she answered.

In the kitchen, she expected! Why should she expect it? Hamlet never used to be in the kitchen. His heart began to beat angrily. The kitchen? That was not the place for a dog like Hamlet. He stumbled down the dark stairs into the basement. Mrs. Hounslow was standing beside the kitchen table, her sleeves rolled up above her elbows; she was pounding and pounding. Jeremy cried, at once challenging:

"I say, where's my dog?"

His dog? Mrs. Hounslow, already too scarlet for further colour, nevertheless crimsoned internally. His dog! She hated little boys. Her sister, the one that married the postman, had had one. Two indeed. She loved Hamlet, who had become now, by the rights both of psychology and environment, hers.

" 'E's lying there right in front of the fire, Master Jeremy—the poor little worm," she added.

"The poor little worm" was indeed stretched out gnawing at a bone.

" He oughtn't to be in front of the fire," said Jeremy. " It's bad for dogs. It gives them rheumatism."

She stopped her pounding. They had not met before, but it was one of those old hostilities born in the air, fostered by the crystal moon, roughened by the golden sun.

Jeremy stood, his legs apart, looking down upon his dog. He saw how fat he was, how deeply engrossed in his bone, how dribbling at the jaws.

"Hamlet! " he said. He repeated the name three times. At the third call the dog looked up, then went back to his bone. Mrs. Hounslow sniffed.

Meanwhile in Hamlet's soul something was stirring—memories, affections, sentiments. . . . He licked the bone again. It no longer tasted so sweet as before. He looked up at Mrs. Hounslow imploringly.

She declared herself. "He do love the kitchen. If there's one place where he loves to be, it's the kitchen. Only last night I was saying to my sister, 'Anne,' I said, 'it's a most curious thing how that dog do love the kitchen.' A little kindness goes a long way with animals, poor things. As I said to my sister——"

"But he oughtn't to love the kitchen!" Jeremy burst out indignantly. "He isn't a kitchen dog!"

Mrs. Hounslow had received the Last Insult. Her face darkened *sub rosa*. She to be reproached, she who had been the only one to show affection to the poor deserted lamb, she who had protected him and fed him and given him warm places in which to sleep. A kitchen dog! And her kitchen the cleanest, shiniest, most bescoured kitchen in Polchester!

She had, however, her dignity.

"That's as may be, Master Jeremy," she said. "But it's natural, both in dogs and humans, that they should go to them as cares for them best and takes trouble over them."

She went on with her pounding, breathing deeply.

Jeremy looked at her. He had hurt her feelings. He was sorry for that. After all, she had been kind to the dog—in her own way. She naturally could not understand the point of view that he must take.

"Thank you very much," he said huskily, "for having been so kind to Hamlet all this time. . . . He's going to live upstairs now—but it was very good of you to take so much trouble."

Hamlet was deep in his bone once more. When Jeremy put his hand on his collar he growled. That roused Jeremy's temper. He dragged the dog across the floor; Hamlet pushed out his legs, and behind his hair his eyes glared. The door closed on them both.

IV

Upstairs in his own room he squatted on the floor and drew Hamlet in between his legs. Hamlet would not look at his master. He sulked as only dogs and beautiful women can.

"Hamlet, you *must* remember. You can't have forgotten *everything* so quickly. You *can't* have forgotten the fun we had last year, out at the farm, and when I rescued you after Mary shut you up, and biting Aunt Amy and everything.

"I know I've been away, and you must have thought I was never coming back, but I couldn't help that. I had to go to school, and I couldn't take you with me. And now I'm going to be home for weeks and weeks, and it will be awfully slow if you aren't with me. Nobody seems really excited about my coming back, and Uncle Samuel's away, and everything's rotten—so you must stay with me and go out with me for walks and everything."

Hamlet was staring down at the floor through his hair. His master was scratching his head in exactly the way that he used to do, in the way that no one else had ever done. Three, four, five scratches in the middle, then slowly towards the right ear, then slowly towards the left, then both ears pulled close together, then a piece of hair twisted into a peak, then all smoothed down again and softly stroked into tranquillity. Delicious! His soul quivered with sensuous ecstasy. Then his master's hands smelt as they had always done, hard and rough, with the skin suddenly soft between the fingers. Very good to lick! His tongue was half out. In another moment he would have rolled over on to his back, his legs stuck stiffly out, his eyes closed, waiting for his belly to be tickled. In another moment! But there was a knock on the door, and Mary appeared.

Mary's eyes were red behind her spectacles.

She had the sad, resigned indignation of a Cassandra misunderstood.

"Jeremy, aren't you coming down to tea? We're half finished."

He rose to his feet. He knew that he must say something.

"I say, Mary," he stammered, "it was most awfully decent of you to make that poetry up. I did like it."

"Did you really?" she asked, gulping.

"Yes, I did."

"Would you like a copy of it?"

"Most awfully."

"I did make a copy of it. But I thought nobody cared—or wanted to hear. . . ." Fearful lest she should begin to cry again, he said hurriedly :

"Here's Hamlet. He's always been in the kitchen. He's not going to be any longer."

Hamlet followed him downstairs, but still with reluctant dignity. The moment of his surrender had been covered, and he did not know that he would now surrender after all. He would see. Meanwhile he smelt food, and where food was he must be.

Tea was in the schoolroom. Miss Jones, the governess, was away on her holiday, and Jeremy saw at once that the worst thing possible had occurred : his Aunt Amy, whom he did not love, was in charge of the tea-table. He had fantastic thoughts when he saw his aunt, thinking of her never as a human being, but as an animal, a bird, perhaps. A crow. A vulture. Something hooked and clawed. But to-day she was determined that she would be friendly.

" Sit down, Jeremy dear. You're very late, but on the first day we'll say nothing about it."

His mother should have been here. Where was his mother?

" Have you washed your hands? Mother has callers. . . . There is blackberry jam and also strawberry. Your welcome home, Jeremy."

He would have neither. He loved blackberry. Still more he loved strawberry. But he would have neither. Because Aunt Amy had asked him. His eye was on Hamlet, who was sulking by the door.

"I do hope, dear, that you're not going to have that dog with you everywhere again. All the time you were away he was in the kitchen. Very happy there, I believe."

Jeremy said nothing.

Aunt Amy, who was, I think, to be applauded for her efforts with a sulky boy, bravely persevered.

" Do tell us, dear, about this last time at school. We are all so eager to know. Was it cricket or football, dear, and how did your work go? "

He mumbled something, blushing to the eyes as he caught his sister Helen's ironical supercilious glance.

" I hope your master was pleased with you, dear."

He burst out : " I was whacked twice."

Aunt Amy sighed. " The less about that, dear, the better. We want to know what you did well ! "

How strange that in the train he had eagerly desired this moment—and now he had nothing to say.

" I don't know," he murmured. " There was a chap called Bates got bunked for stealing."

Aunt Amy sighed again. " Yes, Helen dear, you can go if you've really finished. Wipe your mouth, Mary."

Hamlet was watching his master. More than ever now were recollections stealing upon him. His master was unhappy, just as he used to be unhappy. He was hating that dark, strange-smelling animal (smelling of soap, the smell that Hamlet most avoided) whom Hamlet also hated.

Yes, everything was returning. . . .

V

Later on they were down in the drawing-
room. Mrs. Cole was reading " The Dove in
the Eagle's Nest," the children grouped about
her feet. Jeremy, his rough bullet head against
his mother's dress, was almost asleep. He had
had a long, exhausting day; he was happy at
last, seeing the colours fold and unfold before
his eyes. That other world that was sometimes
so strangely close to him mingled with the world
of facts—now he was racing in the wagonette,
leaning over and shouting triumphantly against
those left behind; now the path changed to a
pool of gold, and out of it a bronze tower rose
solemn to heaven, straight and tall against the
blue sky, and the windows of the tower opened
and music sounded, and his mother's voice came
back to him like the sudden rushing of the train,
and he saw Mary's spectacles and the flickering
fire and Helen's gleaming shoes.

For the moment he had forgotten Hamlet.
The dog lay near the door. It opened, and
Aunt Amy came in.

At once the dog was through the door, down
the stairs, and into the kitchen. This was habit.
Something had acted in him before he could
stop to think. It was natural for him to be in
the kitchen at this hour, when it was brilliantly
lit, and the cook and the housemaid and the

kitchenmaid were having their last drop of tea.
. . . Always things for him at this moment,
sweet things, fat things, meaty things. He sat
there, and they dropped bits into his mouth,
murmuring " Poor worm," " Little lamb,"
" Sweet pet."

Mrs. Hounslow was to-night quite especially
affectionate, delighted with his return to her.
She patted him, pulled him into her ample lap,
folded his head against her yet ampler bosom,
confided to the maids what that limb of a boy
had dared to say to her—" kitchen dog! "
indeed. As though it weren't the finest kitchen
in Glebeshire, and who'd looked after the poor
animal if she hadn't—and then—and why—but
of course.

The maids agreed, sipping the tea from
their saucers.

But Hamlet was not happy. He did not
care to-night for Mrs. Hounslow's embraces.
He was not happy. He struggled from her lap
on to the floor, and sat there scratching himself.

When ten struck he was taken to his warm
corner near the oven. She curled him up, she
bent down and kissed him. The lights were
turned out, and he was alone. He could not
sleep. The loud ticking of the kitchen clock,
for so many months a pleasant sleepy sound,
to-night disturbed him.

He was not happy. He got up and

wandered about the kitchen, sniffing. He went
to the door. It was ajar. He pushed it
with his nose. Something was leading him.
He remembered now—how well he remembered! Up these dark stairs, under that hissing
clock, up these stairs again, along that passage,
the moon grinning at him through the window
(but, of course, he did not know that it was
the moon). Up more stairs, along this wall,
then this door! He pushed with his nose; it
moved; he squeezed himself through.

He hesitated, sniffing. Then—how familiar
this was—a spring, and he was on the bed; a
step or two, and he was licking his master's
cheek.

A cry: "Hamlet! Oh, Hamlet!" He
snuggled under his master's arm, licking the
cheek furiously, planting his paw, but with the
nails carefully drawn in, on his master's neck.
Once more that hand was about his head, the
scratch first to the left, then to the right, then
the pulling of the ears. . . .

With a sigh of satisfaction he sank into the
hollow of his master's body, and in another
second was asleep.

CHAPTER II

CONSCIENCE MONEY

I

THESE Christmas holidays had begun badly. Jeremy's mood was wrong from the very start. He had not wished it to be wrong. He had come determined to find everything right and beautiful. Now nothing was right and nothing was beautiful.

For one thing, there was nothing to do. It was not the custom nearly thirty years ago to invent games, occupations and employments for your young as it is to-day. Mrs. Cole, loving her children, had nevertheless enough to do to make the house go round, and Mr. Cole was busy in his study. The children would amuse themselves—who could doubt it—but at the same time there were so many things that they must not do that as the days passed they were more and more restricted and confined.

" Mary, what are you reading? . . . Oh, I wouldn't read that quite yet, dear. A little later, perhaps." Or, " Helen, you're sitting in the sun. Go and get your hat." Or, " Not

c
25

on the carpet, dear. It will make your clothes
so dusty. Why don't you sit down and read
a little?"

Before his departure schoolwards Jeremy
had been accustomed to those inhibitions, and
had taken them for granted as inevitable. Then
in that other world he had discovered a new
row of inhibitions as numerous and devastating
as the first series, but quite different, covering
in no kind of way the same ground. These new
inhibitions were absolute, and the danger of
disobeying them was far graver than in the
earlier case. He fitted, then, his life into
those and grew like a little plant, upwards and
outwards, as that sinister gardener, school
tradition, demanded. Then came the return
to home, and behold those old early childish
inhibitions were still in force! It was still
" Don't, Jeremy. You'll tear your trousers."
Or, " No, not now, dear. Mother's busy."
Or, " No, you can't go into the tower now.
Perhaps to-morrow." Or, " Once is enough,
Jeremy. Don't be greedy."

And, on the other side, there was nothing
to do—*Nothing to Do.*

He could no longer play with Mary or
Helen. Mary was too emotional, and Helen
too conceited. And who wanted to play with
girls, anyway? Barbara was rather fascinating,
but was surrounded by defences of nurses,

mothers and mysterious decrees. Hamlet was
his only resource. Without him he would
surely have fallen sick and died. But a dog is
limited within doors. For Hamlet's own sake
Jeremy longed that they should be for ever in
the open. Oh! why did they not live in the
country? Why in this stupid and stuffy town?

But then, again, was it stupid and stuffy?
Jeremy longed to investigate it more intimately,
but was prevented at every turn. It might be
an enchanting town. Certainly there were
sounds and lights and colours that, now that he
was older and knew what life was, suggested
themselves as entrancing.

He simply was not allowed to discover for
himself—hindered, inhibited everywhere.

Had only Uncle Samuel been here things
would have been better. Uncle Samuel was
queer and strange and said most disconcerting
things, but he did understand Jeremy. As it
was, no one understood him. To-day, had
anyone seen a small thick-set boy with a stocky
figure and a snub nose standing half-way down
the stairs lost and desolate, there would be a
thousand things to suggest. Then it was not
the hour for the afternoon walk, or the hour
was past. Children must not be in the way.

Matters were not improved by a little conversation that he had with Aunt Amy. She
found him one morning standing before the

dining-room window staring into Orange Street.

"Well, Jeremy"—she paused in the quick, rattle-rattle walk that she always had in the morning when she was helping her sister over household duties—"nothing to do?"

He neither answered nor turned round. "You should reply when spoken to." Then, more softly, because there was something desolate in his attitude that she could not but feel, "Well, dear—tell me."

He turned round, and as he looked at her she was conscious, as she had often been before, almost with terror, of the strange creatures that little boys were and how far from her understanding.

"I want to go out and buy a football," he said.

"A football!" she repeated, as though he had said a gorilla.

"Yes," he said impatiently. "The little ones are only ten and sixpence, and I've got that over from the pound Uncle Samuel gave me on my birthday—and father says I mustn't go out."

"Well, that settles it, then," said Aunt Amy cheerfully.

"I don't see why," said Jeremy slowly. "He's let me go out alone when I was ever so small before I went to school."

" You can be sure he has his reasons," said Aunt Amy. She suddenly sat down on one of the dining-room chairs and said, " Come here, Jeremy."

He came to her reluctantly. She put him in front of her and laid her hands on his shoulders and stared at him. He wriggled uncomfortably, wishing to escape from her projecting tooth and her eyes that were here grey and there green. Herself meanwhile felt a sudden warmth of sentiment. She wanted to be kind to him; why, she knew not.

" You're getting a big boy now, Jeremy." She paused.

" Yes," said Jeremy.

" And you don't want to be a sulky big boy, do you? "

" I'm not sulky," said Jeremy.

" No, dear, I'm sure you're not. But you're not being quite the bright willing boy we'd like to see you. You know that we all love you, don't you? "

" Yes," said Jeremy.

" Well, then, you must repay our love and show us that you are happy and willing to do what your father and mother wish."

Jeremy said nothing.

" You do love your father and mother, don't you? "

" Yes," said Jeremy.

"Well, then," said Aunt Amy triumph- antly, as though she had been working out a problem in Euclid, "you must show it. No more sulking, dear; but be the bright little boy we all know you can be."

She left Jeremy puzzled and confused. Was it true that he was sulky? He did love his father and mother, but deeply distrusted scenes of sentiment. Nevertheless, Christmas was approaching, and he felt warm towards all the world—even Aunt Amy. Often and often he went up to his bedroom, closed the door behind him, looked under his bed to make quite sure that no one was in the room, then very cautiously opened the lid of his play-box and peered inside. At the bottom of the box were a number of odd-shaped parcels; he picked them up one after another and stroked their paper, then laid them carefully in their places. He sighed as of a man who has accomplished a great and serious task. Many times a day he did this. He had himself unpacked his play- box on his return from school. No one in the house save only he had beheld those strange parcels.

II

Christmas approached nearer and nearer— now it was only four days before Christmas Eve.

There was no snow, but frost and a cold, pale blue sky; the town was like a crystallized fruit, hard and glittering and sharply coloured.

The market was open during the whole of Christmas week, and there was the old woman under her umbrella and the fur-coated man with the wooden toys, and the fruit stalls with the holly and mistletoe, and the Punch and Judy under the town clock, where it had been for ever so many years, and the man with the coloured balloons, and the little dogs on wheels that you wound up in the back with a key and they jumped along the cobbles as natural as life.

The children were deeply absorbed over their presents. Mary looked at Jeremy so often from behind her spectacles in a mysterious and ominous way that at last he said:

"All right, Mary, you'll know me next time."

"I was wondering," she said, with a convulsive choke in her throat, "whether you'll like my present."

"I expect I will," he said, busy at the moment with the brushing of Hamlet.

"Because," she went on, "there were two things, and I couldn't make up my mind which, and I asked Helen, and she said the first one, because you might have a cold any time and it would be good in the snow; but we don't have snow here much, so I thought the other would be better, because you do like pictures, don't you, Jeremy, and sometimes the pictures are lovely—so I got that, and now I don't know whether you'll like it.''

Jeremy had no reply to make to this.

'' Oh, now you've guessed what it is.''

'' No, I haven't,'' said Jeremy quite truthfully.

'' Oh, I'm so glad,'' Mary sighed with relief. '' Have you got all your presents? ''

'' Yes, all of them,'' said Jeremy, drawing himself up and gazing with dreamy pride over Hamlet's head.

'' Shall I like mine? '' asked Mary, her eyes glistening.

'' Awfully,'' said Jeremy. '' You'll like it,'' he said slowly, '' better than anything you've ever been given.''

'' Better than the writing-case Uncle Samuel gave me? ''

'' Much better.''

'' Oh, Jeremy! '' She suddenly flung her arms round his neck and kissed him. Hamlet barked and escaped the brush and comb, then seized Mary's hair ribbon, that had, as usual, fallen to the floor, and ran with it to a distant corner. Incidents followed that had nothing to do with presents.

Then when Christmas Day grew very near

indeed, those parcels at the bottom of his play-box became an obsession. He went up a hundred times a day to look at them, to take them out and stroke them, to feel their knobs and protruding angles, to replace them, first in this way and then in that. Sometimes he laid them all out upon the bed, sometimes he spread them in a long line across the carpet. He brought up Hamlet and made him look at them. Hamlet sniffed each parcel, then wanted to tear the paper wrappings; finally, he lay on the carpet and rattled in his throat, wagging his tail and baring his teeth.

Christmas Eve arrived, a beautiful, clear, frosty day.

III

Jeremy came in from his morning walk, his cheeks crimson, looking very nautical in his blue reefer coat. He went straight up to his room, locked the door, and opened the play-box. The parcels were all there. He counted them, felt them, sighed a sigh of satisfaction and pride, then closed the play-box again.

He took off his coat and went downstairs. Helen, meeting him in the hall, cried :

" Oh, Jeremy, father wants to see you."

" Where? "

" In the study."

Jeremy paused. The word "study" had always a strangely disagreeable sound. Their father never wished to see any of them there unless for some very unpleasant purpose. He threw his mind back. What had he been doing? What sin had he within the last day or two committed? He could think of nothing. His parcels had kept him quiet. Both he and Hamlet had been very good.

Only Aunt Amy had spoken to him about sulking. But that had been over a week ago. No, he had been very good. There could be nothing. Nevertheless, he walked down the hall with slow and hesitating step. Hamlet wanted to come with him. He had to stop him. Hamlet sat down near the door and watched him enter with anxious eyes. He did not like Mr. Cole.

The study was a close, dark room lined with book-shelves, rows and rows of theological works all dusty and forlorn. In the middle of the left wall between the book-shelves hung a large photograph of the Forum, Rome, and on the similar space on the other wall a photograph of the Parthenon. Behind a large desk sat Mr. Cole, very thin, very black, very white. His small son stood on the other side of the desk and looked at him.

"Well, my boy, what is it?"

"Helen said you wanted me." He shifted

from one foot to the other and looked anxiously at the Forum.

"Did I? Ah, let me see. . . . What was it? Hum, ha. Ah, yes. Of course. It's your journey-money. I should have asked you many days ago. I thought your mother had taken it. She had apparently forgotten."

Journey-money? Of what was he talking? Journey-money?

"What journey-money, father?" Even as he spoke his voice faltered, because, although he still did not know in the least of what his father was speaking, danger hovered suddenly near him like a large black bird, the wings obliterating the dusty light. Mr. Cole, who had much to do, grew a little impatient.

"Yes, yes. The money that we sent to your master for your journey home. Your mother fancied, from what Mr. Thompson wrote to her, that she had not sent quite enough on earlier occasions, that the former sum had not been quite sufficient. This time we sent at least a pound more than the fare demanded."

The bird came closer. Even now he did not understand, but his throat was dry and his heart was beating violently.

"The money that Mr. Thompson gave me the day before the end of term?"

"Yes, yes, my boy."

"He gave me fifteen shillings and the ticket."

"Well, let me have it."

"I spent it."

There was a pause. Mr. Cole stared at his son.

"What do you say?"

"I spent it, father."

"What?"

"I spent it."

Fright now was upon him—terror, panic. But behind the panic, like the resolution under torture not to betray one's friend, was the resolve never, never to say upon what the money had been spent.

"*What?*"

"I haven't got it, father. I thought it was for me."

"You thought it was for you?"

"Yes. Mr. Thompson didn't say anything about it—only that it was for the journey."

"And did you spend it on the journey?"

There was no answer.

"Will you kindly tell me how, having already your ticket, you managed to spend one pound between your school and your home?"

He felt the tears rising, and desperately beat them back. How he hated those tears that came always, it seemed, when one least wished to cry.

"It wasn't a pound." One tear came, hesitated and fell. "It was—fifteen shillings."

"Very well, then. Will you kindly explain to me how you spent fifteen shillings?"

No answer.

"Jeremy, how old are you?"

"Ten—and a—half."

"Ten and a half. Very well. You have been a year and a half at school. You are quite old enough to understand. Do you know what you have done?"

Tears now were falling fast.

"You have stolen this money."

No word.

"Do you know what they call someone who steals money?"

No answer.

"They call him a thief."

Through convulsive sobs there came:

"I didn't steal it."

"Do not add lying to the rest." Mr. Cole got up. "Come with me to your room."

They walked into the hall. Hamlet was waiting, and sprang forward. At once he saw in the sobbing figure of his master trouble and disaster. His head fell, his tail crept between his legs. He slowly followed the procession, only looking at Mr. Cole's black legs with longing. Upstairs they went, up through the tranquil and happy house. Barbara was being bathed; gurgling and applause and the splash of water came from the bathroom. They were in Jeremy's room, the door closed—Hamlet on the other side.

Jeremy stood, the tears drying on his face, his sobs coming in convulsive spasms.

"I am determined to know what you have done with this money—on what you have spent it."

There was no answer.

"It is of no use to be obstinate, Jeremy. Tell me—on what have you spent this money?"

He looked about him. There must be something in the room that would show him. Not many things here. The little case with some books, the pictures of "Napoleon on the *Bellerophon*" and "The Charge of the Light Brigade," the white bed and wash-hand stand, the chest of drawers. . . . Then his eye fell on the play-box. He went to it and opened it.

Jeremy gave a long, convulsive sigh. Then, between his sobs: "Father—please. I'll get the money. I will really. I didn't know it was wrong. Those are mine—they break, two of them. I'll get the money. I will really. Please, father."

A word here is needed in defence of Mr. Cole. A word is not in truth necessary. His action was inevitable. He truly loved his son, and because of that very love he was now shocked to the depth of his soul. His son was a thief. His son had lied and stolen. He was

old enough to know what he was about. To
himself, who had been brought up in a poverty
that was martyrdom and an honesty that was
fanatical, no sin could be worse than this save
only the sins of the flesh. For more than two
years now he had been troubled by Jeremy, seeing many signs in him of a nature very different
from his own, signs of independence, rebellion
and, as it seemed to him, hardness of heart
and selfishness. Now the boy was a thief,
deliberately spending money that did not belong
to him in the hopes that his parents would
forget. . . .

He bent over his play-box, saw the parcels
so neatly laid out there, took one up in his hand.
He looked back at his son.

" What *is* this, Jeremy? "

There was no answer.

" Did you get these things with the
money? "

" Yes, father." Then he said, " They're
presents for Christmas."

" Presents! "

Mr. Cole took up first one parcel, then
another, holding them up to the light. Then,
very slowly, with that deliberation with which
he did everything, he undid the parcels. Jeremy
said nothing, only stood there, his face white
and dirty where the tears had left marks, his
legs apart, his fists clenched.

One after another they were laid bare and placed upon the bed; rather pitiful they looked. A white-backed hair brush, a coral necklace, a little brooch of silver-gilt, a pair of woollen gloves, a baby's coral, a story book, a dog collar, two handkerchiefs, a work-box, a cheap copy in a cheap frame of "Dignity and Impudence," a tea caddy. Obviously all the servants had been included in this—no one had been forgotten. Had not Mr. Cole been so wholly and so truly shocked by his son's wickedness he must have been touched by the thought that had plainly gone to the buying of each gift. But imagination was not Mr. Cole's strongest part.

Jeremy watched him. Suddenly he broke out:

"Father, don't take them away. Let me give them to-morrow. You can punish me any way you like. You can beat me or take away my pocket money for ever or anything you like —but let me give them to-morrow. Please, father. Please, father."

"That must be part of your punishment, my son," Mr. Cole said very sorrowfully and finding it difficult to balance the things one upon another in his arms.

In another second of time, Jeremy was upon him, screaming, beating with his fists, scratching with his hands, crying:

"You shan't take them! You shan't take

them! They're mine! You're wicked! You're
wicked! They're my things! You shan't take
them!"

He was mad, wild, frantic. His hands were
round his father's thigh, his head beating against
his father's chest, his legs kicking against his
father's calves.

He screamed like something not human.

For a moment Mr. Cole was almost carried
off his balance. The things that he was carrying
—the hair brush, the necklace, the picture—
went tumbling on the floor.

Then Jeremy was picked up and, still kicking
and breathless, flung on to the bed.

Then the door closed and the boy was alone.

IV

The first real agony of Jeremy's young
life followed. Two years before, just at this
time, he had been in disgrace for telling a
lie. His misery had been acute for an hour
or two, and then, with the swift memory of
eight years old, it had been forgotten and
covered up. This was another business. When,
after lying stunned for a long time, thoughts
came to him, his first emotion was one of
blind, mad rage—an emotion quite new to him,
never felt before. Injustice! Injustice! That

D

was a new word written on the pages of his life's book, never again to be eradicated. There came before him at once, as though it were being presented to him by some new friend who was with him in the room for the first time, the picture of the afternoon when he had bought the presents. The group of boys who had gone into the little neighbouring town to buy things that they were " taking home," his consciousness of the fifteen shillings as absolutely his own, his first thought that he would buy sweets with some of it and keep the rest for the holidays, then the sudden flash of inspiration, presents for everybody, Christmas presents for everybody ; and with that the sudden flooding of his heart with love for home, for Polchester, for everyone, even Aunt Amy and the kitchenmaid, and then his delighted discovery in the general shop where they were, that there were so many different things to buy and so many so cheap.

The half-hour that he had and the wonderful excitement of taking back his parcels, himself packing them in his play-box—and it ends in this !

He hadn't *known* that the money was not for him ; he hadn't thought for a moment that it was not !

He sat up on the bed and looked about the room and saw the things scattered about the floor—the brush, the necklace. The glass of the

picture was broken. At the sight of that he
suddenly began to cry again, kneeling on the
bed, rubbing his knuckles into his eyes. He felt
sick—his head was aching, his eyes were red hot
—and he felt anger, furious, rebellious anger.
He hated his father, hated him so that it made
him sick to think of him. What would his
father do to him? He didn't care. He would
like to be terribly punished, beaten to within an
inch of his life, because then he could with more
justice than ever devote his life to hating his
father. He would hate him for ever, for ever
and ever. And all this time he was crying in a
snivelling sort of way, like a little animal whose
limb is broken.

The house was utterly silent about him. No
sound at all. Then he caught a thin, feeble
scratching at the door. He climbed off the bed
and went to it. Opening it cautiously, he
peered out. Hamlet was there wagging his tail.
He pulled him into the room, shut the door,
dragging him on to the bed, folded him into
himself, suffering himself to be licked from one
ear to the other.

v

How terrible the time that followed! None
of the Cole children could remember anything
at all like it. Even Helen, who was nearly

grown up now because she was at the Polchester High School and had won last term a prize for callisthenics, was impressed with the tragedy of it all. How awful that Christmas Day, never by any of them to be forgotten for the rest of their lives!

Jeremy came downstairs and there was a pretence of gaiety. Presents were distributed on Christmas evening. Turkey and plum pudding were eaten. A heavy cloud enveloped everyone.

The fanatic that then was in Mr. Cole began now to flower. For the first time his son appeared to him as a conscience-developing individual; for the first time he really loved him; and for the first time he felt that there was a soul to be saved and that he must save it. For the first time also in their married lives a serious difference of opinion divided the father and mother. Mrs. Cole yearned over her boy who was now in some strange way escaping her. She was no psychologist, and indeed thirty years ago parents never conceived of analysing their children. She was only discovering, what every mother discovers, that a year's absence had taken her boy away from her, had given him interests that she could not share, taught him ambitions, confided to him secrets, delivered him over to hero-worshippings that would never be hers. Not for ten years would he

return to her. To be a mother you must have
infinite patience.

Secretly she rebelled against her husband's
policy; outwardly she submitted to it.

During all the week following Christmas the
Coles were a miserable family, and in the middle
of them Jeremy moved, a figure of stone. They
wished him to be an outcast; very well then,
he would be an outcast. They thought him a
criminal and not fit for their society; very well
then, he would be apart and of himself. The
presents were there, at the bottom of his play-
box. His only definite punishment was that he
should receive no pocket-money throughout the
holidays—but he was a pariah—and a pariah he
would be.

Once his mother talked to him, drawing him
to her, putting her arms around him.

"Jeremy, dear, just go to father and say
you're sorry and then it will all be over."

"I'm not sorry."

"Well, if you're not sorry about spending
the money, because you didn't know that you
oughtn't to, say you're sorry because you kicked
father."

"I'm not sorry I kicked father."

"But father loves you. He was only doing
what he thought was right."

"Father doesn't love me or he would have
known I didn't steal the money."

"But, Jeremy dear, father wants you to realize that you mustn't spend other people's money as though it were your own. You're too young to understand now——"

"I'm not too young to understand."

Mrs. Cole sighed. This Jeremy was utterly strange to her, so old, so oddly different from the boy of a year ago, so hard and so hostile. She was very unhappy. And Jeremy, too, was unhappy—desperately unhappy. It was no fun being a rebel. Sometimes he was on the very edge of surrender, longing to go and submit to his father, fling his arms round his mother, listen to Mary's silly stories, play and shout and sing and laugh as he used to do.

Something kept him back. It was as though he were in a nightmare, one of those nightmares when you can't speak, a weight is on your chest, you move against your will.

He was so unhappy that he told Hamlet that he was going to run away to sea. He had serious thoughts of this.

Then suddenly Uncle Samuel returned from Paris.

VI

It was a wet, windy evening. The rain was blowing in streaky gusts up Orange Street, sending the lamps inebriated, and whipping at windows as though it would never find outlet

sufficient for its ill temper. Out of the storm
came Uncle Samuel in a black cape and a floppy
black hat, straight from that mysterious, unseen,
unfathomed country, Paris. As usual, he was
casual and careless enough in his greetings,
kissed his sister quickly, nodded to his brother-
in-law, grinned at the children, and was in a
moment transported to that strange region at
the back of the house where was his studio, that
magical place into which none of the children
had even entered. He did not that evening
apparently notice Jeremy's desolate figure.

On the following afternoon Jeremy, Hamlet
at his heels, was hanging disconsolately about the
passage when his uncle suddenly appeared.

" Hallo ! " he said.

" Hallo ! " said Jeremy.

Uncle Samuel was in his blue painting smock.
Whereas the other members of the family were
so well known to Jeremy that they were almost
like the wallpaper or the piano, Uncle Samuel's
appearance was always new and exciting. With
his chubby face, the grey hair that stood up
rather thinly about his crimson pate, his fat
stumpy body, ironical blue eyes and little,
rather childish, mouth, he always seemed nearer
to Jeremy than the others—younger, more
excitable, more easily surprised. He had the
look of an old baby, Jeremy sometimes thought.
He looked at Jeremy consideringly.

" Got anything to do? "

" No."

" Come on into the studio."

" Oh, may I? "

" Well, I wouldn't ask you if I didn't want
you. . . . Yes, you may bring the dog."

Jeremy's excitement was intense. Once,
long ago, his uncle had said that he might go
into the studio, but he had never dared to
venture. He walked carefully like Agag. The
door was opened, a curtain pulled aside. A long,
empty room with wide high windows overlooking
meadow and hill, a low bookcase running the
length of the room, a large sofa with cushions,
two rugs, some pictures with their faces to the
wall, some other pictures hanging, funny ones,
a girl with a green face, a house all crooked, a
cow (or was it a horse?) . . .

Uncle Samuel went to the sofa and sat down.
He called Jeremy over to him and pulled him in
between his knees.

" Been having a row? " he said.

" Yes," said Jeremy.

" Kicked your father? "

" Yes."

" What was it all about? "

Jeremy told him. Uncle Samuel listened
attentively, his eyes no longer ironical. He put
his hand on Jeremy's shoulder, and the boy,
feeling the unexpected kindness, burst into

tears. The misery of the last week overflowed from his heart.

" I didn't—know. . . . I didn't really—I wanted to give them the things—I wasn't wicked."

The man bent down and picked the boy up and held him tight. Then he talked to him.

" Look here, you've not got to mind this. You were wrong, too, you know. Your father was right from *his* way of seeing things. His way isn't yours, that's all. When you get older you'll find people often don't see things the way you do, won't like the work you're proudest of, simply won't understand it. There are as many different opinions as can be in this old world, and you've simply got to face it. You've just got to be ready for anything—not to get angry and kick. Don't let yourself be too sensitive. You'll go up and you'll go down, and when you're up people will say you ought to be down, and when you're down there'll be a few kind souls will help you up again. Misunderstood! Why, bless my soul, you'll be misunderstood a million times before you're done. If you've got work you like, a friend you can trust and a strong stomach you'll have enough to be thankful for.

" You won't understand all I'm saying yet, but you soon will. You come along in here and be kind to your old uncle, who's never had anything right all his life—largely through his own fault, mind you. There, there! Bless me, you're as soppy as a shower of rain. Fond of your uncle?"

Jeremy hugged him.

"That's right. Well, mind you keep it up. I can do with some. Will you say you're sorry to your father?"

Jeremy nodded his head.

"That's right. . . . Now listen. This studio is for you to be in when you like. Not your beastly sisters, mind you; but you—*and* your dog, if he'll behave himself. . . ."

Hamlet promised. Jeremy ceased to cry. He looked about him.

When they had come in the room had been in dusk. Now it was too dark to see. He felt for his uncle's hand and held it. Nothing so wonderful as this had yet happened in his life. He did not know, however, how wonderful in reality that evening would afterwards seem to him. All his after life he would look back to it, the dark room, the dog quiet at their feet, the cool strength of his uncle's hand, the strange, heating excitement, the happiness and security after the week of wild loneliness and dismay. It was in that half-hour that his real life began; it was then that, like Alice in her looking-glass, he stepped over the brook and entered into his inheritance.

CHAPTER III

THE DANCE

I

A FORTNIGHT after Christmas a bomb, partly of apprehension, partly of delight, fell upon the Cole family—an invitation to a dance in the house of Mrs. Mulholland, of Cleek.

The invitation arrived at breakfast, and the children would in all probability have known nothing at all about it had it not been in an envelope addressed to "Miss Cole." Helen, therefore, opened it, and, never having received anything like it before, thought at first that it was a grown-up invitation to a grown-up tea party.

Miss Cole
Miss Mary Cole
Master Jeremy Cole

MRS. JAMES MULHOLLAND
AT HOME, JANUARY 10, 1895

Dancing, 6.30—10.
The Manor House,
Cleek.

She was flattered by this, of course, but
it was not until the word "*Dancing*" caught
her eye that she realized the true significance of
the invitation.

"Dancing!" She adored it. At the High
School she was recognized as the best dancer of
all the younger girls. She was! She knew she
was! She was adorable, fascinating, wonderful
when she danced. She was! She knew she
was!

She gave her mother the invitation and in
a voice trembling with emotion said: "Oh,
mother, may we go? May we?"

Mary and Jeremy, who saw that they also
were concerned in this mysterious affair, stopped
eating.

Mrs. Cole looked at the card. "Mrs. Mulholland! How good of her! And she really
hardly knows us! We've only exchanged
calls."

"Mrs. Mulholland! That's the woman out
at Cleek," said Aunt Amy, who always liked
to feel that she was the real directress of
the Cole family affairs. "Has she asked the
children to a party?"

"Yes—to a dance on the tenth!"

"Well, of course they can't go," said Aunt
Amy decisively. "Cleek's much too far."

Now it happened that on that particular
morning Mr. Cole was feeling considerably

irritated by his sister-in-law. He often felt like this and spent many half-hours in wondering why his sister-in-law and his brother-in-law—neither of them at all sympathetic to him—occupied his house. And then he remembered that his sister-in-law at least shared in the expenses of the family, and that without that share finances would be difficult.

But this morning even this thought did not overcome his dislike of his sister-in-law. He was ready to contradict anything that she said.

He looked over the top of his egg at his wife. "I don't see why they shouldn't go. We can have a cab from Poole's."

Aunt Amy, who, like Mrs. Norris, was very careful with other people's money, burst out:

"But think, Herbert—all the expense of a cab! And it will have to wait to take them back again. And Poole's charges go up and up. I'm sure the children will do very nicely at home."

How gladly at that moment would Helen, Mary and Jeremy have put poison in Aunt Amy's tea or stabbed her in the back with a bread-knife! However, little as they realized it, she was doing everything to help their cause.

Mr. Cole, looking at Aunt Amy very severely, said:

"Thank you, Amy, but that's my affair.

Poor as we are, we can still afford a cab. I think it will be good for the children to go. Mrs. Mulholland's kindness must not be rejected."

At that moment in came Uncle Samuel, late and unshaven as usual, and the conversation was not continued. The affair was settled by the kindness of a neighbour, Mrs. Carstairs, who, having been also invited to take her small boy, offered to share a cab and chaperon the Cole children.

No child of to-day can possibly conceive what it was to us children in the old days in Polchester to be invited to a dance. For the grown-ups in Polchester there were a great many balls—more, perhaps, than there are to-day—but for the children there was very little—some afternoon parties, perhaps one pantomime, little more.

To the Cole children an evening dance—a dance out of Polchester with a drive at both ends of it—was wonder beyond wonder. Life was instantly at the merest murmur of its name transformed into something exquisite, rainbow-coloured, fantastical.

Helen's transports were all selfish. She was not a bad girl did you grant her her devastating egotism; she cared for her family, she was neither vindictive nor mean, not too greedy, and not too vain; but she drove towards her

purpose with the cold, clean-cut assurance of
a steel knife cutting paper—and that purpose
was the aggrandizement and public splendour
of Helen Cole.

Mary was the romantic one of the family,
and this ball was as marvellous to her as were
ever the coach and wand to Cinderella. Full of
tremors, she nevertheless allowed her imagination full play. Soon Mrs. Mulholland, her
house, her grounds, her family, her servants,
were scattered with star-dust ablaze with
diamonds, glittering with pearls and rubies.
She sat for hours, motionless, picturing it.

Jeremy's attitude was mixed. He was
deeply excited, but hid his emotion from
everyone save Uncle Samuel, of whom in the
strictest privacy he asked many searching
questions. He had a habit just at this time,
which was found irritating by his elders, of
asking questions and himself answering them.
As, for instance, " Will it be the same cab both
ways? Yes." " Will it be mostly girls that
will be there? No."

" If you know the answers to the questions,
what do you ask them for? " said Uncle
Samuel.

But he didn't know the answers to his
questions; it was a habit into which he had
fallen. He would try and stop it. Uncle
Samuel gave him his view of dances in general;

it was a poor one. Jeremy, who was adoring his uncle just now, tried to feel superior.

"Uncle Samuel says dances are rotten," he announced to Helen.

"Mother says you're not to use that word," said Helen.

Nevertheless in his heart he was excited—desperately.

II

The Day arrived—which for a whole week it had seemed that it would never have strength sufficient to do. All the afternoon they were being dressed. The young assistant of Mr. Consett, the hairdresser, came up to attend to Helen and Mary. This had never happened before. The dresses of Helen and Mary were alike, white silk, with pink ribbons. Helen looked lovely with her black hair, big black eyes and thick eyelashes, her slender white neck, tall slim body and lovely ankles. She was one upon whom fine clothes settled with a sigh of satisfaction, as though they knew that they were in luck. With Mary it was precisely the opposite; the plainer you dressed her the better. Fine clothes only accentuated her poor complexion, dusty hair and ill-shaped body. Yes, Helen looked lovely. Even Jeremy would have noticed it had he not been absorbed by his own clothing. For the first time in his life he was wearing a white waistcoat; he was, of course, uncomfortably clean. He hated the sticky feeling in his hair, the tightness of his black shoes, the creaking of his stiff white shirt—but these things must be. Had he only known it, his snub nose, his square, pugnacious face, and a certain sturdy soundness of his limbs gave him exactly the appearance of a Sealyham puppy—but Sealyhams were not popular thirty years ago. Hamlet smelt the unusual cleanliness of his master and was excited by it. He stuck closely to his heels, determining that if his master were going away again, this time he would not be left behind, but would go too. When, however, Poole's cab really arrived, he was given no chance, being held, to his infinite disgust, in the bony arms of Aunt Amy.

All the grown ups were there to watch them go, and Mrs. Hounslow and Minnie the parlourmaid in the background. Mr. Cole was smiling and looking quite cheerful. He felt that this was all his doing.

"Now, children," cried Aunt Amy, as though it were *her* family, *her* cab and *her* party, " mind you enjoy yourselves and tell Mrs. Carstairs that mother doesn't want you to stay too late. . . ."

They were to pick up Mrs. Carstairs, who lived higher up the terrace, who was a nice rosy-

E

faced woman, a widow with a small boy called
Herbert. Because Herbert was their father's
name it had a solemn, grown-up air to the
children, and they felt the contrast to be very
funny indeed when a small, pale-faced mouse of
a boy was piloted into the cab. He was so deeply
smothered in shawls and comforters that there
was little to be seen but a sharply peaked nose.
He was, it seemed, a serious-minded child. Soon
after getting into the cab he remarked :

"I do hope that we all enjoy ourselves this
evening, I'm sure."

Mrs. Carstairs, although she was stout and
jolly, was so nervous about the health of
her only child that she made all the children
nervous too.

"You aren't feeling cold, Bertie darling, are
you? . . . You haven't got a headache, have
you? Lean against mother, darling, if you're
tired. Are you tired?"

To all of which Herbert answered very
solemnly :

"I am not, mother."

He was, however, it seemed, a child with a
considerable sense of humour, because he suddenly pinched Jeremy in the fatty part of his
thigh, and then looked at him very severely as
though challenging him to say anything about it,
and it suddenly occurred to Jeremy that you had
a great advantage if you looked old and solemn,

because no one would ever believe anything
wicked of you.

His thoughts, however, of young Herbert
were soon lost in the excitement of the adventure of the cab. Nothing that he had ever
known was more wonderful than this, the rolling
through the lighted town, the background so
dark like the inside of a box, the tearing through
the market-place now so silent and mysterious,
down through North Street, over the Pol bridge,
and so out into the country. The silence of the
high road, rhythmed by the clamp-clamp of the
horse's hoofs, the mysterious gleam of white
patches as the road was illumined by the light
from the carriage lamps, the heavy thick-set
hedges, watching as though they were an army of
soldiers drawn up in solemn order to let the
carriage pass through, the smell of the night
mingled with the smell of the cab, the rattle of
the ill-fitting windows, the excited, half-
strangled breathing of Mary—all these together
produced in Jeremy's breast a feeling of exalta-
tion, pride and adventure that was never to be
forgotten.

They were all packed very closely together
and bounced about like marionettes without
self-control.

Jeremy said in a voice hoarse with bumping
and excitement: " Shall I put my gloves on
yet? " He had never had white gloves before.

Mrs. Carstairs said : " You might try them on, dear, and see. Be careful not to split them "—which, of course, he immediately did ; not a very bad split and between the thumb and finger of the left hand, so that perhaps it would not be seen.

While with some concern he was considering this, they drove through park gates and along a wide drive. To Jeremy's excited fancy silver birds seemed to fly past the windows and sheets of stars bend down and flash to the ground and rise swinging up to heaven again. They passed a stretch of water on their right, dark like a blind mirror, but with a crack of light that crossed it and then faded into splashing gold where the lamps and shining windows of the house reflected in it. They were there ; other carriages also ; children like ghosts passing up the stone steps, the great house so strangely indifferent.

He saw as he got out of the carriage dark spaces beyond the splash of light where the garden was hidden, cold and reserved and apart. It was like him to notice that, the only child that evening who saw.

Inside the house there was a sudden noise of laughter and voices and people moving, and two large footmen with white powdered hair waiting to take your coats. Without his coat, waiting for a moment alone, he felt shivery and shy and very conscious of his white waistcoat. Then he

saw young Ernest, son of the Dean of Polchester, and Bill Bartlett and the Misses Bartlett, children of one of the canons, and Tommy
Winchester, son of the precentor. He winked
at Tommy, who was a fat, round boy with a face
like an apple, but pretended not to see when
Ernest caught his eye, because he hated Ernest,
and having fought him once nearly two years
ago, hoped very much to have the pleasure of
fighting him again soon and licking him. He
advanced into the big, shining, dazzling room,
behind his two sisters, as on to a field of battle.

"The Misses Cole and Master Cole,"
shouted a large stout man with a face like an
oyster; and then Jeremy found himself shaking
hands with a beautiful lady, all white hair, black
silk and diamonds, and an old gentleman with
an eyeglass; and then, before he knew it, he
was standing against the wall with Mary and
Helen surveying the scene.

As he watched, a sudden desperate depression
fell upon him. It was all like a painted picture
that he was outside; he was an outcast and
Mary was an outcast and Helen. They had
arrived at an interval between the dances, and
the gleaming floor was like a great lake stretching
from golden shore to golden shore. From the
ceiling hung great clusters of light, throwing
down splashes like dim islands, and every once
and again someone would cross the floor very

carefully, seeming to struggle to reach the
islands, to pause there for a moment as though
for safety. . . .

Against the wall, right round the ballroom,
figures were ranged, some like Chinese idols,
silent and motionless, others animated and
excited. Voices rose like the noise of wind or
rain.

Everyone, even the Chinese idols, seemed to
be at home and at their ease; only Jeremy and
his sisters were cared for by no one. Then
suddenly a stout, smiling woman appeared as
though out of the floor, and behind her a very
frightened boy. She spoke to Helen.

" You're Helen Cole, are you not? Well,
dear, here's Harry Preston wants you to have a
dance with him." Then, turning to Mary:
" Are you dancing the next, dear? No? We
must alter that. Here's Willie Richmond—
Willie," catching hold of a long and gawky boy,
" you're not dancing the next, are you? I'm
sure Miss Cole will be delighted,"—then departed like a train that has picked up its passen-
gers and is hurrying on to its next station.

The small boy gazed distressfully at Helen,
but she was quite equal to him, smiling with that
sweet smile that was kept entirely for strangers
or important visitors and saying :

" What is it? Oh, a polka. . . . That will
be lovely. I do like polkas, don't you? "

At that moment the band struck up, and in another instant the floor was covered with figures. The tall, gawky boy dragged off Mary, who had said not a word, but stared at him with distressed eyes through her spectacles.

Helen took absolute charge of her partner, moving away with such grace and elegance that Jeremy was suddenly proud of her and seemed to see her as she really was for the first time in his life.

Then he realized that he was alone, absolutely alone, stuck against the wall, a silly gawk, for all the world to look at and despise.

III

He set his chin, squared his shoulders, and tried to look as though he were there by preference. No one now paid any attention to him; the music swung on, and although he had never danced in his life, his toes kept time inside his shoes. He gazed haughtily around him, stared at the dancers as they passed him, and was miserable.

Then the stout lady who had carried off Mary and Helen suddenly appeared again and said:

"What! Not dancing? You're Jeremy Cole, aren't you? Come along. I'll find you a partner."

He was led away and precipitated at the feet of a very stout lady who stared at him in a frozen way and a frightened little girl. He had a programme in his hand and was going to ask her for some future polka, when the mountainous lady said in a deep bass voice:

"You'd better take her now. She's been waiting long enough," staring at the genial introducer as she spoke.

Jeremy led away his victim. He was acutely miserable, but the agony of stumbling, bumping and incoherent whirling did not last long because the band suddenly stopped, and before he knew it he was sitting on the steps of a staircase with his partner and staring at her.

She said not a word; then he saw that she was terrified and pity held him.

"Do you like dances?" he asked hoarsely.

"I've never been to one before," she answered in a convulsive whisper, looking as though she were about to cry.

"Where do you live?" he asked.

"Five, Pemberton Terrace, Polchester," she answered breathlessly.

"Was that your mother?"

"No. Auntie."

"How many aunts have you?"

"Five."

"What a lot! I've only one, and it's quite enough. How many uncles have you?"

" I haven't got an uncle."

" I have—a splendid one. Do any of your aunts paint? "

" Auntie Maude does."

" What does she paint? "

" I don't know."

He felt this conversation so stupid that he looked at her in disgust. What was it about girls? Why was there something the matter with all of them? If this was what dances were, he didn't want any more of them. And it was just then, at that most distressing moment, that the wonderful, the never-to-be-forgotten event occurred. Someone was coming down from the stairs above them and wanted to pass them.

A voice said softly : " Do you mind? Thank you so much."

Jeremy rose and then looked up. He was staring at the most beautiful lady he had ever conceived of—indeed, far more than he had ever conceived of, because his dreams had not hitherto been of beautiful ladies. He had never thought of them at all. She was very tall and slender, dressed in white ; she had black hair and a jewel blazing in the front of it. But more than everything was her smile, the jolliest, merriest, twinkliest smile he had ever seen. He could only smile too, standing against the banisters to let her pass. Perhaps there was something in his snub nose, and the way his mouth curled at the corners that struck her. She stopped.

"Enjoying yourself?" she asked.

"Yes," he answered, staring at her with all his soul.

"Well, come on," she said. "There's the music beginning again."

That appeal may have been made to the general stair-covered company, but he felt that it was to him.

"Come on," he said to his partner. At the door of the ballroom he found, to his relief, the massive aunt. "Thank you so much for the delightful dance," he said, bowing as he had seen others do; then he bolted.

Heaven was on his side because just inside the room, and standing for a moment alone, gazing happily about her, was the lovely lady. Could he? Did he dare? His heart was beating in his breast. His knees trembled. He felt as he did when he was summoned to old Thompson's study. But the fear lest she should move away or someone should come and speak to her, drove him forward. He was at her side.

"I say," he muttered huskily, "is anybody dancing with you just now?"

She swung round and looked down at him.

"Hallo!" she said. "It's you!"

"Yes," he answered, still choking. "I would like to dance with you."

"Well, you shall," she said, and suddenly picked him up and whisked him round. What happened after that he never knew. Once, years before, he had escaped from home, gone to the Polchester Fair and ridden on the merry-go-round, ridden on a wonderful coal-black horse all alone under the stars. Something like that earlier experience was this exquisite happiness, delicious movement in which the golden walls, the blazing lights, the glittering, shining floor had their parts. His feet kept no time, they seemed scarcely to touch the floor, but as the music dipped and swung, so he also, floating like a bird, falling like the dying strain of a song, rising like the flight of a star. Suddenly it ceased; he came to earth, breathless, hot and most wonderfully happy. She led him away, holding his hand, to a corner where there was a palm and a little tinkling fountain ; they seemed to be quite by themselves.

"Was that all right?" she asked, laughing and fanning herself with a great fan of white feathers.

He could not speak; he gulped and nodded.

"What's your name?" she asked.

He told her.

She smiled. "Jeremy. That's a pretty name." He blushed with pleasure. "Do you go to school yet? I expect you're good at football."

How wonderful of her to know that, to ask about the one game that was near his heart. He told her eagerly about it, how he had played half-back twice for the school and had been kicked in the eye and hadn't cared, and how next year he hoped to be the regular half-back because Trefusis, who had been half for three years, was going to Eton, and he was very young to be half; he'd only be eleven then—and if he stayed on until he was thirteen——

I'm afraid that he boasted a little.

"Have you got any brothers and sisters?" she asked him.

He told her all about Mary and Helen, and his mother and father and Aunt Amy and Uncle Samuel—especially about Uncle Samuel. And while he talked he stared and stared and stared, never taking his eyes from her face for a single moment. She was laughing all the time and suddenly she said:

"Shall I tell you something, Jeremy?"

He nodded his head.

"This is the very happiest day of my life. I'm so happy that it's all I can do not to sing."

"I'm very happy too," he said. "I didn't think I'd like dances till you came, but now they're splendid."

The cruel music suddenly began, and there, standing in front of them, was a tall, dark man, very fine and straight. The lady rose.

"This is Jeremy," she said. "And this is Major——"

Jeremy didn't catch the name. He would wish to hate him for taking her away had he not looked so fine, just, in short, what Jeremy would like to look when he grew up.

"I tell you what," the lady said, turning round. "Jeremy, you shall take me down to supper. Yes, he shall, Michael. After all, it's their evening, not ours. Four dances from this. That's right. Number eleven. Got it? Good-bye."

She was gone, and Jeremy was staring around him as though in a dream.

IV

Four dances from now! What should be do meanwhile? To dance with anyone else would be desecration. Suddenly Tommy Winchester appeared.

"I say," he wheezed in his funny voice like a miniature organ-blower's. "Have you been down to supper yet? I've been down four times. You should see the ices they've got."

Ices after the experience he'd been having! Nevertheless he was interested.

"Where are they?" he asked.

"Down there," said Tommy, pointing to

some stairs. "That's the back stairs, and you can go down as often as you please and nobody sees."

At that moment there came round the corner the supercilious figure of the Dean's Ernest. He was very elegant, more elegant—as Jeremy was forced to confess—than himself would ever be.

"Hallo, you fellows," said Ernest. He was twelve, and was going next year to Rugby. It was irritating the way that he was always a year ahead of Jeremy in everything. "I call it pretty rotten," he said, smoothing his gloves. "The band's not first class and the floor's awful."

"Well, I think it's splendid," said Jeremy.

"Oh, do you?" said Ernest scornfully. "*You* would! Ever been to a dance before?"

"Yes, lots," said Jeremy, and it is to be hoped that Heaven will forgive him that lie.

"Well, it's my belief that it's his first," said Ernest confidentially to Tommy. "What a kid like that's doing away from his nurse I can't think." Nevertheless he moved away, because Jeremy had grown remarkably thick and sturdy during the last year, and had already in Polchester a pugnacious reputation.

"I say," said Tommy, who seemed to have been long ago forced by his appearance of good-natured chubbiness into the rôle of perpetual peacemaker, "you can get to the supper down there," pointing to the stairs. "You should see the ices they've got. I've been four times."

"Have they?" said the Dean's Ernest, his sallow countenance freshening. "Can you get down that way?"

"You bet!" said Tommy.

"Come on, then." They disappeared.

Jeremy was rather distressed by this encounter. Ernest had had the last word. He wished that he had been able to say "Sucks to you!" which, in addition to being the cry of the moment, was applicable to almost every occasion. Never mind. The opportunity would undoubtedly return. Such an episode should not cloud his happiness.

He seemed to be moving, clouded by the great white fan that she had used. That hid him from the rest of the world. He did indeed dance with Helen (and would have danced with Mary could he have found her); he danced also with a little girl with spots; but in these dances he was blinded and stunned with the light from Juno's eyes. It was an utterly new experience to him. He could compare it with nothing at all save the day when Stevens, the football captain, had said he "had stood it well over his eye," and once when he had gone to have a tooth out and the dentist hadn't taken it after all. And this again was different from those. It was like hot coffee and summer lightning and chestnuts bursting as they fell from the autumn trees; not that he made those comparisons consciously, of course.

Most of all it was like a dream, the most wonderful of all his nights. The third dance was over. He must go and find her.

V

He stepped along the floor, looking about him from side to side; he thought he saw her, started forward, and felt someone touch him on the arm. He turned round. Mary was at his shoulder.

" Hallo! " he said. " I'm in a hurry."

" Oh, Jeremy, do wait a moment." She looked at him piteously.

" Well, what is it? "

" Come out here for a moment. Please do."

He did not want to hurt her, but this pause was an agony to him.

" What is it? " he asked crossly when they were in the hall outside the ballroom.

" Oh, Jeremy, it's all so horrid. Do dance with me. One little boy danced with me and then his mother tried to make him dance again and he wouldn't, and I'm sure it wasn't my fault, because I danced much better than he did. And then Herbert said he could dance and he couldn't, and we fell down and he didn't seem to mind at all; but *I* minded because everyone laughed and I tore my dress. And there hasn't been anybody to dance with for ever so long, and Helen's been dancing all the time. . . . Oh, Jeremy, do dance with me! I do love dancing so, and you haven't danced with me all the evening.''

It was true that he had not, but oh! how he wished her at the other end of England at that moment! She looked so foolish with her hair all over the place and her dress untidy, her sash pulled round the wrong way and her stockings wrinkled. And every moment was precious. *She* would be looking for him, wondering where he was, thinking him mean thus to break his promise when she had given him so especial a favour.

At that thought he started away.

"No, no, Mary. Later on we'll have a dance, two if you like. But not now. I can't, really.''

But Mary was desperate.

"Oh, Jeremy, you must! I can't sit there any more and be looked at by everyone. Oh, please, Jeremy. I'll give you my mother-of-pearl box, if you will.''

"I don't want your old box,'' he said gruffly. He looked at her, looked away, looked back at her, said:

"All right, then. Come on.''

F

His heart was like lead. The evening was ruined for him, and not only the evening, but perhaps his whole life. And yet what was he to do? Mary would cry if he left her. She had had a miserable evening. Something in him was touched, as it always was, by her confident belief that he, and he alone in all the world, could always put things right. It was just his cursed luck! His evening was ruined; he hoped that after this they would go home.

They had what seemed to him the most miserable of dances, but he could see that Mary was what Uncle Samuel called " seventh heavened." She bounced about, stamping her heels on Jeremy's toes, bumping into him, suddenly pushing back her wild hair from her frenzied face, giving little snorts of pleasure, humping her shoulders, tossing her head. Round and round they went, dancing what they imagined to be a polka, Jeremy with his face grimly set, agonized disappointment in his heart. When it was over they sat out on the stairs and Mary panted her thanks.

" That was—lovely, Jeremy—we do dance —well together—don't we? That was the nicest—I've ever had—I do hope—we'll have another."

" I expect it's awfully late," said Jeremy gloomily. " We'll be going home soon."

Soon the music began again and at the

bottom of the stairs, to Jeremy's immense relief, they met Mrs. Carstairs with the serious-faced Herbert.

"That's right, Mary, dear," Mrs. Carstairs said. "I've been looking for you. It's time we went down to supper. Herbert shall take us down. Have you had supper, Jeremy?"

He muttered some excuse and was off. With beating heart he searched the crowds. Nowhere. Nowhere. He searched the fast-emptying ball-room, then the hall; then, with tears in his eyes and a choked, strangling in his throat, was turning back, when he caught sight of the diamond star high above the other heads, and the lovely soft black hair and the jolly smile.

"Traitor!" she said. "You forgot, after all."

"No, I didn't forget. It was my sister."
But there was no time for explanation.

"Did you go with someone else to supper?"

"Yes; I've had supper."

"Oh!" He half turned away. A tear was near its fall. "I suppose you couldn't——"

"Yes, I could." She twirled him round. "I can have any number of suppers. I can have supper all day and supper all night. Come along. You shall take me down in style. I put my arm through yours like that—see? No, the right. Now we lead the way. Who's coming down to supper?"

His pride and his happiness! Who shall describe them? His back was so straight as they walked down the stairs that he almost fell backwards. The supper-room was a clatter of noise, but he was not so proud but that he was suddenly hungry—wildly, savagely hungry. She piled his plate with things, watching him, laughing at him.

"Nobody's cut the cake yet," she cried. "You shall cut it, Jeremy!"

An old stout servant with white hair, who had been watching her with smiling eyes, brought a huge castle, with towers and battlements and flags, and placed it in front of her. She made Jeremy stand on his chair. She gave him a great knife and showed him where to cut. Everyone at the other tables stopped eating and turned round to see. Then they shouted and clapped.

"One, two, three!" he cried, and cut into the cake.

Then they all cheered.

"Bravo," she said. "You did that very well. Now Janet will cut the rest. You must have a piece and I must have a piece. Perhaps one of us will get the ring or the thimble."

And, miracle of miracles, he got the ring, the silver ring! She put it on his finger herself. He flushed, his lip trembled. He felt that he wanted everything to end just then, at that moment—for nothing more ever to happen again.

When he had had three ices, one after the other, she decided that supper was over. They walked out of the room as they had walked into it, in stately fashion, her arm through his.

Then at the top of the stairs there was Mrs. Carstairs.

"Come, Jeremy dear," she said. "It's time to go home. The carriage is there."

He saw that the tall major was also there.

"Hullo, young 'un," he said. "Had a good supper?"

He nodded his head. But he had eyes only for her.

"I'm glad I got that ring," he whispered, "because you put it on my finger. And I'll never take it off till I die."

"Not even when you wash?" she asked, laughing.

"I won't wash that finger," he said.

The major put his hand on his shoulder.

"Here, I've got a secret for you. Shut your eyes." Jeremy shut them. The major's hands were at his white waistcoat pocket. "Now don't you look till you're on your way home. And I'll tell you something. You've shown excellent taste to-night. You couldn't have shown better if you were a hundred."

She bent down and kissed him.

"Good night," she said. "Will you write and tell me about the football?"

"You bet your life," he answered, staring at her. That was the favourite oath just then at Thompson's.

She laughed again. Then, bending down, whispered in his ear dramatically: "If I'm ever in trouble and need you, will you come, wherever you are, whatever you're doing?"

"Yes," he said, his eyes never leaving her face.

She kissed him again.

VI

They were all in the cab rolling homewards. He felt in his pocket; something there in paper. He could tell by the feel of it that it was a sovereign or a shilling. Cautiously he lifted it to the light of the lodge gates.

It was *Gold*. He sighed with satisfaction—but the real thing was the silver ring. He sat there, making calculations.

"Mrs. Carstairs," he said suddenly, "if I have threepence a week for eight years, and save it all, could I have enough to be married?"

There was no answer. She was apparently sleeping—so he added sotto voce:

"And perhaps father will give me sixpence a week after I'm fifteen."

CHAPTER IV

SALADIN AND THE BLACK BISHOP

I

THE old town, like human beings, had its moods of excited reminiscence. Why should it not? Now brooding, now suddenly waking into lightning flashes of dramatic history, so that everyone in the place, scarcely knowing why, began to dream of the old days when armoured men fought all the way down the High Street and up again, and the Black Bishop rode on his great horse to the edge of the rock where the cloisters now are and saw the beggarly heretics flung over far down into the waters below; and the peasants had their fair up on the hill above the Pol (and were all so be-drunken that they set the town on fire, so that three-quarters of it was burnt to the ground in 1457, as everyone knows, and the cathedral itself only saved by a miracle); and the meeting of the maidens in the market-place, who brought a flag which they had worked to send to Monmouth in Bridgewater; and the last drowning of a witch—old Mother Huckepinch—in the Pol in 1723; and so farther and farther and farther. History, history, history —it lay thick as dust about the town, and only needed a little stirring of the town's soil to send the dust up into people's eyes, making them think of times dead and gone and ghosts closer still about them, perhaps, than they cared to think.

It must have been during one of these moods of the town that Jeremy was caught. He was, as all readers of these reminiscences of his early days will have discovered, a two-sided boy, and he had already a strange, secret interior life within his very healthy and normal exterior one. There is nothing harder, perhaps, in our own experience than to look back and discover when it was that that secret life was as it were first confirmed and strengthened by something in the real world that corresponded to it. For some of us that actual moment was so dramatic, so strangely concrete and definite, so friendly (as though it were someone suddenly appearing out of the dark and speaking to us and showing us that we were not alone, either in experience or desire as we had supposed) that we cannot possibly forget its precise time and colour. With others, two or three occasions can claim to have worked the miracle; with others again that confirmation was gradual, arising out of no definite incident, but rather creeping forward like a finger of the rising sun, slowly lighting one's path and showing one where to go.

With Jeremy there had been already definite signs—his adventure years ago with the sea captain, his days on the beach at Rafiel, his friendship with Uncle Samuel; but his actual realization of something strange and mysterious, ancient and yet present, friendly and yet hostile, reassuring and yet terrifying, active and yet quiescent, his recognition of " that life beyond the wall," dated quite definitely from his discovery of Saladin and his strange adventure in the cathedral.

As I have already said on that particular week—the last week of his Christmas holidays— the town was up to its tricks. Had it not been, Jeremy would surely never have felt the spirit of adventure so strongly, never gone into the old bookshop, never—but you shall hear.

He was very quiet and behaving beautifully during that last week—yes, beautifully, until the last three days when the devil (who is always on the wait for young gentlemen when they are about to return to school), or the town, or Uncle Samuel or something or somebody suddenly got hold of him and led him the strangest dance. It must have been the devil that led to the adventure of the night raiders (and that is quite another story); but again it *might* have been the old town—nobody knows. How can anybody

know thirty years after it was all over and done
with?

Until those last three days Jeremy behaved
like an angel—that is, he listened to Aunt Amy
and washed his hands when she told him to; he
did not tease his little sister Barbara, nor hide
Helen's hair ribbons; he allowed Mary to go
walking with him and gave Miss Jones a present
when she returned from her holiday. He felt,
perhaps, that as the holidays had begun so
awfully with that terrible disaster of the Christmas presents, it was up to him to see that they
ended properly. And then he was truly a good
little boy who wanted things to go well and
everyone to be comfortable and happy, only so
strangely moods *would* creep in, and desires and
ambitions, and grown-up people would have such
an amazing point of view about boys and mis-
understand their natural impulses so dreadfully
—what he meant was that if he were grown up
and had a boy " he wouldn't be such an ass! "

The trouble of these last three days all began
by his suddenly remembering that he had never
read his holiday task. He did not remember of
himself, but was reminded by Bill Bartlett,
whom he met in the High Street, who said that
the last two days had been miserable for him by
having to swot at his rotten holiday task and that
he didn't know anything about it now!

Jeremy had completely forgotten his. He

hurried home and dragged it forth from its deserted corner. "The Talisman: A Tale of the Crusades," by Sir Walter Scott, Bart.

It was a horrible-looking book with a dark green cover, no pictures, and rows of notes at the end. Jeremy was not as yet a very great reader of anything, being slow and lazy about it and very eager to skip the difficult words.

His favourite two books were "Robinson Crusoe" and "The Swiss Family Robinson," simply because, in those books, people invented things in a jolly way. And after all, any day one might be on a desert island, and it *was* useful to know what to do. Of "Sir Walter Scott, Bart.," he had never in his life heard, nor did he wish to hear of him. Nevertheless, something must be done. Old Thompson took holiday tasks very seriously indeed. Jeremy's report last term had not been a very good one, and father's eye was upon him.

His first idea was that he would get Uncle Samuel to tell him the story; but when he showed his uncle the book, that gentleman waved his paint-brush in the air and said that "Walter was a fine old gentleman who died game, but a rotten writer, and it was a shame to make kids wade through his abominable prose." There was, then, no hope here. Jeremy looked at the book, read half a page, and then threw it at Hamlet.

But the stern truth of the matter was that in such a matter as this, and indeed in most of the concerns of his daily life, he resembled a spy working his way through the enemy's camp, surrounded on every side by foes, compelled to consider every movement, doomed to death and dishonour if he were caught. It had come to it now that there was in practical fact nothing that he desired to do that he was not forbidden to do, and because his school life had given him rules and standards that did not belong to his home life, he criticized at every turn. There was, for instance, this affair of walking in the town by himself. He could understand that Helen and Mary should not go by themselves because there was apparently something mysterious and precious in girls that was destroyed were they left alone for a single moment. But a boy! a boy who had travelled by himself all those miles to a distant county; a boy who, in all probability would be the half-back for the school next term, a boy who in another two years would be at a public school!

What it came to, of course, was that he was continually giving his elders the slip; was, indeed, like the spy in the enemy's country, because every move had to be considered and, at the end, all the excuses ranged in a long row and the most serviceable carefully chosen. And threadbare by now they were becoming!

On this particular afternoon—the first of the last three days of the holidays—he gave Miss Jones and Helen the slip in the market-place. This was to-day easy to do, because it was market day; he knew that Helen was too deeply concerned with herself and her appearance to care whether he were there or no, and that Miss Jones, delighted as she always was with the shops (knowing them by heart and yet never tired of them), would optimistically trust that he would very soon reappear, and at any rate he knew his way home.

He was always delighted with the market on market days. Never, although so constantly repeated, did it lose its savour for him. He adored everything—the cattle and the sheep in their pens, the farmers with their thick broad backs and thick broad sticks talking in such solemn and serious clusters, the avenue down the middle of the market-place where you walked past stall after stall—stalls of vegetables, stalls of meat, stalls of cups and saucers, stalls of china ornaments, stalls of pots and pans, and, best—far best of all—the flower-stalls with their pots of beautiful flowers, their seeds and their tiny plants growing in rows in wooden boxes. But it was not the outside market that was the most truly entrancing. On the right of the market-place there were strange mysterious passages—known to the irreverent as the Catacombs—and here, in a dusk that would, you would have supposed, have precluded any real buying or selling altogether—the true business of the market went on.

It was here, under these dark ages, that in his younger days the toy-shop had enchanted him, and even now, although he would own it to no one alive, the trains and the air-guns seemed to him vastly alluring. There was also a football —too small for him; not at all the football that he wanted to buy—but nevertheless better than nothing at all. He looked at it. The price was eight and sixpence, and he had in his pocket precisely fivepence halfpenny. He sighed, fingered the ball that was hanging in mid-air, and it revolved round and round in the most entrancing manner. The old woman with the moustache who had, it was reputed, ever since the days of Genesis managed the toy-shop, besought him in wheedling tones to purchase it. He could only sigh again, look at it lovingly, twirl it round once more and pass on. He was in that mood when *he must buy something*—an entrancing, delicious and intoxicating mood, a mood that Helen and Mary were in all the time and would continue to remain in it, like the rest of their sex, until the end, for them, of purses, money and all earthly hopes and ambitions.

Next to the toy-stall was a funny old book-stall. Always hitherto he had passed this; not that it was uninteresting, because the old man who kept the place had coloured prints that he stuck, with pins, into the wooden sides of his booth, and these prints were delightful—funny people in old costumes, coaches stuck in the snow, or a number of stout men tumbling about the floor after drinking too much. But the trouble with Mr. Samuel Porter was that he did not change his prints often enough, being, as anyone could see, a man of lazy and indifferent habits; and when Jeremy had seen the same prints for over a year, he naturally knew them by heart.

On this particular day, however, old Mr. Samuel had changed his prints, and there were some splendid new ones in purples and reds and greens, representing skating on the ice, going up in a balloon, an evening in Vauxhall and the fun of the fair. Jeremy stared at these with open mouth, especially at the fun of the fair, which was most amusing because in it a pig was running away and upsetting everybody, just as it might quite easily do here in the market-place. He stood looking, and Mr. Porter, who wore a faded green hat and large spectacles and hated little boys because they never bought anything, but only teased him and ran away, looked at him out of the corner of his eye and dared him to be cheeky. He had no intention whatever of being cheeky; he stared at the

books, all so broken and old and melancholy,
and thought what a dreary thing having to read
was, and how unfortunate about his holiday task,
and how silly of him to have thought of it just
at that moment and so spoiled his afternoon.

He would then have passed on had it not
been by the strangest coincidence that at that
very instant his eye fell on a little pile of books
at the front of the stall, and the book on the
top of the pile had the very name of his holiday
task : "The Talisman," by Sir Walter Scott,
Bart. It was the strangest looking book, very
different indeed from the book at home.

He stared at it as though it was a lucky
charm. How strange that it should be there
and appearing so oddly different from the
book at home. It was dressed in shabby and
faded yellow covers; he picked it up. On the
outside he read in large letters : "Stead's Penny
Classics !" Penny ! Could it be that this book
was only a penny ? Why, if so, he could buy it
and four others like it ! This sudden knowledge
gave him a new proprietary interest in the book,
as when you discover that a stranger at an hotel
lives, when at home, in your own street ! Opening the little book he saw that the print was very
small indeed, that the lines were crooked and
irregular, here very black and there only a dim
grey. But in the very fact of this faint print there
was something mysterious and appealing. No

notes here, of course, and no undue emphasis on
this "Scott, Bart." man, simply "The Talisman," short and sweet.

Old Mr. Porter, observing the unusual sight
of a small boy actually taking a book in his hands
and reading it, was interested. He had seen the
small boy often enough, and although he would
never admit it to himself, had liked his look of
sturdy independence and healthy self-assurance.
He had not thought that the boy was a reader.
He leaned forward :

"Only a penny," he wheezed (he suffered
terribly from asthma, and the boys of the town
used to call after him "Old Barrel Organ"),
"and just the story for a boy like you."

"I'll have it," said Jeremy with sudden
pride. He was of half a mind to buy some of the
others—he saw that one more was by "Scott,
Bart."—but no. He would see how this one was
before he ventured any farther.

He walked off with his prize.

II

That night he did what he had never done
before, he read in bed.

He was doing as he well knew what was absolutely forbidden, and the novelty of the event,
the excitement of his disobedience, the strange

G

wobbly light that the candle flung as it shifted when his movements were very impetuous, in its insecure china saucer, the way the lines of the printed page ran tumultuously together, all these things helped his sense of the romantic.

He had found every line a difficulty in the other edition, now the sense of indulging the forbidden carried him across the first page or two, and then he was fairly inside it! The little book was very difficult to read; not only was it vilely printed, but also the words ran in a kind of cascade down into the very binding of the book, and you had to pull the thing apart as wide as it would go and then peer into the very depths of darkness and obscurity. Nevertheless it was his book, bought with his own money, and he read and read on and on. . . . And in the morning he read again, and in the evening . . . and on the fourth day, late in the night, the candle very low in its china socket, the room lit with sudden flashes of bizarre brilliance, the book was finished.

III

He was dazzled, bewildered. He could think of nothing else at all. The very first meeting of the knights in the desert had marvellously caught his fancy. He had never imagined any-

thing like that, so courteous, so amiable and so
fierce! Just so would he entertain the Dean's
Ernest did he meet him in the desert, sharing
his food and drink with him, complimenting
him on his armour and his horse (he would be
very showy would the Dean's Ernest), and the
next day sticking his spear through his vitals.
Yes, that would be intensely pleasing, but the
trouble would be that the Dean's Ernest would
most certainly not play fair, but would seize
some mean advantage (steal all Jeremy's dates
when he wasn't looking, or give him one in the
back).

Then the visit to the hermit's cave and the
silence of the chapel and the procession of the
wonderful ladies and the dropping of the rose
at Sir Kenneth's feet.

From that point forward Jeremy dwelt
under enchantment. Nothing could take him
from it. And he believed every word of it!
Just as true to him these men and deeds of the
Eastern desert as were the men and deeds of
Orange Street, Polchester. Truer indeed! He
never quite believed in Uncle Samuel and Aunt
Amy and Barbara—but in Sir Kenneth and
King Richard and Edith and Saladin—how
could he not utterly believe?

Saladin! His was the figure that ultimately
emerged from the gilded background of the
picture. Saladin! He became at once Jeremy's

ideal of everything that was beautiful and "like
a man" and brave. He haunted Jeremy's
dreams, he followed him in his walks, came
before him as he ate and drank. He must know
more about him than "Scott, Bart.," told you;
and once again Uncle Samuel was sought.
Jeremy had formed a habit now of dropping into
Uncle Samuel's studio whenever it pleased him.

The other children watched him with eyes
of wonder and desire. Even Aunt Amy was
surprised. She said a little but sniffed a lot, and
told her brother that he "would regret the
day." He laughed and told her that Jeremy
was "the only artist among the lot of them,"
at which Aunt Amy went to Jeremy's father
and told him to be careful because her brother
"was filling the child's head with all sorts of
notions that could do him no possible good."

Jeremy behaved like a saint in his uncle's
studio. He had his own corner of the shabby
sofa where he would sit curled up like a dog.
He chattered on and on, pouring out the whole
of his mind, heart and soul, keeping nothing
back, because his uncle seemed to understand
everything and never made you feel a fool. He
attacked him at once about Saladin and would
not let him alone. In vain Uncle Samuel protested that he knew no history and that Saladin
was a coloured devil as wicked as sin—Jeremy
stuck fast to his ideal—so that at length Uncle

Samuel in sheer self-defence was compelled to turn to a subject about which he did know something, namely the history of the town Polchester in which they were living.

Never to any living soul had Uncle Samuel confided that he cared in the least about the old town; in his heart, nevertheless, he adored it, and for years had he been studying its life and manners. To his grave his knowledge would have gone with him had not Jeremy, in the secrecy of the studio, lured him on.

Then, as though they were dram-drinking together, did the two sit close and talk about the town, and under the boy's eyes the streets blossomed like the rose, the fountains played, the walls echoed to the cries and shouts of armoured men, and the cathedral towers rose ever higher and higher, gigantic, majestic, wonderful, piercing the eternal sky.

Best of all he liked to hear about the Black Bishop, that proud priest who had believed himself greater than the High God, had defeated all his enemies, lived in the castle on the hill above the town like a king, and was at last encircled by a ring of foes, caught in the Cathedral Square, and died there fighting to the end.

Jeremy would never forget one afternoon when he sat on the floor, his head against the shabby sofa, and Uncle Samuel, who was doing something to his paint-box, became carried

away with the picture of his story. He drew for
Jeremy the old town with the gabled roofs and
the balconies and the cobbled roads, and the
cathedral so marvellously alive above it all. As
he talked the winter sun poured into the room
in a golden stream, making the whitewashed
walls swan-colour, turning some old stuffs that
he had hanging over the door and near the
window into wine-red shadow and purple light;
and the trees beyond the high windows were
stained copper against the dusky sky.

Uncle Samuel's voice stopped and the room
slided into grey. Jeremy stared before him and
saw Saladin and the Black Bishop, gigantic
figures hovering over the town that was small
and coloured like a musical box. The cathedral
was a new place to him, no longer somewhere
that was tiresome and dreary on Sunday and
dead all the rest of the week. He longed to go
there by himself, alone, nobody to see what he
would do and hear what he would say. He
would go! He would go! He nodded to himself in the dark.

IV

All very well, but he must be quick about it
if these holidays were to see him bring it off.
Only three days!

Then Aunt Amy announced that she intended on this fine afternoon to pay a call on Miss Nightingale who lived in the Precincts, and to her great surprise Jeremy suggested that he should accompany her.

She was rather flattered, and when it was discovered that Miss Jones and Helen were also going that way and could pick Jeremy up and bring him home, she agreed to the plan. Jeremy and she were old, old enemies; he had insulted her again and again, played jokes upon her, had terrible storms of temper with her; but once, when a wretched little boy had laughed at her, he had fought the little boy and she had never forgotten that. As he grew older something unregenerate in her insisted on admiring him; he was such a thorough boy, so sturdy and manly. She adored the way that his mouth went up at the corners when he laughed; she liked his voice when it was hoarse with a serious effort to persuade somebody of something. Then, although he had so often been rude to her, she could not deny that he was a thorough little gentleman in all that she meant by that term. His manners, when he liked, could be beautiful, quite as good as Helen's and much less artificial. If you cared for boys at all—which Aunt Amy must confess that she did not—then Jeremy was the sort of boy to care for. She had, in fact, both a family and an individual pride in him.

He was very funny to-day walking up the High Street; she could not understand him at all.

"Would you jump, Aunt Amy, if you suddenly saw the Black Bishop on his coal black horse, with his helmet and suit of mail, riding along down the High Street?"

"The Black Bishop? What Black Bishop?"

Was the boy being impertinent to dear Bishop Crozier, whose hair was in any case white, who had certainly never ridden a coal-black horse. . . .

Jeremy carefully explained.

"Oh! the one in the cathedral! Oh! but he was dead and buried long ago!"

"Yes; but if *he should* come to life! He was strong enough for anything."

"What an idea!" She couldn't think where the boy got those strange irreligious ideas from—from her brother Samuel, she supposed!

"The dead don't come back like that, Jeremy dear," she explained gently. "How do you do, Miss Mackenzie? Oh, much better, thank you. It was only a little foolish tooth-ache. It isn't right of us to suppose they do. God doesn't mean us to."

"I don't believe God could stop the Black Bishop coming back if he wanted to," said Jeremy.

Aunt Amy would have been terribly shocked had she not seen a most remarkable hat in Forrest's window that was only thirteen and eleven.

"What did you say, dear? With a little bit of blue at the side. . . . Oh, but you mustn't say that, dear. That's very wicked. God can do everything."

"Saladin didn't believe in God," said Jeremy, winking at Tommy Winchester who was in charge of his mother on the other side of the street. "At least not in your God, or father's. His God. . . ."

"Oh, there's Mrs. Winchester! Take off your hat, Jeremy. I'm sure it's going to snow before I get back. Perhaps Miss Nightingale will be out and I'm sure I shan't be sorry. You mustn't say that, Jeremy. There's only one God."

"But if there's only one God——" he began, then broke off at the sight of a dog, strangely like Hamlet. Not so nice though— not nearly so nice.

He was returning to his consideration of the Deity, the Black Bishop and Saladin, when, behold, they were already in the Precincts.

"Now, you'll be all right, Jeremy dear, won't you, just for a minute or two? Miss Jones can't be long."

All right! Of course he would be all right!

"If you like to wait here and just see, perhaps Miss Nightingale won't be in, and then we could go back together."

No, he thought he wouldn't wait because he had promised Miss Jones who would be on the other side of the cathedral. Very well, then.

He watched his aunt ring Miss Nightingale's very neat little door bell, and saw her then admitted into Miss Nightingale's very neat little house. At that moment the cathedral chimes struck a quarter past four. He stepped across the path, pushed up the heavy leather flap of the great door and entered. Afternoon service, which began at half past three, was just ending. Some special saint's day. Far, far away in the distance the canon's voice beautifully echoed. The choir responded. "The peace of God that passeth all understanding. . . . Passeth all understanding! Passeth all understanding," repeated the thick pillars and the high-arched roof, dove-coloured now in the dusk, and the deep, black-stained seats. "Passeth all understanding! All understanding!" The flagstones echoed deep, deep into the ground. The organ rolled into a voluntary; white flecks of colour splashed for a moment against the screen and were gone. Two or three people, tourists probably, came slowly down the nave, paused for a moment to look at the garrison window with the Christ and the little children, and went out

through the west end door. The organ rolled
on, the only sound now in the building.

Jeremy was suddenly frightened. Strange
that a place which had always seemed to him the
last word in commonplace should now terrify
him. It was different, alive, moving in the
heart of its shadows, whispering.

He walked down the side aisle looking at
every tablet, every monument, every window,
with a new interest. The aliveness of the church
walked with him; it was as though, as he passed
them, they gathered themselves and followed in
a long, grey, silent procession after him. He
reached the side chapel where was the tomb of
the Black Bishop. There he lay, safely enclosed
behind the golden grill, his gauntleted hands
folded on his chest, his spurs on his heels, angels
supporting his head, and grim defiance in his
face.

Jeremy stared and stared and stared again.
About him and around him and above him the
cathedral seemed to grow vaster and vaster.
Clouds of dusk filled it; the colour from the
windows and the tombs and the great gold
trumpeting angels stained the shadows with
patches of light.

Jeremy was cold and shivered; he looked up,
and there, opposite him, standing on the raised
steps leading to the choir, was the Black Bishop.
He was there just as Jeremy had fancied him,

standing, his legs a little apart, one mailed fist resting on his sword, his thick black beard sweeping his breast-plate. He was staring at Jeremy and seemed to be challenging him to move.

The boy could only stare back. Some spirit in him seemed to bid him remember that this was true, whatever soon might disprove it, that the past was the present and the present the past, that nothing ever died, that nothing must frighten him because it survived, and that he must take his share in his inheritance.

All that he really thought was : " I wonder if he'll come nearer." But he did not. Jeremy himself moved and suddenly the whole cathedral stirred, the mist breaking, steps sounding on the flags, voices echoing. No figure was there—only shadow. But here was that horrid fat man, the precentor, who sometimes came to their house to tea.

" Why, my boy, what are you doing here? " he asked in his big superior voice.

" I came in," said Jeremy, still staring at the steps of the choir, " just for a moment."

The precentor put his hand on Jeremy's shoulder. " That's right, my lad," he said. " Study our great church and all its history. You cannot begin too young. Father well, and mother well? "

" Yes," said Jeremy, looking back behind him as he turned away. Oh! but his face had been fine! So strong, like a rock, his sword had shone and his gauntlets! How tall he had been, and how mighty his chest.

"That's right! That's right. Remember me to them when you get home. You must come up and play with my little girls one of these afternoons."

"I'm going back to school," Jeremy said, "day after to-morrow."

"Well, well. That's a pity, that's a pity. Another day, perhaps. Good day to you. Good day."

Chanting, he went along, and Jeremy stood outside the cathedral staring about him. Lights were blowing in the wind; the dusk was blue and grey. The air was thick with armoured men marching in a vast procession across the sky. The wind blew, they flashed downwards in a cloud, wheeling up into the sky again as though under command.

The air cleared; the huge front of the cathedral was behind him, and before him, under the Precinct's lamp, Miss Jones and Helen.

"Why, Jeremy, where have you been? We've been looking for you everywhere. We were just going home."

"Come on," Jeremy growled. "It's late."

CHAPTER V

POODLE

I

I HATE to confess it, but truth forces me—
Hamlet was a snob. With other dogs. Not
with humans. With humans you never could
tell—he would cling to the one and cleave from
the other without any apparent just reason. He
loved the lamplighter of Orange Street, although
he was a dirty, dishevelled rabbit of a man; he
hated Aunt Amy, who was as decent and cleanly
a spinster as England could provide. But with
dogs he was a terrible snob. This, of course, he
had no possible right to be, himself an absolute
mongrel with at least five different breeds peep-
ing now here, now there out of his peculiar body
—nevertheless he did like a dog to be a gentleman, and openly said so. It may have been that
there was in it more of the snobbery of the artist
than of the social striver. What he wanted
was to spend his time with dogs of intelligence,
dogs with *savoir faire*, dogs of enterprise and
ambition. What he could not abide was your
mealy-mouthed, lick-spittle, creeping and crawl-

Poodle 103

ing kind of dog. And he made his opinion very
clear indeed.

Since his master's return for the holidays and
his own subsequent restoration to the upper part
of the house, I am sorry to say that his conceit, already sufficiently large, was considerably
swollen. His master was the most magnificent,
stupendous, successful, all-knowing human to be
found anywhere, and he was the favourite, best-
beloved, most warmly-cherished object of that
master's affections. It followed then that he was
a dog beyond all other dogs.

When he had been a kitchen dog he had
affected a superiority that the other kitchen
dogs of the neighbourhood had found quite
intolerable.

He would talk to none of them, but would
strut up and down inside the garden railings,
looking with his melancholy, contemptuous eyes
at those who invited him without, suffering
himself to be lured neither by lust of food nor
invitation to battle nor tender suggestions of
love. When he became an upstairs dog again,
the other upstairs dogs did not, of course, allow
him to forget his recent status.

But Hamlet was not like other dogs; he had
a humour and sarcasm, a gift of phrase, an enchanting cynicism which very few dogs were able
to resist. He was out of doors now so fre-
quently with Jeremy that he met dogs from

quite distant parts of the town, and a little while
before Christmas made friends with a fine, aristocratic fox-terrier who lived in one of the villas
beyond the high school. This fox-terrier found
Hamlet exactly the companion he desired,
having himself a very pretty wit, but being lazy
withal and liking others to make his jokes for
him.

His name was Pompey, which, as he confided
to Hamlet, was a silly name; but then his mistress was a silly woman, her only merit being
that she adored him to madness. He had as fine
a contempt for most of the other dogs of the
world as Hamlet himself. It passed his com-
prehension that humans should wish to feed and
pet such animals as he found on every side of
him.

He saw, of course, at once, that Hamlet was
a mongrel, but he had, I fancy, an idea that he
should play Sancho Panza to his own Quixote.
He often told himself that it was absurdly beneath his dignity to go about with such a fellow,
but for pretty play of wit, agility in snatching
another dog's bone and remaining dignified as
he did so, for a handsome melancholy and gentle
contempt, he had never known Hamlet's equal.

Hamlet counted it as one of his most successful days when he brought Pompey into the
Orange Street circle. There was not a dog there
but recognized that Pompey was a cut above

them all, a dog who had won prizes and might win prizes yet again (although, between you and me, self-indulgence was already thickening him). All the sycophants in Orange Street (and there, as elsewhere, there were plenty of these creatures) made up at once to Pompey and approached Hamlet with disgusting flatteries. A pug, known as Flossie, slobbered at Hamlet's feet, telling him that she had long been intending to call on him, but that her mistress was so exacting that it was very difficult to find time "for all one's social duties." Hamlet regarded the revolting object (glistening with grease and fat) with high contempt, his beard assuming its most ironical point.

"I had a very nice bone waiting for you in the kitchen," he said.

Flossie shivered. "A bone with you anywhere would be a delight," she wheezed.

Hamlet was, of course, in no way deceived by these flatteries. He knew his world. He watched even his friend Pompey with a good deal of irony. He would have supposed that his friend was too well-bred to care what these poor creatures should say to him; nevertheless Pompey was more pleased than he should have been. He sat there, round the corner, just by the monument, and received the homage with a pleasure that was most certainly not forced. He was himself a little conscious of this. "Awful

H

bore," he explained afterwards to Hamlet, "having to listen to all they had to say. But what's one to do? One can't be rude, you know. One doesn't want to be impolite. And I must say they were very kind."

Hamlet was now restored into the best Orange Street society—all received him back— all with one very important exception. This was a white poodle, the pride and joy of a retired military colonel who lived at 41 Orange Street, and his name was Mephistopheles—Mephisto for short. Ever since Hamlet's first introduction to the Cole family he and this dog had been at war. Mephisto was not a dog of the very highest breed, but his family was quite good enough. And then, being French, he could say a good deal about his origins and nobody could contradict him. He did not, as a fact, say very much. He was too haughty to be talkative, too superior to be familiar. He had no friends. There *was* a miserable Dachs, Fritz by name, who claimed to be a friend, but everyone knew how Mephisto laughed at Fritz when he was not there, calling him opprobrious names and commenting on his German love of food.

From the very first Mephisto had seemed to Hamlet an indecent dog. The way that he was here naked and there over-hairy had nothing to be said for it. His naked part was quite pink.

Then Mephisto had the French weakness of

parsimony. Never was there a meaner dog. He stored bones as no dog had a right to do, and had never been known to give anything to anybody. Then he had the other French weakness of an incapacity for friendship. The domestic life might perhaps appeal to him strongly (no one knew whether he were married or not), but friendship meant nothing to him.

He was as are all the French, practical, unsentimental, seeing life as it really is and allowing no nonsense. If he had those French defects he had also the great French virtue of courage. He was afraid of nothing and of no one. No dog was too big for him, and he once had a fight with a St. Bernard who happened to stroll down his way that was historic.

He was no coward, as Hamlet very well knew —but how Hamlet hated him! All his fur bristled if Mephisto was within half a mile. Mephisto's superior smile, his contempt at the rather sentimental enthusiasms to which Hamlet occasionally gave vent (that went, as they often do, with his cynicism), these made a conflict inevitable.

II

The actual cause of the conflict was Pompey. We all know how very trying it is to make a fine friend, to introduce him into our own circle,

and then to discover him, when he is nicely
settled, making more of others than of ourselves
—neglecting us, in fact.

This was exactly what Pompey did. He
grew a little weary of Hamlet's humour (he
became very quickly tired of experiences), and he
was not at all sure that Hamlet was not laughing at himself. He was flattered by Mephisto's
attitude that at last he had found a dog in the
town worthy to be his companion. He did not
care very much for Mephisto—he found his
French conceit very trying—but it *was* true
that Hamlet was a mongrel of the mongrels,
and that it was absurd that he, a dog who had
taken prizes, should be with him so continually
in public.

Obviously, it was impossible that he should
be friends *both* with Mephisto and Hamlet, so
quite simply he chose Mephisto.

Hamlet was most deeply hurt. He was hurt
not only for himself (he had a sensitive and
affectionate nature), but also that so well-bred
a dog as Pompey should take up with a French
animal who had all the faults of his race and
very little of its intelligence. He had one short,
sharp altercation with Pompey, told him one
or two home truths, and left him.

For a week or two he avoided the company
of his kind and devoted himself to his master.
All this occurred at Christmas-time, when

Jeremy was in disgrace for the buying of
Christmas presents with money not really his
own. Jeremy thought, of course, that Hamlet
had noticed his misfortunes, and was trying in
his own way to express his sympathy for them.
Master and dog were very close together during
those weeks. While Hamlet sat at his master's
feet, pressing his thick body close up against
his master's leg, staring in front of him, half
asleep, half awake, seeing bones and cats and
rabbits, and near these Mephisto with his naked
patches and the treacherous Pompey, Jeremy
thought that he was considering only his
master's unhappiness. He was thinking a
little of that, but for the most part he was
meditating revenge.

He must fight Mephisto. For a long time
now it had been coming to that. He was
compelled to confess that at the first positive
thought of the definite fact he shivered with
apprehension. After all, no one is truly brave
who has not known fear, and Hamlet, sitting
staring into the schoolroom fire, knew fear in
no half measure. Then the thoughts of the
insults he had received stirred him—let him
only be angry enough and he would forget his
fear—and the very thought of Mephisto made
him angry.

He had one staunch, unfaltering little friend
among the dogs of the neighbourhood. This

was an unimportant nondescript little fox-terrier, the property of the hairdresser at the bottom of Orange Street. His name was Bobby. There was nothing at all to distinguish Bobby from all the dogs in the world—he was one of those ill-bred, colourless fox-terriers who are known to their masters only by sterling character. He had suffered every sort of indignity in his time : stones had been thrown at him, kettles had been tied to his tail, cats had scratched his eyes, his master (who often drank too much) kicked and abused him; but he had an indomitable spirit, an essential gaiety of heart that no troubles could quench. He was not admitted into the hierarchy of Orange Street dogs—even Flossie did not permit herself to be aware of his existence—but he hung about always in a good humour, always ready to do anyone a good turn, and often just rolling over and over in the road at the sheer joy of life. At the first glimpse of Hamlet he had lost his heart to him. Hamlet had not been so kind to him as he should have been, but he had not rebuffed him as the other dogs had done, and had gone with him once all the way down to the hairdresser's to see the hairdresser's baby, of whose strength and appearance Bobby was inordinately proud. Now, in these days of Hamlet's trouble Bobby showed the true mettle of his pasture. He longed that

Pompey might speak to him so that he might show him what he thought of him.

"You mustn't let this worry you too much," he said to Hamlet. "I've been through far worse things than this. It simply shows that Pompey, in spite of his high breeding, is worth nothing at all."

"I'm going to fight Mephisto," said Hamlet.

Bobby's eyes opened wide at that and he looked up from the old and very dirty bone that he was investigating.

"Fight Mephisto!" he repeated. "That's a tall order."

"Never mind," said Hamlet firmly. "It's got to be done, and you've got to help me."

III

When Fate intends something to occur she very quickly provides the opportunity. The opportunity in this instance was Bobby.

His was a most sociable soul. We all know dogs whose whole interest in life is social; they are not as a rule very popular with their masters, it being said of them that they care for one as much as another, and will leap with friendly gestures upon the hostile burglar as eagerly as they will upon the most important person in the household.

Bobby was not that kind of dog; he really did care for his hairdresser and his hairdresser's wife and baby and for Hamlet more than any other humans or any other dog in the world. But he was miserable when he was alone; he must have company. His only family was a very busy and preoccupied one, and he did not wish to bore Hamlet with too much of his own society.

The Orange Street dogs had their most accustomed meeting-place at a piece of deserted garden just behind the monument at the top of the hill. Here it was shady in hot weather and comfortable and cosy in chill; they were secure from rude boys and tiresome officials, and there was no large house near enough to them for servants to come out and chase them away. It was, it was true, on the whole the second-class dogs who gathered there; Mephisto but seldom put in an appearance, and therefore those sycophants, Flossie and Fritz, hinted that it was a commonplace crowd and beneath them. Moreover, it was never very easy for Mephisto to escape far from his own home, as his master, the colonel, was so proud of him and so nervous of losing him that he could not bear to let him out of his sight.

It happened, however, one fine morning, a few days after Christmas, that the colonel was in bed with a catarrh (he was a very hypochondriacal gentleman), and Mephisto, meeting Pompey in the street, they wandered amicably together in the direction of the monument. Mephisto was very ready to show himself in public, having been to the barber's only the day before. He was inordinately proud of the second tuft at the end of his tail, at the gleaming white circle of hair round his neck, and the more the pink skin showed through in his naked parts the happier he was. He really thought there was not such another dog in the world as himself this fine morning, being a provincial and narrow-minded dog in spite of his French origin.

Mephisto and Pompey trotted up Orange Street together, and Flossie, who was always on the look-out from behind her garden railing for the passing of Mephisto, was graciously allowed to join them. She wheezed along with them, puffing herself up and swelling with self-importance. The conversation chanced to turn upon Hamlet. Mephisto said that now that he and Pompey were friends, he would really like to ask him a question that had been often in his mind, and that was how it came about that Pompey could ever have allowed himself such a common, vulgar friend as Hamlet. Pompey replied that he felt that that was a just and fair question for his friend to ask him, and he could only reply that the fellow had seemed at

first to have a coarse sort of humour that was
diverting for the moment. One tired naturally
of the thing very quickly, and the trouble was
with these coarse-grained creatures that when
you tired of them, having given them a little
encouragement at first out of sheer kindness,
it was exceedingly difficult to shake them off
again. The fellow had seemed lonely, and
Pompey had taken pity upon him; he would
see to it that it should be a long time before
he did such a thing again. Mephisto said that
he was glad to hear this. For himself, he had
never been able to abide the creature, and
he could only trust that he would soon be
ridden over by a cart or poisoned by a
burglar or thrown into the river by a couple
of boys.

When they arrived at the monument they
found several dogs among the trees flattering
and amusing an elegant creature called Trixie,
who was young and handsome and liked flirta-
tions. Bobby also was there, rolling about on the
grass, performing some of his simple tricks, like
snapping at three imaginary flies at once, tossing into the air a phantom bone, and lying stiff
on his back with his four legs stiffly in the air.
He had been happy until the two aristocrats
arrived; now he knew that his good time was
over. He should have gone away, but something kept him—he did so hate to be alone—

and so he sat on, a silly grin on his rather foolish face, listening to the conversation.

While several of the dogs continued to wander about after the idiotic Trixie, who was as arch and self-conscious as a dog could very well be, the conversation of the rest belaboured poor Hamlet. It is well for us that we do not hear the criticism that goes on behind our backs; one and all of us, we are in the same box. Did we hear we should watch the gradual creation of so strange and unreal a figure that we should rub our eyes in amazement, crying, "Surely, surely this cannot be us!"

Not the tiniest shred of character was soon left to Hamlet. He was a thief, a drunkard, a wanton and upstart, a coward and a mongrel. Bobby listened to all of this, growing with every word of it more uncomfortable. He hated them all, but it would need immense pluck to speak up for his friend, and he did not know whether by so venturing he might not effect more harm than good.

The sight, however, of Mephisto's contemptuous supercilious face, his tufted tail, his shining patches drove him on. He burst out, barking that Hamlet was the bravest, the finest of all the dogs in the town, that he was honourable to a fault, loyal and true, that he was worth all the dogs there together.

When he had finished there was an explosion

of derisive barks; as he heard them internally
he trembled. For a large fortune of bones he
would have wished to sink his pride and run.
He stood his ground, however. With one
directing bark from Mephisto they set upon him.
They rolled him over. Their teeth were in his
ears, his eyes, his belly. He gave himself up for
lost. At that very instant Hamlet appeared
upon the scene.

IV

He had not intended to go that way, but
finding that his master was occupied with those
two supremely unattractive and uninteresting
humans, his sisters, he thought that he would
pursue an interesting smell that he had noticed
in the direction of the High School during the
last two days. Far behind him were his childish
times when he had supposed that rabbit lurked
round every corner, and he had succeeded now in
analysing almost every smell in his consciousness.
As we are raised to the heights of our poor
imagination by great poetry, great music and
great pictures, so is the dog aroused to his divine
ecstasy by smell. With him a dead mouse
behind the wainscot may take the place that
Shelley's "Skylark" assumes with us, and
Bach's fugues are to us what grilled haddock
was to Hamlet—*Tot homines tot. . . .*

He had not, however, gone far towards the
High School when he recognized Bobby's bark,
and Bobby's bark appealing for help. When
he turned the corner he saw that his fate was
upon him. Mephisto was a little apart, watching the barking and struggling heap of dogs,
himself uttering no sound, but every once and
again pretending to search for a fly in the tuft
of his tail that he might show to all the world
that he was above and beyond vulgar street rows.

And at sight of him Hamlet knew that
what he had hoped would be was. The sight
of Mephisto's contempt, combined with the
urgency of poor Bobby's appeals, roused all the
latent devil in him. Twitching his beard, feeling no fear, knowing nothing but a hatred and
loathing for his enemy, he walked across the
grass and approached Mephisto. The poodle
paused for a moment from his search for the
fly, looked round, saw whom it was (he had, of
course, known from the first) and resumed his
search.

Hamlet went up to him, sniffed him deliberately and with scorn, then bit his tail in
its tenderest and most naked part. The other
dogs, even in the most dramatic moment of their
own scuffle, were at once aware that something
terrible had occurred. They allowed Bobby to
rise, and turned towards the new scene.
Mephisto was indeed a fearful sight; every hair

on his head seemed to be erect, the naked
patches burned with a curious light, his legs
were stiff as though made of iron, and from his
throat proceeded the strangest, most threatening
growl ever uttered by dog.

And now Hamlet, pray to the gods of your
forefathers, if indeed you know who any of them
were! Gather to your aid every principle of
courage and fortitude you have ever collected,
and, better than they, summon to yourself all
the tricks and delicacies of warfare that during
your short life you have gained by your experience, for indeed to-day you will need them
all! Think not of the meal that only an hour
ago you have, in the event, most unwisely eaten,
pray that your enemy also may have been con-
suming food; remember that you are fighting
for the weak and the undertrodden, for the
defenceless and humble-hearted, and better still
than that, you are fighting for yourself because
you have been insulted and the honour of your
very nondescript family called in question!

The other dogs recognized at once that this
was no ordinary contest, and it was difficult for
them to control their excitement. This they
showed with little snappy barks and quiverings
of the body, but they realized that too much
noise would summon humans on to the scene and
stop the fight. Of them all Bobby was the most
deeply concerned. Bleeding though he was in

one ear, he jumped from foot to foot, snivelling with terror and desire, yapping hysterically to encourage his friend and hero, watching every movement with an interest so active that he almost died of unnatural repression.

To Hamlet, after the first moment of contact, impressions were confused. It was, unfortunately, the first important fight of his life, and he had not, alas, very much experience to guide him. But somewhere in his mixed and misty past there had been a bulldog ancestor, and his main feeling from the beginning to the end was that he must catch on with his teeth somewhere and then hold and never let go again. This principle at first he found difficult to follow. Tufts of white hair disgustingly choked him, his teeth slipped on the bare places, and it seemed strangely difficult to stand on his own feet. The poodle pursued a policy of snap, retreat, and come again. He was always on the stir, catching Hamlet's ear, wrenching it, then slipping away and suddenly seizing a hind leg. He was a master of this art, and it seemed to him that his victory was going to be very easy. First he had one of his enemy's ears, then the other, now a foot, now the hair of his head, now one of his eyes. . . . His danger was, as he knew, that he was not in good condition, being overfed by his master the colonel, and loving a soft and lazy life. He recognized that he had been

in a far better state two years before when he
had fought the St. Bernard.

But poor Hamlet's case was soon very bad
indeed. He was out of breath and panting;
the world was swinging round him, the grass
seeming to meet the sky, and the audience of
dogs to float in mid-air. All his attacks missed;
he could no longer see; blood was flowing from
one eye and one ear; he suddenly realized that
the poodle meant to kill and it did not seem at
all impossible but that he should achieve that.
The love of life was strong upon him. Behind
his fighting there was his dear master and his love
for him, the world with its hunts and smells and
soft slumbers and delicious food, the place where
he slept, the rooms of the house where he lived,
the lights and the darks, the mists and the flashing stars—all these things ranged through his
sub-conscious mind, only consciously forming
behind his determination not to die and, in any
case, to hold on to the last, if only, yes, if only
he could find something on to which he might
hold.

The poodle's teeth were terribly sharp, and
Hamlet seemed to be bitten in a thousand places.
Worst of all, something had happened to one of
his hind-legs so that it trembled under him, and
he was afraid lest soon he should not be able to
stand. Once down, he knew that it would be
all over with him. His throat was dry, his head

a burning fire, his heart a recording hammer, and the world was now, in very truth, reeling round and round like a flying star. He knew that Mephisto was now certain of victory; he could feel the hot breath of that hated triumph upon his face. Worst of all there was creeping upon him a terrible lassitude, so that he felt as though nothing mattered if only he might lay him down and sleep. Sleep . . . sleep. . . . His teeth snapped feebly. His body was one vast pain. . . . Now he was falling. . . . His legs were trembling. He was done, finished, beaten.

At that last moment he heard, as though from an infinite distance, Bobby's encouraging bark.

"Go on! Go on!" the bark cried. "You're not finished yet. He's done too. One more effort and you'll bring it off."

He made one more effort, something colossal, worthy of all the heroes, bracing the whole of his body together, beating down his weakness, urging all the flame and fire of his spirit. He launched out with his body, snapped with his teeth, and at last, at last they fastened upon something, upon something wiry and skinny, but also soft and yielding.

If this time his teeth had slipped it would indeed have been the end, but they held. They held, they held, *they held*—and it was the poodle's tail that they were holding.

I

He felt Mephisto's body swing round—
so weak was he that he swung round with it.
His teeth clenched, clenched and clenched.
Mephisto screamed, a curious, undoglike, almost
human scream. Hamlet's teeth clenched and
clenched and clenched; tighter and tighter they
held. They met. Something was bitten
through.

Mephisto's whole body seemed to collapse.
His fund of resistance was gone. Something
white was on the ground. The end of the tail,
with its famous, magnificent, glorious, superb,
white tuft was no longer attached to Mephisto's
body.

The poodle gave one cry, a dreadful, un-
earthly, ghostly cry of terror, shame and aban-
donment, then, his tail between his legs, ran
for his very life.

v

Ten minutes later Jeremy, looking out of
the schoolroom window, beheld, tottering up
the garden, a battered, dishevelled dog. A little
trail of blood followed his wavering course.

Hamlet looked up at the window, saw his
master, feebly wagged his tail and collapsed.

But as he collapsed he grinned.

CHAPTER VI

THE NIGHT RAIDERS

I

IT will be always difficult to understand what drove Jeremy into this adventure. That on the very last night but one of his Christmas holidays, when he had every good reason for placating the powers and when he did, of his own nature, desire that he should leave everything behind him in the odour of sanctity, that at such a time he should take so wild and unnecessary a risk will always and for ever be a deep mystery.

The end of these holidays he especially desired to clothe in tranquillity because of the painful manner in which they had begun. He really did wish to live at peace with his fellow men, and especially with his mother and father. His mother was easy, but his father!

How were they ever to see the same way about anything? And yet he detected in himself a strange pathetic desire to be liked by his father and himself to like in return; had he only known it, his father felt precisely the same towards himself—but the gulf of two generations was between them.

Indeed, on that very morning Mr. Cole had had a conversation with his brother-in-law Samuel about his son Jeremy. Mr. Cole was never at ease with his brother-in-law. He distrusted artists in general—his idea was that they were wasting the time that God had given them —and he distrusted his brother-in-law in particular because he thought that he often laughed at him, which indeed he often did.

"I'm unhappy about Jeremy," he said, looking at Samuel's blue smock with dissatisfaction. He did wish that Samuel wouldn't wear his painting clothes at breakfast-time.

"Why?" asked Samuel.

"I don't think the boy's improving. School seems to be doing him no good."

"Take him away, then," said Samuel.

"Really," said Mr. Cole, "I wish you wouldn't joke about these things. He must go to school."

"Send him to another school if this one isn't satisfactory."

"No. Thompson's is a good school. I'm afraid it's in the boy, not the school, that the fault lies."

Samuel Trefusis said nothing.

"Well, don't you see what I mean about the boy?" Mr. Cole asked irritably.

"No, I don't. I think the boy perfectly delightful. I don't as a rule like boys. In fact, I detest them. I've come slowly to Jeremy, but now I'm quite conquered by him. He's a baby in many ways still, of course, but he has extraordinary perceptions, is brave, honest, amusing and delightful to look at."

"Honest," said Mr. Cole gloomily, "that's just what I'm not sure about. That affair of the money at the beginning of the holidays."

"Really, Herbert," Samuel broke in indignantly, "if you'll allow me to say so— and even if you won't—you were wrong in that affair from first to last. You never gave the boy a chance. You concluded he was guilty from the first moment. The boy thought he had a right to the money. You bullied and scolded him until he was terrified, and then wanted him to apologize. Twenty years from now parents will have learnt something about their children—the children are going to teach them. Your one idea of bringing up Jeremy is to forbid him to do everything that his natural instincts urge him to do.

"He is a perfectly healthy, affectionate, decent boy. He'll do you credit, but it won't be your merit if he does. It will be in spite of what you've done—not because of it."

Mr. Cole was deeply shocked.

"Really, Samuel, this is going too far. As

you've challenged me, I may say that I've
noticed, and Amy also has noticed, that you're
doing the boy no good by petting him as
you are. It's largely because you are always
inviting the boy into that studio of yours and
encouraging him in the strangest ideas that he
has grown as independent as he has. I don't
think you're a wholesome influence for the boy.
I don't indeed."

Samuel's face closed like a box. He was
very angry. He would have liked, as he would
have liked on many other occasions, to say,
"Very well, then, I leave your house in the
next five minutes," but he was lazy, had very
little money, and adored the town, so he simply
shrugged his shoulders.

"You can forbid him to speak to me if
you like," he said.

Mr. Cole was afraid of his brother-in-law,
so all he said was : "I shall write to Thompson
about him."

II

Meanwhile this awful adventure had suddenly
leaped up in front of Jeremy like a Jack-in-
the-box. Like many of the most daring
adventures, its origin was simple. Four days
earlier there had been a children's afternoon
party at the Dean's. The Dean's children's

parties were always dreary affairs because of Mrs. Dean's neuralgia and because the Dean thought that his share of the affair was over when he had poked his head into the room where they were having tea, patted one or two innocents on the head (they became instantly white with self-consciousness), and then said in a loud, generous voice: "Well, my friends, enjoying yourselves? That's right"—after which he returned to his study. The result of this was that his guests were as sheep without a shepherd. The Dean's children were too young to do much, and the girls' governess too deeply agitated by her fancy that children's parents were staring at her arrogantly to pull herself together and be amiable. It was during one of those catch-as-catch-can intervals, when children were desultorily wandering, boys sticking pins into stout feminine calves, girls sniggering in secret conclave together, infants howling to be taken home, that Jeremy overheard Bill Bartlett say to the Dean's Ernest: "I dare you!"

Jeremy pricked up his ears at once. Anything in which the Dean's Ernest (his foe of foes) was concerned incited him to rivalry. He was terribly bored by the party; not only was it a bad, dull party, but ever since his first real evening ball children's afternoon parties had seemed to him stupid and without reason.

" I don't care," said the Dean's Ernest.

" I dare you," repeated Bill Bartlett.

" I'm not frightened," said Ernest.

" Then do it," said Bill.

" You've got to come too."

" Pooh ! " said Bill, " that's nothing. I've done lots more than that."

Ernest quite plainly disliked the prospect of his daring, and, catching sight of Jeremy, he shifted his ground.

" Young Cole wouldn't dare," he said.

" Yes, he would," said Bartlett; " he dares more than you dare."

" No, he doesn't," said the Dean's Ernest indignantly.

" Yes, he does."

" You dare more than Sampson dares, don't you, Cole? " said Bill.

" Of course I do," said Jeremy, without a moment's hesitation.

" Well, do it then," said the Dean's Ernest swiftly.

It appeared on further examination that Bartlett had dared young Sampson to walk round the cathedral twice just as the clocks were striking midnight. It was obvious at once that this involved quite terrifying dangers. Apart altogether from the ghostly prospect of walking round the cathedral at midnight, there was the escape from the house, the danger of

the police and the return to the house. Jeremy
saw at once all that was involved, but because
the Dean's Ernest was there and staring at
him from under his pale eyebrows with
arrogant contempt, he said at once :

" I dare."

Tommy Winchester, who was complaining
bitterly about the food provided, was soon
drawn into the challenge, and although his
stout cheeks quivered at the prospect (Major
Winchester, his father, was the sternest of
disciplinarians) he had to say : " I dare."

Details were then settled. It was to be
three nights from that day; they were to meet
just outside the west door as the clock struck
twelve, to walk or run twice round the
cathedral, and then find their way home again.

" I bet young Cole doesn't come," Jeremy
heard Ernest say loudly to Bill as they parted.

Of course after that he would go, but when
he reached home and considered it he was
miserable. To end the holidays with such a
risk truly appalled him. From every point of
view it was madness. Even though he escaped
through the pantry window (he knew that he
could push up the catch and then drop into the
garden without difficulty), there was all the
danger of his absence being discovered while he
was away. Then there was the peril of a policeman finding them and reporting them; then

there was the return, with the climb back into
the pantry and the noisy crawl (you never knew
when a board was going to creak) back into
his room again. He had no illusion at all as
to what would happen if his father caught
him : that would simply sign and seal his
disgrace once and for ever. But worse—far
worse to him—was what Uncle Samuel would
feel. Uncle Samuel had simply been wonderful
to him during these holidays. He adored
Uncle Samuel. Uncle Samuel had, as it were,
" banked " on his honour and integrity, when
all the rest of the world doubted it. Uncle
Samuel loved him and believed in him. He
had a momentary passionate impulse to go to
Uncle Samuel and tell him everything. But
he knew what the consequence of that must be;
Uncle Samuel would persuade him not to go,
would, indeed, make him give his word that he
would not go; then for ever would he be
disgraced in the eyes of Bill Bartlett, Tommy
Winchester and the others, and the Dean's
Ernest would certainly never allow him to hear
the last of it. It was possible that the others
would fail at the final moment and would not
be there, but he must be there. Yes, he must,
he must—even though death and torture awaited
him as the consequence of his going.

Had he not trusted Bartlett he might have
thought the whole thing a plot on the part of

the Dean's Ernest to put him into a dangerous position, but Bartlett was a friend of his and the challenge was genuine.

As the dreadful hour approached he became more and more miserable. Everyone noticed his depression, and thought it was because he was going back to school. Aunt Amy was quite touched.

" Never mind, Jeremy dear," she said ; " it will soon be over. The weeks will pass, and then you will be home with us again. It won't seem so bad when you're there."

He said, " No, Aunt Amy," quite mildly. One of the worst things was deceiving his mother. She had not played so great a part in his life since his going to school, but she was always there, quiet and sensible and kind, helping him about his clothes, soothing him when he was angry, understanding him when he was sad, laughing with him when he was happy, comfortable and consoling always ; like Uncle Samuel, believing in him. He remembered still with the utmost vividness the terror that he had been in two years ago, when she had nearly died just after Barbara's arrival. Because she was so safely there he did not think much about her, but when a crisis came, when things were difficult at school, she was always the first person who came to his mind.

The evening arrived, and as he went up to

bed his teeth positively chattered. It seemed
a fine night, but very dark, he thought, as he
looked out through the landing window.
Hamlet gaily followed him upstairs. He was
only now recovering from the terrific fight that
he had had a week or so ago with the poodle,
and one of his ears was still badly torn and he
limped a little on one foot. Nevertheless, he
was in high spirits and gambolled all the way
up the stairs, suddenly stopping to bark under
the landing window, as he always did when he
was in high spirits, chasing an imaginary piece
of paper all the way up the last flight of stairs,
and pausing outside Jeremy's bedroom door,
panting and heaving, his tongue hanging out
and a wicked look of pleasure in his sparkling
eyes.

Here indeed was a new problem. Hamlet!
What would happen if he suddenly awoke,
discovered his master's absence, and began to
bark? Or suppose that he awoke when Jeremy
was leaving his room, and determined to follow
him? Jeremy, at these thoughts, felt his spirits
sink even lower than they had been before.
How could he in this thing escape disaster?
He was like a man doomed. He hated the
Dean's Ernest at that moment with a passion
that had very little of the child in it.

He took off his coat and trousers and
climbed into bed. Hamlet jumped up, moved

round and round for some moments, scratching and sniffing as he always did until he had found a place to his mind; then, with a little contented sigh, curled up and went to sleep. Jeremy lay there with beating heart. He heard half-past nine strike from St. John's, then ten, then half-past. For a little while he slept, then awoke with a start to hear it strike eleven. No sound in the house save Hamlet's regular snores. A new figure leapt in front of him. The policeman! A terrible giant of a man, with a great stick and a huge lantern.

"What are you doing here, little boy?" he cried. "Come with me to the police station!"

Jeremy shivered beneath the bedclothes. Perspiration beaded his forehead, and his legs gave curious little jerks from the knees downwards as though they had a life of their own with which he had nothing to do.

Half-past eleven struck. Very carefully he got out of bed, watching Hamlet out of the corner of his eye, put on his coat, his trousers and his boots, stole to the door and paused. Hamlet was still snoring peacefully. He crept out, then remembered that to do this properly one must take off one's boots and carry them in one's hand. Too late now for that. Downstairs he went; at every creak he paused; the house was like a closed box around him. From some room far away came loud, impatient snores. Once he stumbled and nearly fell; he stayed there, his hands on the banisters, a dead man save for the beating of his heart.

His hand was on the pantry window, he had pushed back the catch, climbed through, and in another moment was in the garden.

III

It was a very dark night. The garden gate creaked behind him as though accusing him of his wicked act; the darkness was so thick that you had to push against it as though it were a wall.

At first he ran, then the whole world seemed to run after him, trees, houses and all, so he stopped and walked slowly. The world seemed gigantic; he was not as yet conscious of fear, but only suspicious of the presence of that gigantic policeman taking step with him, inch by inch, flicking his dark lantern, now here, now there, rising like a Jack-in-the-box suddenly above the trees and peering down upon him.

Then, when for the moment he left the houses behind him and began to walk up Green Lane towards the cathedral, his heart failed him. How horrible the trees were! All shapes and sizes; towers of castles, masts of ships,

animals, pigs and hens and lions blowing a little
in the night breezes, becking and bowing above
him, holding out horrible, long, skinny fingers
towards him, sometimes closing in upon him,
then moving, fan-wise, out again. In fact, he
was now completely miserable. With the dreadful finality of childhood he saw himself as con-
demned for life. By this time Hamlet, having
discovered his absence, had barked the house
awake. Already, perhaps, with lanterns they
had started to search for him. The awful
moment of discovery would come. Even Uncle
Samuel would abandon him; nobody would ever
be kind to him again.

At this point it was all that he could do to
keep back the tears. His teeth were chattering,
he had a crick in his back, he was very cold, the
heel of one shoe rubbed his foot. And he was
frightened! Bet your life but he was frightened!
He hadn't known that it would be like this, so
silent and yet so full of sound, so dark and yet
so light and alive with strange quivering lights,
so cold and yet so warm with an odd, pressing
heat! There were no lamps lit in the town
below him (all lights out at ten o'clock in the
Polchester of thirty years ago), and the cathedral loomed up before him a heavy black mass,
threatening to fall upon him like the mountain
in the Bible. Now the trees were coming to
an end—here was a house and there another. A

light in one window, but, for the rest, the
houses quite dead like coffins. He came into
Bodger Street, past the funny old-fashioned
turnstile that led into Canon's Yard over the
cobble-stones of that ancient square, through
the turnstile at the other end and into the
Precincts. He was there! Shivering and
frightened, but there! He had kept his word.

As he crossed the grass a figure moved forward from the shadow of the cathedral and came
to meet him. It was Tommy Winchester. It
immensely cheered Jeremy to see him; it also
cheered him to see that if he was frightened
Tommy was a great deal more so. Tommy's
teeth were chattering so that he could scarcely
speak, but he managed to say that it was
beastly cold, and that he had upset a jug of
water getting out of his bedroom, and that a
dog had barked at him all the way along the
Precincts, and that he was sure his father would
beat him. They were joined a moment later
by another shivering mortal, Bartlett. A more
unhappy trio never met together in the world's
history. They were too miserable for conversation, but simply stood huddled together
under the great buttress by the west door and
waited for the clock to strike.

The only thing that Bartlett said was: " I
bet Sampson doesn't come! " At that Jeremy's
heart gave a triumphant leap. How splendid

it would be if the Dean's Ernest funked it!
Of course he *would* funk it, and would have
some long story about his door being closed or
having a headache, some lie or other!

Nevertheless, they strained their eyes across
the dark wavering lake of the Precincts watching
for him.

" I'm so cold," Tommy said through his
chattering teeth. Then suddenly, as though
struck by a gun: " I'm going to sneeze! "

And he did sneeze, an awful shattering,
devastating sound with which the cathedral,
and indeed the whole town, seemed to shake.
That was an awful moment. The boys stood,
holding their breath, waiting for all the black
houses to open their doors and all the townsmen
to turn out in their nightshirts with lanterns
(just as they do in the *Meistersinger*, although
that, of course, the boys did not know) crying:
" Who's that who sneezed? Where did the
sneeze come from? What was that sneeze? "

Nothing happened save that the silence was
more awful than before. Then there was a
kind of whirring noise above their heads, a
moment's pause, and the great cathedral clock
began to strike midnight.

" Now," said Bartlett, " we've got to walk
or run round the cathedral twice."

He was off, and Tommy and Jeremy after
him.

J

Jeremy was a good runner, but this was like
no race that he had ever engaged in before.
As he ran the notes boomed out above his
head and the high shadow of the great building
seemed to catch his feet and hold him. He
could not see, and, as before, when he ran the
rest of the world seemed to run with him, so
that he was always pausing to hear whether
anyone were moving with him or no.

Then quite suddenly he was alone, and
frightened as he had never in his life been
before; no, not when the horrible sea captain
had woken him in the middle of the night, not
when he thought that God had killed Hamlet,
not when he had first been tossed in a blanket
at Thompson's, not when he had first played
second-half in a real game and had to lie down
and let ten boys kick the ball from under him!

His body was turned to water. He could
not move. The shadows were so vast around
him, the ground wavered beneath his feet, the
trees on the slopes below the cathedral all
nodded as though they knew that terrible things
would soon happen to him—and there was no
sound anywhere. What he wanted was to creep
close to the cathedral, clutch the stone walls,
and stay there. That was what he nearly did,
and if he had done it he would have been there,
I believe, until this very day. Then he remembered the Dean's Ernest who had been too

frightened to come, he remembered that he had been "dared" to run round the cathedral twice, and that he had only as yet run half round it once. His stockings were down over his ankles, both his boots now hurt him, he had lost his cap; he summoned all the pluck that there was in his soul and body combined and ran on.

When he had finished his first round and was back by the west door again, there was no sign of the other two boys. He paused desperately for breath; then, as though pursued by all the evil spirits of the night, started again. This time it did not seem so long. He shut his ears to all possible sound, refused to think, and the physical pain of the stitch in his side and his two rubbed heels kept him from grosser fear. Then, just as he completed the second round, the most awful thing happened. A figure, an enormous figure it seemed to poor Jeremy, rose out of the ground, a figure with flapping wings; a great light was flashed in the air; a strange, high voice screamed aloud. The figure moved towards him. That was enough for his courage. As though death itself were behind him, he took to his heels, tore across the grass, plunged through the stile into Parson's Yard.

The little shadow had been like a curve of wind on the grass. High in the air rose the cry:

" A windy night and all clear! A windy
night and all clear! " and the night-watchman,
his thoughts upon the toasted cheese that would
in another half-hour be his reward, pressed
round the corner of the cathedral.

IV

And Jeremy ran on! How he ran! He
stumbled, nearly fell, recovered himself, felt
no pain in his legs or side, only fear, fear,
fear! As he ran he was saying :

" I must get back! Oh, I must get back!
I must be home. . . . I must get back! " and
did not know that he was saying anything
at all.

Then suddenly in the middle of Grass Lane
he recovered himself and stood. How still and
quiet everything was! A few stars were breaking through the clouds. The rustling of the
trees now was friendly and reassuring, and
there was a soft undertone in the air as though
a thousand streams were running beneath his
feet.

He stood, panting, loving to feel the stroke
of the little wind against his hot cheek. What
was that that had frightened him? Whom
could it have been?

But gradually the centre of interest was

shifting. The past was the past. He had done what he had said he would do. Now for the future. He shivered as it came to him in its full force, then squared his shoulders and marched on. He would meet whatever it might be, and anyway he was going to school the day after to-morrow. . . .

Time moved quickly then. He was soon passing the High School, the world completely dead now on every side of him; then there was his old friend the monument; then the row of houses in which his own home stood. He closed the garden gate very carefully behind him, stole up the path, found the ledge stone below the pantry window, then felt for the ledge.

His heart ceased to beat: the catch was fastened. Someone, then, *had* discovered his absence! The house seemed to be dark and silent enough, but they were lying in wait for him inside!

Well, he was going on with it now. All that he wanted was the quiet and comfort of his room and to be warm and cosy again in bed. He was suddenly quite horribly tired. He pushed with his fingers between the ledges and found then that the catch was *not* securely fastened after all. The upper part of the window suddenly jerked upwards, moving awkwardly and with a creaking noise that he had not known before. He pulled himself on to the window-ledge, then very carefully let himself down on the other side. The first thing that he knew was that his feet touched a chair, and there had been no chair there before; then, that his fingers were rubbing against the corner of a table!

He was not in their own pantry, he was not in their own house! He had climbed in through the wrong window! And even as he realized this and moved in an agony of alarm back to climb out of the window again, his arm brushed the table *again*, he pushed something, and with the noise of the Niagara Falls a thousand times emphasized echoing in his ears, the china of all the pantries of heaven fell clattering to the ground.

V

After that things happened quickly. A light instantly cleaved the darkness, and he saw an open door, a candle held aloft, and the strangest figure holding it. At the same time a deep voice said:

" Stand just where you are! Move another step and I fire! "

" Don't fire, please," said Jeremy. " It's only me! "

The figure confronting him was a woman's. It was, in fact, quite easily to be recognized as that of Miss Lisbeth Mackenzie, who had lived next door to the Coles for years and years and years—ever since, in fact, Jeremy could remember—and waged, like Betsy Trotwood, incessant warfare on boys, butchers and others who walked across her lawn, whose only merit had been that she hated Aunt Amy, and told her so. She was an eccentric old woman, eccentric in manners, in habits and appearance, but surely never in her life had she looked so eccentric as she did now. With her white hair piled untidily on her head, her old face of a crow pallid behind her hooked and piercing nose, over her nightdress she had hurriedly gathered her bed-quilt—a coat, like Joseph's, of many and varied colours—and on her feet were white woollen stockings.

In the hand that did not hold the candle she flourished a pistol that, even to Jeremy's unaccustomed and childish eyes, was undoubtedly a very old and dusty one.

They must have been a queer couple to behold had there been any third person there to behold them : the small boy, dishevelled, hatless, his collar burst, his stockings down over his ankles, and the old woman in her patchwork quilt. Miss Mackenzie, having expected to behold a hirsute and ferocious burglar, was considerably surprised. She held the candle closer, then exclaimed:

"Why, you're a little Cole from next door."

"Yes," said Jeremy. "I thought this was our pantry and it was yours. Wait a minute. I'm going to sneeze." This he did, and then hurried on breathlessly: "Please let me go now and I'll come in to-morrow and explain everything and pay for the cups and saucers. But I don't want them to know that I've been out."

"Here, pick the bits up at once," she said, "or somebody will be cutting themselves. It's just like that maid, having it out on the table. That settles it. She shall leave to-morrow."

She put down the candle and pistol on the table, and then watched him while he picked up the pieces. They were not very many.

"And now please may I go?" said Jeremy again. "I didn't mean to come into your house. I didn't really. I'll explain everything to-morrow."

"No, you won't," said Miss Mackenzie grimly. "You'll explain here and now. That's a pretty thing to come breaking into somebody's house after midnight, and then thinking you can go out just as easily as you came in. . . . You can sit down," she said as a kind of afterthought, pointing to a chair.

"It isn't anything really," said Jeremy very quickly. "I mean that it isn't anything you need mind. They dared me to run round the cathedral twice when the clock struck twelve, and I did it, and ran home and climbed into your house by mistake."

"Who's they?" asked Miss Mackenzie, gathering her quilt more closely about her.

"Bill Bartlett and Ernest Sampson," he said, as though that must tell her everything. "The Dean's son, you know; and I don't like him, so when he dares me to anything I must do it, you see."

"I don't see at all," said Miss Mackenzie. "It was a very wicked and silly thing to do. There are plenty of people I don't like, but I don't run round the cathedral just to please them."

"Oh, I didn't run round it to *please* him!" Jeremy said indignantly. "I don't want to please him, of course. But he said that I wouldn't do it and he would, whereas, as a matter of fact, I did and he didn't."

"As a matter of fact," picked up from the drawing-room, was just then a very favourite phrase of his.

"Well, you'll get it hot from your father," said Miss Mackenzie, "when he knows about it."

"Oh, but perhaps he won't know," said

Jeremy eagerly. " The house looks all dark, and perhaps Hamlet didn't wake up."

" Hamlet? " repeated Miss Mackenzie.

" Yes; that's my dog."

" Oh, that hateful dog that sometimes looks through the railings into my garden as though he would like to come in and tear up all my flowers. He'd better try, that's all."

" He isn't hateful," said Jeremy. " He's a splendid dog. He had a fight a little while ago, and was nearly killed, but he didn't care. He just grinned."

" He won't grin if I get hold of him," said Miss Mackenzie. " Now what are you going to do about it when your father knows you've been out like this? "

"Oh, he mustn't know! " said Jeremy. " You're not going to tell him, are you? "

" Of course I am," said Miss Mackenzie. " I can't have little boys climbing into my house after midnight and then do nothing about it ! "

" Oh, please, please! " said Jeremy. " Don't do anything this time. I promise never to do it again. It would be dreadful if father knew. It's so important that the holidays should end well. They began so badly. You won't tell him, will you? "

" Of course I will," said Miss Mackenzie. " First thing in the morning. I shall ask him to whip you and to allow me to be present during the ceremony. There's nothing that I love like seeing little boys whipped—especially naughty little boys."

For a moment Jeremy thought that she meant it. Then he caught sight of her twinkling eye.

"No, you won't," he said confidently. "You're just trying to frighten me. But I'm not frightened. I go back to school day after to-morrow, so they can't do much anyway."

"If I let you off," she said, "you've got to promise me something. You've got to promise me that you'll come and read to me twice every day during next holidays!"

"Oh, Lord!"

Jeremy couldn't be quite sure whether she meant it or not. How awful if she did mean it! Still, a bargain was a bargain. He looked at her carefully. She seemed very old. She might die before next holidays.

"All right," he said; "I promise. I don't read very well, you know."

"All the better practice for you," she answered. Her eye mysteriously twinkled above the bed-quilt.

She let him go then, even assisting him from behind out of the pantry window. He had a look and a smile at her before he dropped on the other side. She looked so queer, with her crabbed face and untidy hair, under the jumping candle. She nodded to him grimly.

Soon he was at his own window and through it. Not a sound in the house. He crept up the stairs. The same wild snore met him, rumbling like the sleeping soul of the house. Everything the same. To him all those terrors and alarms, and they had slept as though it had been one moment of time.

He opened his own door. Hamlet's even, whining breathing met him. Not much of a watchdog. Never mind. How tired he was! *How* tired! He flung off his clothes, stood for a moment to feel the cold air on his naked body, then his nightshirt was over his head.

The bed was lovely, lovely, lovely. Only as he sank down a silver slope into a sea of red and purple leaves a thought went sliding with him. The Dean's Ernest had funked it! The Dean's Ernest had funked it! Let us never forget! Let us . . . *Plunk!*

CHAPTER VII

YOUNG BALTIMORE

I

JEREMY was miserable. He was sitting on the high ground above the cricket field. The warm summer air wrapped him as though in a cloak; at his feet the grass was bright shrill green, then as it fell away it grew darker, tumbling into purple shadow as it curved to the flattened plateau. Behind him the wood was like a wall of painted steel. Far away the figures of the cricketers were white dolls moving against the bright red brick of the school buildings. One little white cloud shaped like an elephant, like a rent torn in the blue canvas of the sky, hung motionless above his head; and he watched this, waiting for it to lengthen, to fade into another shape, formless, until at last, shredded into scraps of paper, it vanished. He watched the cloud and thought: " I'd like to roll him down the hill and never see him again."

He was thinking of young Baltimore, who was sitting close to him. He was doing nothing but stare and let his mouth hang slackly open.

Because he did nothing so often was one of the reasons why Jeremy hated him so deeply. Baltimore was not an attractive-looking boy. He was perhaps ten years of age, white faced, sandy haired, furtive eyed, with two pimples on his forehead and one on his nose. He looked as though quite recently he had been rolled in the mud. And that was true. He had been.

From near at hand, from the outskirts of the wood, shrill cries could be heard singing:

> " Stocky had a little lamb,
>   Its fleece was white as snow,
>   And everywhere that Stocky went
>   That lamb was sure to go."

Jeremy, hearing these voices, made a movement as though he would rise and pursue them, then apparently realized his impotence and stayed where he was.

"Beasts!" said Baltimore, and suddenly broke into a miserable crying, a wretched, snivelling, gasping wheeze.

Jeremy looked at him with disgust.

"You do cry the most awful lot," he said. "If you didn't cry so much they wouldn't laugh at you."

He gloomily reflected over his fate. The summer term, only a week old, that should have been the happiest of the year, was already the worst that he had known at Thompson's.

On his arrival, full of health, vigour and plans, old Thompson had taken him aside and said :

"Now, Cole, I've something for you to do this term. I want you to be kind to a new boy who has never been away from home before and knows nothing about school life. I want you to be kind to him, look after him, see that no one treats him harshly, make him feel that he is still at home. You are getting one of the bigger boys here now, and you must look after the small ones."

Jeremy was not displeased when he heard this. It gave him a sense of importance that he liked; moreover he had but recently read "Tom Brown," and Tom, whom he greatly admired, had been approached in just this way about Arthur, and Arthur, although he had seemed tiresome at first, had developed very well, had had a romantic illness and become a first-class cricketer.

His first vision of Baltimore had been disappointing. He had found him sitting on his play-box in the passage, snivelling in just that unpleasant way that he had afterwards made so peculiarly his own. He told Jeremy that what he wanted to do was to go home to his mother at once, that his name was Percy, and that he had been kicked on the leg twice.

"You mustn't tell the others that your

name's Percy," said Jeremy, " or you'll never
hear the last of it."

It appeared, however, from certain cries
heard in the distance, that Baltimore had already
done this.

Jeremy wondered then why he had been
selected for this especial duty. He was not
by any means one of the older boys in the
school, nor one of the more important. He
foresaw trouble.

Baltimore had been informed that Jeremy
was to look after him.

" Mr. Thompson says you're to look after
me," he said, " and not let the boys kick me
or take things out of my play-box; and if they
do I'm to tell Mr. Thompson."

Jeremy's cheeks paled with horror as he
heard this declaration.

" Oh, I say, you mustn't do that," he
declared. " That would be sneaking. You
mustn't tell Thompson things."

" Why mustn't I? " asked Baltimore, producing a large cake of chocolate from his
play-box and proceeding to eat it.

" Oh, because—because—sneaking's worse
than anything."

" My mother said I was to," said Baltimore.

" And you mustn't talk about your mother
either," said Jeremy, " nor any of your people
at home."

" Why mustn't I? " asked Baltimore.

" Because they'll rag you if you do."

Baltimore nodded his head in a determined manner.

" I will if they kick me," he said.

That evening was an unhappy one. Jeremy, kept by the matron over some silly business connected with his underclothes, came late into the dormitory to discover a naked Baltimore being beaten with hair-brushes. That was a difficult moment for him, but he dealt with it in the traditional manner of school heroes. He rushed into the midst of the gang, rescued Percy and challenged the room. He was popular and known for a determined fighter, so there was some laughter and jeering; but Baltimore was allowed to creep into his bed.

Next morning the school understood that young Stocky Cole had a new *protégé* and that it was that terrible new boy Pimply Percy. Jeremy's best friend, Riley minor, spoke to him seriously about it.

" I say, Stocky, it isn't true that you've taken up with that awful new kid? "

" Thompson says I've got to look after him," Jeremy explained.

" But he's the worst of the lot," Riley complained disgustedly.

" Well, I've got to anyway," said Jeremy shortly.

K

The sad part of it was that Baltimore was by no means grateful for Jeremy's championship.

"You might have come in earlier," he said. "I don't call that looking after me."

He now followed Jeremy like a shadow, a complaining, snivelling, whining shadow.

Jeremy expostulated.

"Look here," he said. "We needn't be together all the time. If you're in trouble or anything you just give me a shout. I'm sure to be round somewhere."

But Baltimore shook his head.

"That isn't what Mr. Thompson said," he remarked. "He said that you'd look after me. But how can you look after me if you're not there?"

"He didn't mean us to be together the whole time," said Jeremy.

The thing was impossible. He could keep his own small fry in order, although the jeers and insults of those who had until this term been his admiring friends were very hard to bear. But what was he to do, for instance, about Cracky Brown? Cracky was captain of the cricket, thirteen years of age and going to Eton next term. He was one of three heroes allowed a study, and he was fagged for by several of the new boys, including Baltimore. He had already given young Baltimore several for breaking a cup and saucer. How could Jeremy, aged ten and a half, and in the lower fourth, go up to Cracky and say : " Look here, Brown, you've got to leave Baltimore alone," and yet this was exactly what Baltimore expected Jeremy to do. Baltimore was a boy with one idea.

" Mr. Thompson said you were to see they didn't hit me," he complained.

" Don't call him Mr. Thompson," urged Jeremy. " Nobody does."

Here on the hillside Jeremy moodily kicked the turf and watched the shredding cloud. Another week of this and he would be more laughed at than any other boy in the school. Had it been the winter term his prowess at football might have saved the situation, but he had never been very good at cricket, and never would be. He hated it and was still in third game among all the kids and wasters.

It would all have been so much easier, he reflected, had he only found Baltimore possible as a companion. But he thought that he had never loathed anyone so much as this snivelling, pimply boy, and something unregenerate in him rose triumphant in his breast when he saw Baltimore kicked—and this made it much more difficult for him to stop the kicking.

What *was* he to do about it? Appeal to Thompson, of course, he could not. He had

promised to do his best and do his best he must.
Then the brilliant idea occurred to him that
he would write to Uncle Samuel and ask his
advice. He did not like writing letters—indeed,
he loathed it—and his letters were blotched and
illegible productions when they were finished,
but at least he could make the situation clear
to Uncle Samuel and Uncle Samuel always
knew the right thing to do.

At the thought of his uncle a great wave
of homesickness swept over him. He saw the
town and the High Street with all the familiar
shops, and the Cathedral, and his home with
the dark hall and the hat-rack, and Hamlet
running down the stairs, barking, and Mary
with her spectacles and Uncle Samuel's studio
—he was even for a moment sentimental over
Aunt Amy.

He shook himself and the vision faded. He
would not be beaten by this thing. He turned
to Baltimore.

" I'm not going to have you following me
everywhere," he said. " I'm only looking after
you because I promised Thompson. You can
have your choice. I'll leave you alone and let
everyone kick you as much as they like, and
then you can go and sneak to Thompson. That
won't help you a bit; they'll only kick you all
the more. But if you behave decently and stop
crying and come to me when you want anything

I'll see that none of the smaller boys touch you.
If Cracky wants to hit you I can't help it, but
he hits everybody, so there's nothing in that.
Now, what is it to be?"

His voice was so stern that Baltimore stopped
snivelling and stared at him in surprise.

"All right," he said. "I won't follow you
everywhere."

Jeremy got up. "You stay here till I've
got to the bottom of the hill. I'll sit next you
at tea and see they don't take your grub."

He nodded and started away. Baltimore
sat there, staring with baleful eyes.

II

Then a strange thing occurred; let the
psychologists explain it as they may. Jeremy
suddenly began to feel sorry for Baltimore.
There is no doubt at all that the protective
maternal sense is very strong in the male as
well as the female breast. Jeremy had known
it before even with his tiresome sister Mary.
Now Baltimore did what he was told and only
appeared at certain intervals. Jeremy found
himself then often wondering what the kid was
about, whether anyone was chastising him, and
if so, how the kid was taking it. After the
first week Baltimore was left a great deal alone,

partly because of Jeremy's championship, and
partly because he was himself so boring and
pitiful that there was nothing to be done with
him.

He developed very quickly into that well-
known genus of small boy who is to be seen
wandering about the playground all alone, kicking small stones with his feet, slouching, his
cap on the back of his head, his hands deep in
his trouser pockets, a look of utter despair on
his young face. He was also the dirtiest boy
that Thompson's had ever seen, and that is
saying a great deal. His fingers were dyed in
ink; his boots, the laces hanging from them,
were caked in mud; his collar was soiled and
torn; his hair matted and unbrushed. Jeremy,
himself often dirty, nevertheless with an innate
sense of cleanliness, tried to clean him up. But
it was hopeless. Baltimore no longer snivelled.
He was now numb with misery. He stared at
Jeremy as a wild animal caught by the leg in
a trap might stare.

Jeremy began to be very unhappy. He no
longer considered what the other boys might
say, neither their jeers nor their laughter. One
evening, coming up to Baltimore in the playground, he caught his arm.

"You can come and do prep with me to-
night if you like," he said.

Baltimore continued to kick pebbles.

" Has anyone been going for you lately? "
he asked.

Baltimore shook his head.

" I wish I was dead," he replied.

This seemed melodramatic.

" Oh, you'll be all right soon," said Jeremy.

But he could get nothing out of him. Some
of the boy's loneliness seemed to penetrate his
own spirit.

" I say, you can be as much with me as
you like, you know," he remarked awkwardly.

Baltimore nodded his head and moved away.

Bitterly was Jeremy to regret that word of
his. It was as though Baltimore had laid a
trap for him, pretending loneliness in order to
secure that invitation. He was suddenly once
again with Jeremy everywhere.

And now he was no longer either silent or
humble. Words poured from his mouth, words
inevitably, unavoidably connected with himself
and his doings, his fine brave doings—how he
was this at home and that at home, how his
aunt had thought the one and his mother the
other, how his father had given him a pony
and his cousin a dog. . . .

Now round every corner his besmudged face
would be appearing, his inky fingers protruding,
his voice triumphantly proclaiming :

" I'm coming with you now, Cole. There's
an hour before prep."

And strangely now, in spite of himself, Jeremy liked it. He was suddenly touched by young Baltimore and his dirt and his helplessness. Later years were to prove that Jeremy Cole could be always caught, held and won by something misshapen, abused, cast out by society. So now he was caught by young Baltimore. He did his sums for him (when he could—he was no great hand at sums), protected him from Tubby Smith, the bully of the lower fourth, shepherded him in and out of meals, took him for walks on Sunday afternoons. . . .

He was losing Riley. That hurt him desperately. Nevertheless he continued in his serious, entirely unsentimental way to look after Baltimore.

And was young Baltimore grateful? We shall see.

III

One day when the summer term was about a month old a very dreary game of cricket was pursuing its slow course in third game. The infants concerned in it were sleepily watching the efforts of one after another of their number to bowl Corkery Minimus. Corkery was not, as cricket is considered at Lord's, a great cricketer, but he was a stolid, phlegmatic youth,

too big for third game and too lazy to wake up
and so push forward into second. He stood
stolidly at his wicket, making a run or two
occasionally in order to poach the bowling.
Jeremy was sitting in the pavilion, his cap
tilted forward over his eyes, nearly asleep, and
praying that Corkery might stay in all the
afternoon and so save him from batting. One
of the younger masters, Newsom, a youth fresh
from Cambridge, was presiding over the afternoon and longing for six o'clock.

Suddenly he heard a thin and weedy voice
at his ear:

"Please, sir, do you think I might bowl?
I think I could get him out."

Newsom pulled himself in from his dreams
and gazed wearily down upon the grimy face
of Baltimore.

"You!" he exclaimed. Baltimore was not
beloved by the masters.

"Yes, sir," Baltimore said, his cold, green
eyes fixed earnestly upon Newsom's face.

"Oh, I suppose so," Newsom said wearily;
"anything for a change."

Had anyone been watching Baltimore at
that moment they would have seen a curious
thing. A new spirit inhabited the boy's body.
Something seemed suddenly to stiffen him; his
legs were no longer shambly, his eyes no longer
dead. He was in a moment moving as though

he knew his ground and as though he had first and royal right to be there.

Of course, no one noticed this. There was a general titter when it was seen that Baltimore had the ball in his hand. Corkery turned round and sniggered to the wicket-keeper, and the wicket-keeper sniggered back.

Baltimore paid no attention to anybody. He ran to the wicket and delivered an underhand lob. A second later Corkery's bails were on the ground. Again, had anyone noticed, he would have perceived that the delivery of that ball was no ordinary one, that the twist of the arm as it was delivered was definite and assured and by no means accidental.

No one noticed anything except that Corkery was at length out; although he had been batting for an hour and ten minutes, he had made only nine runs. Baltimore's next three balls took three wickets, Jeremy's amongst them. No one was very enthusiastic about this. The balls were considered " sneaks," and just the kind that Pimply Percy *would* bowl. Corkery, in fact, was extremely indignant and swore he would " take it out " of Pimples in the dormitory that evening.

Very odd was Baltimore over this. No sign of any feeling whatever. Jeremy expected that he would be full that evening of his prowess. Not a word.

Jeremy himself was proud of his young friend. It was as though he had possessed an ugly and stupid puppy who, it was suddenly discovered, could balance spoons on the end of his nose.

He told Riley about it. Riley was disgusted. "You and your Percy," he said. "You can jolly well choose, Stocky. It's him or me. He's all right now. The other fellows leave him alone. Why can't you drop him?"

Jeremy could not explain why, but he did not want to drop him. He liked having something to look after.

Next week something more occurred. Baltimore was pushed up into second game. It was, indeed, very necessary that he should be. Had he stayed in third game that galaxy of all the cricketing talents would have been entirely demoralized; no one could withstand him. Wickets fell faster than ninepins. He gained no popularity for this. He was, indeed, beaten in the box-room with hair-brushes for bowling "sneaks." He took his beating without a word. He seemed suddenly to have found his footing. He held up his head, occasionally washed his face, and stared superciliously about him.

Jeremy now was far keener about young Baltimore's career than he had ever been about his own. Securing an afternoon "off," he went and watched his friend's first appearance

in second game. Knowing nothing about
cricket, he was nevertheless clever enough to
detect that there was something natural and
even inevitable in Baltimore's cricket. Not
only in his bowling, but also in his fielding.
He recognized it, perhaps, because it was the
same with himself in football. Awkward and
ill at ease as he was on the cricket field, he
moved with perfect confidence in Rugby,
knowing at once where to go and what to do.
So it was now with Baltimore. In that game
he took eight wickets for eighteen runs.

The school began now to talk about the
new prodigy. There were, of course, two sides
in the matter, many people declaring that they
were " sneaky," low-down balls that anybody
could bowl if they were dishonest enough to
do so. Others said that there was nothing
low-down about it, and that young Baltimore
would be in first game before he knew where
he was. On his second day in second game
Baltimore took Smith Major's wicket first ball,
and Smith Major had batted twice for the first
eleven. After this the great Cracky himself
came and watched him. He said nothing, but
next day Baltimore was down for first game.

Jeremy now was bursting with pride. He
tried to show Baltimore how immensely pleased
he was.

In a corner after tea he talked to him.

"There's never been a new kid his first term in first game before, I don't think," said Jeremy, regardless of grammar. "They'll play you for the second eleven, I expect."

"They're sure to," said Baltimore calmly; "and then they'll play me for the first."

Strange that Jeremy, who hated above all things "side" in his fellow human beings, was not repelled by this. Here in Baltimore was the *feu sacré*. Jeremy recognized its presence and bowed to it. Small boys are always fond of anything of which they are proud, and so Jeremy now, in spite of the green eyes, the arrogant, aloof attitude, the unpleasant personal habits, had an affection for Baltimore—the affection of the hen whose ugly duckling turns out a swan.

"You don't seem very pleased about it," he said, looking at Baltimore curiously.

"What's there to be pleased about?" said Baltimore coldly. "Of course, I knew I could play cricket. No one in this rotten place can play. I can bat, too, only they always put me in last."

"Will you walk out to Pocker's after dinner to-morrow?" Jeremy asked.

"All right," said Baltimore indifferently.

IV

In the following week Baltimore played for
the second eleven, took eight wickets for twenty
runs, and himself made thirty. A fortnight
later he was down on the boards in the first
eleven for the Lower Templeton match. Now,
indeed, the whole school was talking about
him, masters and boys alike. His batting was
another matter from his bowling. There was
no doubt at all that he was a natural cricketer.
Mr. Rochester, the games master, said he was
the most promising cricketer that he had yet
seen at Thompson's, remarkable style for so
young a boy, an extraordinarily fine eye. The
Lower Templeton match was the match of the
season. Lower Templeton was a private school
some ten miles away, and Thompson's strongest
rivals; they had more boys than Thompson's,
and two times out of three they won the
cricket match. They were entirely above themselves and jeered at Thompson's, implying that
they showed the most wonderful condescension
in coming over to play at all. Consequently
there burned in the heart of every boy in
Thompson's—yes, and in the heart of every
master and every servant—a longing desire that
the swollen-headed idiots should be beaten.

Boys are exceedingly susceptible to atmosphere, and in no time at all the first weeks

of Baltimore's stay at Thompson's were entirely forgotten. He was a new creature, a marvel, a miracle. Young Corkery was heard at tea to offer him his last sardine, although only a fortnight before he had belaboured his posterior with hair-brushes. Cracky Brown took in him now a fatherly interest, and inflicted on him only the lightest fagging and inquired anxiously many times a day about his health. Jeremy surrendered absolutely to this glamour, but it was to more than mere glamour that he was surrendering. He did not realize it, but he had never in all his life before had any friend who had been a success. His father and mother, his sister Mary, his Uncle Samuel—none of these could be said to be in the eyes of the world successes. And at school it had been the same; his best friend, Riley, was quite undistinguished in every way, and the master whom he liked best, old Podgy Johnson, was more than undistinguished—he was derided.

It was not that he liked vulgar applause for his friend and himself enjoyed to bathe in its blinding light. It was, quite simply, that he loved his friend to be successful, that it was " fun " for him, amusing, exciting, and warmed him all over. No longer need he feel any pity for Baltimore; Baltimore was happy now; he *must* be.

It must be confessed that Baltimore showed no especial signs of being happy when the great day arrived. At breakfast he accepted quite calmly the portions of potted meat, marmalade, sardines and pickles offered him by adoring admirers, and ate them all on the same plate quite impassively.

After dinner Jeremy and Riley took their places on the grass in front of the pavilion and waited for the game to begin. Riley was now very submissive, compelled to admit that after all Jeremy had once again showed his remarkable judgment. Who but Jeremy would have seen in Baltimore on his arrival at Thompson's the seeds of greatness? He was forced to confess that he himself had been blind to them. With their straw hats tilted over their eyes, lying full-length on the grass, a bag of sweets between them, they were as happy as thieves.

In strict truth Jeremy's emotions were not those precisely of happiness. He was too deeply excited, too passionately anxious for Baltimore's success to be really happy. He could not hear the sweets crunching between his teeth for the beating of his heart. What followed was what any reader of school stories would expect to follow. Had Baltimore been precisely the handsome blue-eyed hero of one of Dean Farrar's epics of boyhood, he could not have behaved more appropriately. Thompson's went in first, and disaster instantly assailed them. Six wickets were down for ten owing to a diabolical fast bowler whom Lower Templeton had brought with them. Cracky Brown was the only Thompsonian who made any kind of a stand, and he had no one to stay with him until Baltimore came in and (Cracky content merely to keep up his wicket) made thirty-five. Thompson's were all out for fifty-six. Lower Templeton then went in, and, because Cracky did not at once put on Baltimore to bowl, made thirty-four for two wickets. Baltimore then took the remaining eight wickets for seventeen. Lower Templeton were all out for fifty-one.

The excitement during the second innings had to be seen to be believed. Even old Thompson, who was known for his imperturbable temper, was seen to wipe his brow continually with a yellow handkerchief.

Thompson's went in, and four wickets fell for eleven. Baltimore went in at fifth wicket, and made thirty-nine. Thompson's were all out for sixty-one, and were sixty-six ahead of Lower Templeton. This was a good lead, and the hearts of Thompson's beat high. Baltimore started well and took six of the Lower Templeton wickets for twenty; then he obviously tired. Cracky took him off, and Lower Templeton had three-quarters of an hour's pure joy. As

L

the school clock struck half-past six Lower Templeton had made sixty runs for eight wickets. Cracky then put Baltimore on again, and he took the remaining wickets for no runs. Thompson's were victorious by six runs, and Baltimore was carried shoulder-high, amongst the plaudits of the surrounding multitudes, up to the school buildings.

V

Impossible to give any adequate idea of Jeremy's pride and pleasure over this event. He did not share in the procession up to the school, but waited his time. Then, just before chapel, crossing the playground in the purple dusk, he passed Baltimore and another boy.

"Hullo! . . . I say . . ." He stopped.

Baltimore looked back over his shoulder. Jeremy could not precisely see the expression, but fancied it contemptuous. Most curiously, then, for the rest of the evening he was worried and unhappy. Why should he worry? Baltimore was his friend—must be, after all that Jeremy had done for him. Jeremy was too young and too unanalytical to know what it was that he wanted, but in reality he longed now for that protective sense to continue. He must still "have something to look after."

There were lots of things he could do for Baltimore. . . .

Next morning after breakfast he caught him alone, ten minutes before chapel. He was embarrassed and shy, but he plunged in: "I say—it was ripping yesterday. Weren't you glad?"

Baltimore, looking at Jeremy curiously, shrugged his shoulders.

"You're coming out next Sunday, aren't you?" he went on.

Baltimore smiled. "I'm not going to have you following me everywhere," he said, in a rather feeble imitation of Jeremy's voice. "If you behave all right, and don't cry and tell me when anyone kicks you, I'll let you speak to me sometimes. Otherwise you keep off."

He put his tongue out at Jeremy and swaggered off.

Jeremy stood there. He was hurt as he had never been before in his young life; he had, indeed, never known this kind of hurt.

Someone came in.

"Hullo, Stocky! Coming up to chapel?"

"All right," he answered, moving to get his books out of his locker. But he'd lost something, something awfully jolly. . . . He fumbled in his locker for it. He wanted to cry—like any kid. He was crying, but he wasn't going to let Stokoe see it. He found an old fragment of liquorice stick. It mingled in his mouth with the salt taste of tears. So, dragging his head from his locker, he kicked Stokoe in amicable friendship, and they departed chapel-wards, tumbling over one another puppywise as they went.

But no more miserable boy sat in chapel that morning.

VI

Two days later, turning the corner of the playground, he heard shrill crying. Looking farther, he perceived Baltimore twisting the arms of a miniature boy, the smallest boy in the school—Brown Minimus. He was also kicking him in tender places.

" Now will you give it me? " he was saying.

A second later Baltimore was, in his turn, having his arms twisted and his posterior kicked. As Jeremy kicked and twisted he felt a strange, a mysterious pleasure.

Baltimore tried to bite, then he said, " I'll tell Thompson."

" I don't care if you do," said Jeremy.

Yes, he felt a strange wild pleasure, but when that afternoon old Thompson genially said :

" Well, Cole, I think Baltimore's found his feet now all right, hasn't he? "

Jeremy said: "Yes, sir; he has."

He felt miserable. He sat down and kicked the turf furiously with his toes. He had lost something, he knew not what; something very precious. . . .

Someone called him, and he went off to join in a rag. Anyway, "Tom Brown" was a rotten book.

CHAPTER VIII

THE RUFFIANS

I

JEREMY sat on a high cliff overlooking the sea. He had never, since he was a tiny baby, had any fear of heights, and now his short, thick legs dangled over a fearful abyss in a way that would have caused his mother's heart to go faint with terror had she seen it.

The sight before him was superb, not to be exceeded perhaps in the whole world for strength and even ferocity of outline combined with luxuriance and Southern softness of colour.

Here the two worlds met, the worlds of the north and the south; even in the early morning breeze there seemed to mingle the harsh irony of the high Glebeshire uplands and the gentle, caressing warmth of the sheltered coves and shell-scattered shores.

The sea was a vast curtain of silk, pale blue beyond the cove, a deep and shining green in the depths immediately below Jeremy's feet.

That pale curtain was woven both of sea and sky, and seemed to quiver under the fingers of the morning breeze. It was suspended between two walls of sharp black rock, jagged, ferocious, ruthless. Sharp to Jeremy's right, inside the black curve of stone, was a little beach of the palest yellow, and nestling on to it, standing almost within it, was a little old church with a crooked grey tower and a wandering grave-yard.

Behind the church stretched a lovely cham-paign of the gentlest, most English country-side : hills, green as brightly coloured glass, rising smoothly into the blue, little valleys thickly patched with trees, cottages from whose stumpy chimneys smoke was already rising, cows and sheep, and in the distance the joyful barking of a dog, the only sound in all that early scene save the curling whisper of the tide.

Jeremy had arrived with his family at Caerlyon Rectory the night before in a state of rebellious discontent. He had been dis-gusted when he heard that this summer they were to break the habit of years and to abandon his beloved cow farm in favour of a new camping ground.

And a rectory too ! When they always lived so close to churches and had so eternally to do with them ! No farm any more ! No

Mrs. Monk, Mr. Monk and the little Monks, no animals, no cows and pigs, no sheep and no horses; above all no Tim. No Tim with the red face and the strong legs; Tim, perhaps the best friend he had in the world, after, of course, Riley and Hamlet. He had felt it bitterly, and during that journey from Polchester to the sea, always hitherto so wonderful a journey, he had sulked and sulked, refusing to notice any of the new scenery, the novel excitements and fresh incidents (like the driving all the way, for instance, from St. Mary Moor in a big wagon-ette with farmers and their wives), lest he should be betrayed into any sort of disloyalty to his old friends.

The arrival at the Rectory, with its old walled garden, the flowers all glimmering in the dusk, the vast oak in the middle of the lawn, was, in spite of himself, an interesting experience, but he allowed no expression of amusement to escape from him and went to bed the moment after supper.

He awoke, of course, at a desperately early hour, and was compelled then to jump out of bed and look out of the window. He discovered to his excited amazement that the sea was right under his nose. This was marvellous to him.

At Cow Farm you could watch only a little cup of it between a dip in the trees, and that miles away. Here the garden seemed actually to border it, and you could watch it stretch with the black cliffs to the left of it, miles, miles, miles into the sky. The world was lovely at that hour; blackbirds and thrushes were on the dew-drenched lawn. Somewhere in the house a cuckoo-clock announced that it was just six o'clock. Before he knew what he was about he had slipped on his clothes, was down the dark stairs and out in the garden. . . .

As he sat dangling his feet above space and looked out to sea he argued with himself about Cow Farm. Of course Cow Farm would always be first, but that did not mean that other places could not be nice as well. He would never find anyone in Caerlyon as delightful as Tim, and if only Tim were here, everything would be perfect; but Tim could not, of course, be in two places at once, and he had to do his duty by the Monks.

As he sat there swinging his legs and looking down into that perfect green water, so clear that you could see gold and purple lights shifting beneath it and black lines of rock-like liquorice sticks twisting as the shadows moved, he was forced to admit to himself that he was terribly happy.

He had never lived close, cheek-by-jowl, with the sea, as he was doing now. The thought

of five whole weeks spent thus on the very edge
of the water made him wriggle his legs so that
there was very real danger of his falling over.
The juxtaposition of Hamlet who had, of course,
followed him, saved him from further danger.
He knew that he himself was safe and would
never fall, but Hamlet was another matter and
must be protected. The dog was perilously near
the edge, balancing on his fore-feet and sniffing
down; so the boy got up and dragged the dog
back, and then lay down among the sea-pinks
and the heather and looked up into the cloudless
sky.

Hamlet rested his head on the fatty part of
his master's thigh and breathed deep content.
He had come into some place where there
wandered a new company of smells, appetizing,
tempting. Soon he would investigate them.
For the present it was enough to lie warm with
his master and dream.

Suddenly he was conscious of something.
He raised his head, and Jeremy, feeling his
withdrawal, half sat up and looked about him.
Facing them both were a group of giant
boulders, scattered there in the heather, and
looking like some Druid circle of ancient stones.
Hamlet was now on all fours, his tail up, his
hair bristling.

" It's all right," said Jeremy lazily.
" There's nobody there——" But even as he

looked an extraordinary phenomenon occurred.
There rose from behind the boulder a tangled
head of hair, and beneath the hair a round,
hostile face and two fierce interrogative eyes.
Then, as though this were not enough, there
arose in line with the first head a second, and
with the second a third, and then with the third
a fourth. Four round, bullet heads, four fierce,
hostile pairs of eyes staring at Hamlet and
Jeremy.

Jeremy stared back, feeling that here was
some trick played upon him, as when the
conjurer at Thompson's had produced a pigeon
out of a handkerchief. The trick effect was
heightened by the fact that the four heads and
the sturdy bodies connected with them were
graduated in height to a nicety, as you might
see four clowns at a circus, as were the four
bears, a symmetry almost divine and quite
unnatural.

The eldest, the fiercest and most hostile, had
a face and shoulders that might belong to a boy
of sixteen, the youngest and smallest might have
been Jeremy's age. Jeremy did not notice any
of this. Very plain to him the fact that the
four faces, to whomsoever they might belong,
did not care either for him or his dog. One
to four; he was in a situation of some danger.
He was suddenly aware that he had never seen
boys quite so ferocious in appearance; the

street boys of Polchester were milk and water to them. Hamlet also felt this. He was sitting up, his head raised, his body stiff, intent, and you could feel within him the bark strangled by the melodrama of the situation.

Jeremy said rather feebly:

" Hullo! "

The reply was a terrific ear-shattering bellow from four lusty throats; then more distinctly:

" Get out of this! "

Fear was in his heart; he was compelled afterwards to admit it. He could only reply very feebly:

" Why? "

The eldest of the party, glaring, replied:

" If you don't, we'll make you." Then: " This is ours here."

Hamlet was now quivering all over, and Jeremy was afraid lest he should make a dash for the boulders. He therefore climbed on to his feet, holding Hamlet's collar with his hand, and, smiling, answered:

" I'm sorry. I didn't know. I've only just come."

" Well, get out, then," was the only reply.

What fascinated him like a dream was the way that the faces did not move nor more body

reveal itself. Painted against the blue sky,
they might have been, ferocious stares and all.
There was nothing more to be done. He beat
an inglorious retreat, not, indeed, running, but
walking with what dignity he could summon,
Hamlet at his side uttering noises like a kettle
on the boil.

II

He had not to wait long for some explanation of the vision. At breakfast (and it was a
wonderful breakfast, with more eggs and bacon,
cream and strawberry jam than he had ever
known) his father said :

"Now, children, there's one thing here
that you must remember. Jeremy, are you
listening?"

"Yes, father."

"Don't speak with your mouth full.
There's a farm near the church on the sand.
You can't mistake it."

"Is the farm on the sand, father?" asked
Mary, her eyes wide open.

"No, of course not. How could a farm
be on the sand? The farm-house stands back
at the end of the path that runs by the church.
It's a grey farm with a high stone wall. You
can't mistake it. Well, none of you children
are to go near that farm—on no account

whatever, *on no account whatever*, to go near it."

"Why not, father?" asked Jeremy. "Is there scarlet fever there?"

"Because I say so is quite enough," said Mr. Cole. "There's a family staying there you must have *nothing at all* to do with. Perhaps you will see them in the distance. You must avoid them and *never* speak to them."

"Are they *very* wicked?" asked Mary, her voice vibrating low with the drama of the situation.

"Never mind what they are. They are not fit companions for you children. It is most unfortunate that they are here so close to us. Had I known it I would not, I think, have come here."

Jeremy said nothing; these were, of course, his friends of the morning. He could see now straight across the breakfast-table those eight burning, staring eyes.

Later, from the slope of the green hill above the rectory, he looked across the gleaming beach at the church, the road, and then, in the distance, the forbidden farm. Strange how the forbidding of anything made one from the very bottom of one's soul long for it! Yesterday, staring across the green slopes and hollows, the farm would have been but a grey patch sewn into the purple hill that hung behind it.

Now it was mysterious, crammed with hidden life of its own, the most dramatic point in the whole landscape. What had they done, that family that was so terrible? What was there about those four boys that he had never seen in any boys before? He longed to know them with a burning, desperate longing. Nevertheless a whole week passed without any contact.

Once Jeremy saw, against the sky-line on the hill behind the church, a trail of four, single file, silhouetted black. They passed steadily, secretly, bent on their own mysterious purposes. The sky, when their figures had left it, was painted with drama.

Once Mary reported that, wandering along the beach, a wild figure, almost naked, had started from behind a rock and shouted at her. She ran, of course, and behind her there echoed a dreadful laugh. But the best story of all was from Helen, who, passing the graveyard, had seen go down the road a most beautiful lady, most beautifully dressed. According to Helen, she was the most lovely lady ever seen, with jewels hanging from her ears, pearls round her neck, and her clothes a bright orange. She had walked up the road and gone through the gate into the farm.

The mystery would have excited them all even more than, in fact, it did had Caerlyon itself been less entrancing. But what Caerlyon turned out to be no words can describe! Those were the days, of course, before golf-links in Glebeshire, and although no one who has ever played on the Caerlyon links will ever wish them away (they, the handsomest, kindest, most fantastic sea links in all England), yet I will not pretend that those same green slopes, sliding so softly down to the sea-shore, bending back so gently to the wild mysteries of the Poonderry Moor, had not then a virgin charm that now they have lost! Who can decide?

But, for children thirty years ago, what a kingdom! Glittering with colour, they had the softness of a loving mother, the sudden, tumbled romance of an adventurous elder brother; they caught all the colours of the floating sky in their laps and the shadows flew like birds from shoulder to shoulder, and then suddenly the hills would shake their sides, and all those shadows would slide down to the yellow beach and lie there like purple carpets. You could race and race and never grow tired, lie on your back and stare into the fathomless sky, roll over for ever and come to no harm, wander and never be lost. The first gate of the kingdom and the last—the little golden

square underneath the tower where the green
witch has her stall of treasures that she never
sells. . . .

III

Then the great adventure occurred. One
afternoon the sun shone so gloriously that
Jeremy was blinded by it, blinded and dream-
smitten so that he sat, perched on the garden
wall of the rectory, staring before him at the
glitter and the sparkle, seeing nothing but,
perhaps, a little boat of dark wood with a ruby
sail floating out to the horizon, having on its
boards sacks of gold and pearls and diamonds—
gold in fat slabs, pearls in white, shaking heaps,
diamonds that put out the eyes, so bright they
were—going . . . going . . . whither? He does
not know, but shades his eyes against the sun
and the boat has gone, and there is nothing
there but an unbroken blue of sea with the
black rocks fringing it.

Mary called up to him from the garden and
suggested that they should go out and pick
flowers, and, still in a dream, he climbed down
from the wall and stood there nodding his head
like a mandarin. He suffered himself to be led
by Mary into the high-road, only stopping for
a moment to whistle for Hamlet, who came

M

running across the lawn as though he had just been shot out of a cannon.

It can have been only because he was sunk so deep in his dream that he wandered, without knowing it, down over the beach, jumping the hill-stream that intersected it, up the sand, past the church, out along the road that led straight to the forbidden farm. Nor was Mary thinking of their direction. She was having one of her happy days, her straw hat on the back of her head, her glasses full of sunlight, her stockings wrinkled about her legs, walking, her head in the air, singing one of her strange tuneless chants that came to her when she was happy.

There was a field on their right, and a break in the hedge. Through the break she saw buttercups—thousands of them—and loosestrife and snapdragons. She climbed the gate and vanished into the field. Jeremy walked on, scarcely realizing her absence. Suddenly he heard a scream. He stopped and Hamlet stopped, pricking up his ears. Another scream, then a succession, piercing and terrible.

Then over the field gate Mary appeared, tumbling over regardless of all audiences and proprieties, then running, crying, "Jeremy! Jeremy! Jeremy!" buttercups scattering from her hand as she ran. Her face was one

question-mark of terror; her hat was gone, her
hair-ribbon dangling, her stockings about her
ankles. All she could do was to cling to
Jeremy crying, "Oh, oh, oh! . . . Ah, ah,
ah!"

"What is it?" he asked roughly, his fear
for her making him impatient. "Was it a
bull?"

"No—no. . . . Oh, Jeremy! . . . Oh, dear,
oh, dear! . . . The boys! . . . They hit me—
pulled my hair!"

"What boys?" But already he knew.

Recovering a little, she told him. She had
not been in the field a moment, and was bending down picking her first buttercups, when
she felt herself violently seized from behind,
her arms held; and, looking up, there were
three boys standing there, all around her.
Terrible, fierce boys, looking ever so wicked.
They tore her hat off her head, pulled her hair,
and told her to leave the field at once, never
to come into it again, that it was *their* field, and
she'd better not forget it, and to tell all her
beastly family that they'd better not forget it
either, and that they'd be shot if they came in
there.

"Then they took me to the gate and
pushed me over. They were very rough. I've
got bruises." She began to cry as the full
horror of the event broke upon her.

Jeremy's anger was terrible to witness. He took her by the arm.

" Come with me," he said.

He led her to the end of the road beyond the church.

" Now you go home," he said. " Don't breathe a word to anyone till I get back."

" Very well," she sobbed; " but I've lost my hat."

" I'll get your hat," he answered. " And take Hamlet with you."

He watched her set off. No harm could come to her there, in the open. She had only to cross the beach and climb the hill. He watched her until she had jumped the stream, Hamlet running in front of her, then he turned back.

He climbed the gate into the field. There was no one; only the golden sea of buttercups, and near the gate a straw hat. He picked it up and, back in the road again, stood hesitating. There was only one thing he could do, and he knew it. But he hesitated. He had been forbidden to enter the place. And, besides, there were four of them. And such a four! Then he shrugged his shoulders, a very characteristic action of his, and marched ahead.

The gate of the farm swung easily open, and then at once he was upon them, all four

of them sitting in a row upon a stone wall
at the far corner of the yard and staring at
him.

It was a dirty, messy place, and a fitting
background for that company. The farm itself
looked fierce with its blind grey wall and its
sullen windows, and the yard was in fearful
confusion, oozing between the stones with shiny
yellow streams and dank, coagulating pools,
piled high with heaps of stinking manure, pigs
wandering in the middle distance, hens and
chickens, and a ruffian dog chained to his
kennel.

The four looked at Jeremy without
moving.

Jeremy came close to them and said,
" You're a lot of dirty cads."

They made neither answer nor movement.

" Dirty cads to touch my sister, a girl who
couldn't touch you."

Still no answer. Only one, the smallest,
jumped off the wall and ran to the gate behind
Jeremy.

" I'm not afraid of you," said Jeremy (he
was—terribly afraid). " I wouldn't be afraid
of a lot of dirty sneaks like you are—to hit a
girl ! "

Still no answer. So he ended :

" And we'll go wherever we like. It isn't

your field, and we've just as much right to it
as you have!"

He turned to go, and faced the boy at the
gate. The other three had now climbed off the
wall, and he was surrounded. He had never,
since the night with the sea-captain, been in
so perilous a situation. He thought that they
would murder him, and then hide his body
under the manure—they looked quite capable
of it. And in some strange way this farm was
so completely shut off from the outside world,
the house watched so silently, the wall was so
high. And he was very small indeed compared
with the biggest of the four. No, he did not
feel very happy.

Nothing could be more terrifying than their
silence; but, if they were silent, he could be
silent too, so he just stood there and said
nothing.

"What are you going to do about it?"
suddenly asked the biggest of the four.

"Do about what?" he replied, his voice
trembling in spite of himself; simply, as it
seemed to him, from the noisy beating of his
heart.

"Our cheeking your sister."

"I can't do much," Jeremy said, "when
there are four of you, but I'll fight the one my
own size."

That hero, grinning, moved forward to

Jeremy, but the one who had already spoken broke out :

" Let him out. We don't want him. . . . And don't you come back again ! " he suddenly shouted.

" I will," Jeremy shouted in return, " if I want to ! " And then, I regret to say, took to his heels and ran pell-mell down the road.

IV

Now this was an open declaration of war and not lightly to be disregarded. Jeremy said not a word of it to anyone, not even to the wide-eyed Mary who had been waiting in a panic of terror under the oak tree, like the lady in Carpaccio's picture of St. George and the Dragon, longing for her true knight to return, all " bloody and tumbled," to quote Miss Jane Porter's " Thaddeus." He was not bloody nor was he tumbled, but he was serious-minded and preoccupied.

This was all very nice, but it was pretty well going to spoil the holidays : these fellows hanging round and turning up just whenever they pleased, frightening everybody and perhaps —this sudden thought made, for a moment, his heart stand still—doing something really horrible to Hamlet!

He felt as though he had the whole burden of it on his shoulders, as though he were on guard for all the family. There was no one to whom he could speak. No one at all.

For several days he moved about as though in enemy country, looking closely at hedges, scanning hill horizons, keeping Hamlet as close to his side as possible. No sign of the ruffians, no word of them at home; they had faded into smoke and gone down with the wind.

Suddenly, one morning when he was in a hollow of the downs throwing pebbles at a tree, he heard a voice:

" Hands up, or I fire! "

He turned round and saw the eldest of the quartette quite close to him. Although he had spoken so fiercely, he was not looking fierce, but, rather, was smiling in a curious crooked kind of way. Jeremy could see him more clearly than before, and a strange enough object he was.

He was wearing a dirty old pair of flannel cricketing trousers and a grubby shirt open at the neck. One of his eyes was bruised and he had a cut across his nose, but the thing in the main that struck Jeremy now was his appearance of immense physical strength. His

muscles seemed simply to bulge under his shirt,
he had the neck of a prize-fighter. He was a
great deal older than Jeremy, perhaps sixteen
or seventeen years of age. His eyes, which
were grey and clear, were his best feature, but
he was no beauty, and in his dirty clothes and
with his bruises he looked a most dangerous
character.

Jeremy called Hamlet to him and held him
by the collar.

"All right," the ruffian said; "I'm not
going to touch your dog."

"I didn't think you were," said Jeremy,
lying.

"Oh, yes, you did. I suppose you think
we eat dog-flesh and murder babies. Lots of
people do."

The sudden sense that other folk in the
world also thought the quartette outlaws was
new to Jeremy. He had envisaged the affair
as a struggle in which the Cole family only
were engaged.

"Eat babies!" Jeremy cried. "No! Do
you?"

"Of course not," said the boy. "That's
the sort of damned rot people talk. They think
we'd do anything."

He suddenly sat down on the turf, and
Jeremy sat down too, dramatically picturing to
himself the kind of thing that would happen

did his father turn the corner and find him there amicably in league with his enemy. There followed a queer in-and-out little conversation, bewildering in some strange way, so that they seemed to sink deeper and deeper into the thick velvet pile of the green downs, lost to all the world that was humming like a top beyond the barrier.

"I liked your coming into the yard about your sister. That was damned plucky of you."

For some reason hidden deep in the green down Jeremy had never before known praise that pleased him so deeply. He flushed, kicking the turf with the heels of his boots.

"You were cads to hit my sister," he said. He let Hamlet's collar go, and the dog went over and smelt the dirty trousers and sniffed at the rough, reddened hand.

"How old are you?"

"Ten and a half."

"I know. You're called Cole. You're the son of the parson at the rectory."

Jeremy nodded his head. The boy was now sprawling his length, his head resting on his arms, his thick legs stretched out.

"You're awfully strong," Jeremy suddenly said.

The boy nodded his head.

"I am that. I can throw a cricket ball from here to the church. I can wrestle anyone. Box, too."

He didn't say this boastfully, but quite calmly, stating well-known facts. Jeremy opened his eyes wide.

"What are *you* called?" he asked.

"Humphrey Charles Ruthven."

"Where do you go to school?"

"I don't go. I was kicked out of Harrow. But it didn't matter anyway, because my governor couldn't pay the school bills."

Expelled! This was exciting indeed.

Jeremy inquired, but his friend would give no reasons—only looked at him curiously and smiled. Then he suddenly went on in another tone: "You know everyone hates us, don't you?"

"Yes, I know that," said Jeremy. "Why is it?"

"Because we're bad," Humphrey said solemnly. "Our hand is against everyone, and everyone's hand is against us."

"But why?" asked Jeremy again.

"Well, for one thing, they don't like father. He's got, if you were speaking very politely, what you'd call a damned bad temper. By Jove, you should see him lose it! He's broken three chairs in the farm already! I don't suppose we shall be here very long.

We're always moving about. Then another reason is that we never have any money. Father makes a bit racing sometimes, and then we're flush for a week or two, but it never lasts long.

"Why," he went on, drawing himself up with an air of pride, "we owe money all over the country. That's why we came down to this rotten dull hole—because we hadn't been down here before. And another reason they don't like us is because that woman who lives with us isn't father's wife and she isn't our mother either. I should rather think not! She's a beast. I hate her," he added reflectively.

There was a great deal of all this that Jeremy didn't understand, but he got from it an immense impression of romance and adventure.

And then, as he looked across at the boy opposite to him, a new feeling came to him, a feeling that he had never known before. It was an exciting, strange emotion, something that was suddenly almost adoration. He was aware, all in a second, that he would do anything in the world for this strange boy. He would like to be ordered by him to run down the shoulder of the down and race across the sands and plunge into the sea, and he would do it, or to be commanded by him all the way to

St. Mary's, ever so many miles, to fetch
something for him. It was so new an experience that he felt exceedingly shy about it, and
could only sit there kicking at the turf and
saying nothing.

Humphrey's brow was suddenly as black as
thunder. He got up.

"I see what it is," he said. "You're like
the rest. Now I've told you what we are, you
don't want to have anything more to do with
us. Well, you needn't. Nobody asked you.
You can just go back to your old parson and
say to him, 'Oh, father, I met such a *wicked*
boy to-day. He *was* naughty, and I'm never
going to talk to him again.' All right, then.
Go along."

The attack was so sudden that Jeremy was
taken entirely by surprise. He had been completely absorbed by this new feeling; he had
not known that he had been silent.

"Oh, no. I don't care what you are or
your father or whether you haven't any money.
I've got some money. I'll give it you if you
like. And you shall have threepence more on
Saturday—fourpence, if I know my Collect. I
say"—he stammered over this request—"I
wish you'd throw a stone from here and see
how far you can."

Humphrey was immensely gratified. He
bent down and picked up a pebble; then,

straining backwards ever so slightly, slung it. It vanished into the blue sea. Jeremy sighed with admiration.

" You *can* throw," he said. " Would you mind if I felt the muscle on your arm? " He felt it. He had never imagined such a muscle.

" Do you think I could have more if I worked at it? " he asked, stretching out his own arm.

Humphrey graciously felt it. " That's not bad for a kid of your size," he said. " You ought to lift weights in the morning. That's the way to bring it up." Then he added : " You're a sporting kid. I like you. I'll be here again same time to-morrow," and without another word was running off, with a strange jumping motion, across the down.

Jeremy went home, and could think of nothing at all but his adventure. How sad it was that always, without his in the least desiring it, he was running up against authority. He had been forbidden to go near the farm or to have anything to do with the wild, outlawed tenants of it, and now here he was making close friends with one of the worst of them.

He could not help it. He did not want to help it. When he looked round the family supper-table how weak, colourless and

uninteresting they all seemed! No muscles, no
outlawry, no running from place to place to
escape the police! He saw Humphrey standing against the sky and slinging that stone.
He could throw! There was no doubt of it.
He could throw, perhaps, better than anyone
else in the world.

They met, then, every day, and for a
glorious, wonderful week nobody knew. I am
sorry to say that Jeremy was involved at once
in a perfect mist of lies and false excuses.
What a business it was being always with the
family! He had felt it now for a long time,
the apparent impossibility of going anywhere
or doing anything without everybody all round
you asking multitudes of questions. "Where
are you going to, Jeremy?" "Where have
you been?" "What have you been doing?"
"I haven't seen you for the last two hours,
Jeremy. Mother's been looking for you everywhere!"

So he lied and lied and lied. Otherwise, he
got no harm from this wonderful week. One
must do Humphrey that justice that he completely respected Jeremy's innocence. He
even, for perhaps the first time in his young
life, tried to restrain his swearing. They found
the wild moor at the back of the downs a
splendid hunting-ground. Here, in the miles
of gorse and shrub and pond and heather, they

were safe from the world, their companions birds and rabbits. Humphrey knew more about animals than anyone in England—he said so himself, so it must be true. The weather was glorious, hot and gorse-scented. They bathed in the pools and ran about naked, Humphrey doing exercises, standing on his head, turning somersaults, lifting Jeremy with his hands as though he weighed nothing at all. Humphrey's body was brown all over, like an animal's. Humphrey talked and Jeremy listened. He told Jeremy the most marvellous stories, and Jeremy believed every word of them. They sat on a little hummock, with a dark wood behind them, and watched the moon rise.

"You're a decent kid," said Humphrey. "I like you better than my brothers. I suppose you'll forget me as soon as I'm gone."

"I'll never forget you," said Jeremy. "Can't you leave your family and be somebody else? Then you can come and stay with us."

"Stay with a parson? Not much. You'll see me again one day. I'll send you a line from time to time and let you know where I am."

Finally, they swore friendship. They exchanged gifts. Humphrey gave Jeremy a broken pocket-knife, and Jeremy gave

Humphrey his silver watch-chain. They shook hands and swore to be friends for ever.

And then the final and terrible tragedy occurred.

v

It came, just as suddenly, as for a romantic climax it should have come.

On the afternoon that followed the friendship-swearing Humphrey did not appear at the accustomed place. Jeremy waited for several hours and then went melancholy home. At breakfast next morning there were those grown-up, mysterious allusions that mean that some catastrophe, too terrible for tender ears, is occurring.

" I never heard anything so awful," said Aunt Amy.

" It's so sad to me," said Jeremy's mother, sighing, " that people should want to do these things."

" It's abominable," said Mr. Cole, " that they were ever allowed to come here at all. We should have been told before we came."

" But do you really think——" said Aunt Amy.

" I know, because Mrs.——"

" But just fancy if——"

" It's quite possible, especially when——"

N

" What a dreadful thing that——"

Jeremy sat there, feeling as though every-one were looking at him. What had happened to Humphrey? He must go at once and find out.

He slipped off after breakfast, and before he reached the bottom of the downs, heard shouts and cries. He ran across the beach and was soon involved in a crowd of farmers, women, boys and animals all shouting, crying out and barking together. Being small he was able to worry his way through without any attention being paid to him; indeed, everyone was too deeply excited by what was happening in the yard of the farm to notice small boys. When at last he got to the gate and looked through, he beheld an extraordinary scene. Among the cobbles and the manure heaps and the filth many things were scattered—articles of clothing, some chairs and a table, some pictures, many torn papers. The yard was almost filled with men and women, all of them apparently shouting and screaming together. A big red-faced man next to Jeremy was crying over and over again : " That'll teach him to meddle with our women." " That'll teach him to meddle with our women. . . ."

On the steps of the farm-house an extra-ordinary woman was standing, quite alone, no one near to her, standing there, contempt in her eyes and a curious smile, almost of pleasure, on her lips. Even to Jeremy's young innocence she was over-coloured. Her face was crimson; she wore a large hat of bright green and a bright green dress with a flowing train. She did not move; she might have been painted into the stone. But Jeremy's gaze (seen dimly and as it were upwards through a pair of high, widely extended farmer's legs) was soon withdrawn from this highly coloured lady to the central figure of the scene. This was a man who seemed to Jeremy the biggest and blackest human he had ever seen. He had jet-black hair, a black beard, and struggling now in the middle of the yard between three rough-looking countrymen, his clothes were almost torn from the upper part of his body. His face was bleeding, and even as Jeremy caught sight of him he snatched one arm free and caught one of his captors a blow that sent him reeling. For one instant he seemed to rise above the crowd, gathering himself together for a mighty effort; he seemed, in that second, to look towards Jeremy, his eyes staring out of his head, his great chest heaving, his legs straining. But at once four men were upon him and began to drive him towards the gate, the crowd bending back and driving Jeremy into a confusion of thighs and legs behind which he could see nothing. Then suddenly once more the scene cleared, and the boy saw a figure run from the house, crying something, his hand raised. Someone caught the figure and stayed it; for a second of time Jeremy saw Humphrey's face flaming with anger. Then the crowd closed round.

At the same instant the black man seemed to be whirled towards them, there was a crushing, a screaming, a boot seemed to rise from the ground of its own volition and kick him violently in the face and he fell down, down, down, into a bottomless sea of black pitch.

VI

For three days he was in bed, his head aching, one cheek swollen to twice its natural size, one eye closed. To his amazement no one scolded him; no one asked him how he had been caught in that crowd. Everyone was very kind to him.

Once he asked his mother " What had happened ? " She told him that " They were very wicked people and had gone away."

When he was up and about again he went to the farm and looked through the gate. Within there was absolute stillness. A pig was snuffling amongst the manure.

He went out to the moor. It was a perfect

afternoon, only a little breeze blowing. The pools, slightly ruffled, were like blue lace. A rabbit sitting in front of his hole did not move. He threw himself, face downwards on the ground, burying his nose in it, feeling in some strange way that Humphrey was there.

CHAPTER IX

THE PICTURE-BOOK

I

SEPTEMBER 1 was Mary's birthday, and it had always something of a melancholy air about it because it meant that the holidays were drawing to a close. Soon there would be the last bathe, the last picnic, the last plunge across the moor, the last waking to the sharp, poignant cry of the flying, swerving gulls.

Then in strange, sudden fashion, like the unclicking of a door that opens into another room, the summer had suddenly slipped aside, giving place to autumn; not full autumn yet, only a few leaves turning, a few fires burning in the fields, the sea only a little colder in colour, the sky at evening a chillier green; but the change was there, and with it Polchester, and close behind Polchester old Thompson stepped towards them.

Yes, Mary's birthday marked the beginning of the end, and, in addition to that, there was the desperate, urgent question of present-giving. Mary took her present-giving (or rather present-

getting) with the utmost seriousness. No one
in the whole world minded quite so desperately
as she what she got, who gave it her, and how it
was given. Not that she was greedy ; indeed, no.
She was not like Helen, who guessed the price
of everything that she received, and had what
Uncle Samuel called " a regular shop mind."

It was all sentiment with Mary. What
she wanted was that someone (anyone) should
love her and therefore give her something.
She knew that Uncle Samuel did not love her,
and she suffered not, therefore, the slightest
unhappiness did he forget her natal day ; but
she would have cried for a week had Jeremy
forgotten it. She did not mind did Jeremy
only spend sixpence on his gift (but he was a
generous boy and always spent everything that,
at the moment, he had) so that she might be sure
that he had taken a little trouble in the buying
of it.

Jeremy knew all this well enough and, in
earlier years, the question of buying had been
simple, because Cow Farm was miles from anywhere, the nearest village being the fishing cove
of Rafiel, and Rafiel had only one " shop
general," and the things in this shop general
were all visible in the window from year's end
to year's end. Mary, therefore, received on her
birthday something with which, by sight at
least, she was thoroughly familiar.

Now this year there were new conditions.
The nearest village with shops was St. Mary's
Moor, some six miles away. It was there that
the purchase must be made, and in any case
it would be on this occasion a real novelty.
Jeremy tried to discover, by those circumlocu-
tory but self-revealing methods peculiar to
intending present-givers, what Mary would
like. Supposing, just supposing, that someone
one day were to die and, most unexpectedly,
leave a lot of money to Mary, what would she
buy? This was the kind of game that Mary
adored, and she entered into it thoroughly.
She would buy an enormous library, thousands
and thousands of books, she would buy a town
and fill it with sweet shops and then put
hundreds of poor children into it to eat as much
as they liked; she would buy Polchester Cathedral and make father bishop. This was flying
rather too high, and so Jeremy, somewhat pre-
cipitately, asked her what she would do were
she given fifteen shillings and sixpence. She
considered, and being that morning in a very
Christian frame of mind, decided that she would
give it to Miss Jones to buy a new hat with.
Mentally cursing girls and their tiresome ways,
Jeremy, outwardly polite, altered his demand
to : "No; but suppose you were given five
shillings and threepence halfpenny " (the exact
sum saved at that moment by him), "and had

to spend it for yourself, Mary, what would you get with it? ''

She would get a book.

Yes, but what book? She clasped her hands and looked to heaven. Oh! there were so many that she wanted. She wanted '' The Young Stepmother '' and '' Dynevor Terrace '' and '' The Scottish Chiefs '' and '' Queechy '' and '' Sylvie and Bruno '' and '' The Queen's Maries '' and—and—hundreds and hundreds.

Well, she couldn't buy hundreds with five and threepence halfpenny, that was certain, and if she thought that he was going to she was very much mistaken; but at least he had got his answer. It was a book that she wanted.

The next thing was to go into St. Mary's Moor. He found the opportunity ready to his hand because Miss Jones had to go to buy some things that were needed for the family the very next afternoon. He would go with her. Mary thought that she would go too, and when Jeremy told her, with an air of great mystery, that that was impossible, she looked so self-conscious that he could have smacked her.

The journey in the old ramshackle omnibus was a delightful adventure. It happened on this particular afternoon that all the Caerlyon farmers and their wives were going too, and there was a '' fine old crush.'' Hamlet, fixed tightly on

his lead, sat between his master's legs, his tongue
out, his hair on end, and his bright eyes wicked,
darting from place to place. He saw so many
things that he would like to do, parcels that
he would like to worry, legs that he would like
to smell, laps that he would like to investigate.

He gave sudden jerks at the lead, suited
himself to the rolling and jolting of the bus so
that he should be flung as near as possible to
the leg, parcel or lap that he most wished to
investigate. Jeremy then was very busy. Miss
Jones, who was a good woman and by now
thoroughly appreciated by all the members of
the Cole family, including Jeremy himself, who
always took her under his especial protection
when they went out anywhere, had in all her
years never learnt that first of all social laws,
" Never try to talk in a noisy vehicle," and had
a long story about one Edmund Spencer, from
whose mother she had that morning received a
letter. She treated Jeremy as a friend and
contemporary (one of the reasons for his liking
of her), and he was always deeply interested
in her histories; but to-day, owing to the
terrific rumblings, rattlings and screaming of
the bus and to the shrieking and shouting of
the farmers and their ladies, he could only
catch occasional words, and was not sure at the
end of it all whether Edmund Spencer were
animal, vegetable or mineral. His confusion

was complete when, just as they were rattling into St. Mary's one and only street, Miss Jones screamed into his ear, " And so they had to give her boiled milk four times a day and nothing else except an occasional potato."

The omnibus drew up in front of the Dog and Rabbit, and everyone departed on their various affairs. St. Mary's was like a little wayside station on the edge of a vast brindled, crinkled moorland, brown and grey and green rucking away to the smooth, pale, egg-shell blue of the afternoon sky. The sea-wind came ruffling up to them where they stood. What storms of wind and rain there must be in the winter! All the houses of the long straggling street seemed to be blown a bit askew.

Jeremy and Miss Jones looked around them, and at once the inevitable " general " sprang to view. Miss Jones had to go into the hotel about some business for the rectory, and telling Jeremy to stay just where he was, and that she wouldn't be more than " just five minutes," vanished. Having been told to stay where he was, it was natural of him to wander down the street, inspect a greasy pond with some ducks, three children playing marbles and two mongrel dogs, and then flatten his nose against the window of the " general."

Inspection proved very disappointing. There seemed to be nothing here that he could possibly

offer to Mary: bootlaces, cards of buttons,
mysterious articles of underwear, foggy bottles
containing bulls' eyes, sticks of liquorice, cakes
of soap, copies of *Home Chat* and *The Woman's
Journal*, some pairs of very dilapidated looking
slippers, some walking-sticks, portraits of Queen
Victoria and the Prince of Wales, highly
coloured. . . .

None of these. Unless, possibly, the Royal
Family. But no. Even to Jeremy's untrained
eye the colour was a *little* bright; and old
Victoria. . . . No, Mary wanted a *book*. He
stared up and down the street in great agitation.
He must buy *something* before Miss Jones came
out of the inn. He did not want her to see
what it was that he bought. The moments
were slipping by. There was *nothing* here.
The two half-crowns and the threepenny piece
in his tightly clenched palm were hot and
sticky. He looked again. There really was
nothing! Then, staring down the street towards
the open moor and the eventual sea, he saw a
little bulging bottle-glass window that seemed
to have coloured things in it. He turned and
almost ran.

It was the last shop in the street, and a
funny, dumpty, white-washed cottage with a
pretty garden on its farther seaward side. The
bottle-glass window protected the strangest
things. (In another place and at another time

it might not be uninteresting to tell the story of Mr. Redpath, of how he opened a curiosity shop in St. Mary's, of all places! and of the adventures, happy and otherwise, that he encountered there.)

In the shop window there were glasses of blue with tapering stems, and squat old men smoking pipes, painted in the gayest colours, and pottery (jugs to drink out of), and there were old chains of beaten and figured silver, and golden boxes, and the model of a ship with full sails and a gorgeous figure-head of red and gold, and there were old pictures in dim frames, and a piece of a coloured rug, and lots and lots of other things as well.

Jeremy pushed the door back, heard a little bell tinkle above his head, and at once was in a shop so crowded that it was impossible to see t'other from which. A young man with a pale face and carroty hair was behind the very high counter, so high that Jeremy's nose just tipped the level of it.

" Have you got such a thing as a book? " he asked very politely.

The young man smiled.

" What sort of a book? "

" Well, she *said* she wanted ' Queechy ' or ' Sylvie and Bruno ' or—I've forgotten the names of the others. You haven't got those two, I suppose? "

"No, I haven't," said the young man, quite grave now.

"Have you got *any* books?" said Jeremy breathlessly, because time was slipping by and he had to stand on his toes.

"I've got this old Bible," said the young man, producing a thick, heavy volume with brass clasps. "You see it's got rather fine pictures. I think you'd better sit on this," he added, producing a high stool; "you'll be able to see better."

"Oh, that's very nice," said Jeremy, fascinated by Moses twisting a serpent around his very muscular arm as though it were a piece of string. "How much is this?"

"Eight pounds and ten," said the young man, as though he'd said a halfpenny.

"I think I'd better tell you at once," said Jeremy, leaning his elbows confidentially on the counter, "that I've only got five shillings and threepence halfpenny."

The young man scratched his head. "I doubt if we've got any book," he began; then suddenly, "Perhaps this will be the very thing —if you like pictures."

He burrowed deep down in the back somewhere, and then produced two or three long, flat-looking books, dusty and a faded yellow. He wiped them with a cloth and presented them to Jeremy. At the first sight of them he

knew that they were what he wanted. He
read the titles: one was "Robinson Crusoe,"
another "The Swiss Family Robinson," the
third "Masterman Ready." He looked at
"Crusoe," and gave a delighted squeal of
ecstasy as he turned over the pages. The print
was funny and blacker than he had ever seen
print before; the pictures were coloured, and
richly coloured, the reds and greens and
purples sinking deep into the page. Oh! it
was a lovely book! a perfect book! the very,
very thing for Mary.

"How much is it?" he asked, trembling
before the answer.

"Exactly five shillings and threepence halfpenny," said the young man gravely.

"That *is* strange," said Jeremy, almost
crowing with delight and keeping his hand on
the book unless it should suddenly melt away.
"That's just what I've got. Isn't that lucky?"

"Very fortunate indeed," said the young
man. "Shall I wrap it up for you?"

"Oh, yes, please do—and very carefully,
please, so nobody can guess what it is."

The young man was very clever about this,
and when he emerged from the back of the shop
he had with him a parcel that might easily
have been a ship or a railway train. Jeremy
paid his money, climbed down from his stool,
then held out his hand.

"Good-bye," he said. "Thank you. I'll come again one day and look at the other things in your shop.

"Please do," said the young man, bowing.

He went out, the little bell tinkling gaily behind him, and there, coming at that very moment out of the hotel, was Miss Jones.

II

We all know the truth of the familiar proverb that "Distance lends enchantment to the view," and it was never more true of anything in the world than of parcels.

All the way back in the 'bus the book grew and grew in magnificence simply because Jeremy could not see it. He clutched the parcel tightly on his knees and resisted all Miss Jones's attempts to discover its contents. Back in the rectory, he rushed up to his bedroom, locked the door, and then, with trembling fingers, undid the paper.

The first glimpse of "Robinson Crusoe and the Footmark on the Sand" thrilled him so that the white-washed walls of his room faded away and the thin pale evening glow passed into a sky of burning blue, and a scarlet cockatoo flew screaming above his head and the sand lay hot and sugar-brown at his feet. Mystery

was there—the footprint in the sand, and
Crusoe with his shaggy beard and peaked hat,
staring. . . .

Feverishly his fingers turned the pages, and
picture after picture opened for his delight.
He had never before seen a book with so many
pictures, pictures so bright and yet so true,
pictures so real that you could almost touch the
trees and the figures and Crusoe's hatchet. He
knelt then on the floor, the book spread out upon
the bed, so deeply absorbed that it was with a
terrific jolt that he heard the banging on the
door and Mary's voice:

" Aren't you coming, Jeremy? We're half
through supper. The bell went hours ago."

Mary! He had forgotten all about her. Of
course, this book was for her. Just the book
for her. She would love the pictures. He had
forgotten all about . . .

He went down to supper and was bewildered
and absent-minded throughout the meal. That
night his dreams were all of Crusoe, of burning
sands and flaming skies, of the crimson cockatoo
and Man Friday. When he woke he jumped
at once out of bed and ran on naked feet to
the book. As a rule the next morning is the
testing time, and too often we find that the
treasure that we bought the day before has
already lost some of its glitter and shine. Now
it was not so; the pictures had grown better

and better, richer and ever more rich. The loveliest pictures . . .

Just the book for Mary. It was then, standing half stripped before his basin, pausing as he always did ere he made the icy attack with the sponge, that he realized his temptation. He did not want to give the book to Mary. He wanted to keep it for himself.

While he dressed the temptation did not approach him very closely. It was so horrible a temptation that he did not look it in the eyes. He was a generous little boy, had never done a mean thing in all his life. He was always eager to give anything away although he had a strong and persistent sense of possessions so that he loved to have his things near him, and they seemed to him, his books and his toys and his football, as alive as the people around him. He had never felt anything so alive as this book was.

When he came down to breakfast he was surprised to find that the sight of Mary made him feel rather cross. She always had, in excess of others, the capacity for irritating him, as she herself well knew. This morning she irritated him very much. Her birthday would be four days from now; he would be glad when it arrived; he could give her the book and the temptation would be over. Indeed, he would like to give her the book now and have done with it.

By the middle of the day he was considering whether he could not give her something else "just as good" and keep the book for himself. He wrapped the book in all its paper, but ran up continually to look at it. She would like something else just as much; she would like something else more. After all, "Robinson Crusoe" was a book for boys. But the trouble was that he had now no money. He would receive threepence on Saturday, the last Saturday before Mary's birthday, but what could you get with threepence? Five shillings of the sum with which he had bought Mary's present had been given him by Uncle Samuel—and Uncle Samuel's next present would be the tip before he went to school.

That afternoon he quarrelled with Mary—for no reason at all. He was sitting under the oak tree on the lawn reading "Redgauntlet." Mary came and asked him whether she could take Hamlet for a run. Hamlet, as though he were a toy-dog made of springs, was leaping up and down. He did not like Mary, but he adored a run.

"No, you can't," said Jeremy.

"Oh! Jeremy, why can't I? I'll take the greatest care of him and those horrid little boys are gone away now and——"

"You can't because I say you can't."

"Oh, Jeremy, do let——"

He started up from his chair, all rage and indignation.

"Look here, Mary, if you go on talking——"

She walked away down the garden, her head hanging in that tiresome way it had when she was unhappy. Hamlet tried to follow her, so he called him back. He came, but was quite definitely in the sulks, sitting, his head raised, very proud, wrath in his eyes, snapping angrily at an occasional fly.

"Redgauntlet" was spoilt for Jeremy. He put the book down and tried to placate Hamlet who knew his power and refused to be placated. Why didn't he let Mary take Hamlet? What a pig he was! He would be nice to Mary when she came back. But when she did return that face of hers, with its beseeching look, irritated him so deeply that he snapped at her more than before.

After all, "Robinson Crusoe" *was* a book for boys. . . .

Two days later he had decided, quite definitely, that he could not part with it. He must find something else for her, something very fine indeed, the best thing that he had. He thought of every possible way of making money, but time was so short and ways of making money quickly were so few. He thought of asking his father for the pocket-money of many weeks in advance, but it would have to be so very many weeks in advance to be worth anything at all, and his father would want to know what he needed the money for; and after the episode of last Christmas he did not wish to say anything about presents. He thought of selling something; but there was no place to sell things in, and he had not anything that anyone else wanted. He thought of asking his mother; but she would send him to his father who always managed the family finances.

He went over all his private possessions. The trouble with them was that Mary knew them all so well.

Impossible to pretend that there was anything there that she could want! He collected the most hopeful of them and laid them out on the bed—a pocket-knife, three books, a photograph frame (rubbed at the edges), a watch chain that had seemed at first to be silver but now most certainly wasn't, a leather pocketbook, a red blotting pad—not a very brilliant collection.

He did not now dare to look at the book at all. He put it away in the bottom of the chest of drawers. He thought that perhaps if he did not see it nor take it out of its brown paper until the actual day that it would be easier to give. But he had imagination as, in later years, he was to find to his cost, and the

book grew and grew in his mind, the pictures
flaming like suns, the spirit of the book smiling
at him, saying to him with confidential friendship : " We belong to one another, you and I.
No one shall part us."

Then Helen said to him :

" What are you going to give Mary on her
birthday ? "

" Why ? " he asked suspiciously.

" I only wanted to know. I've got mine.
Everyone knows you went into St. Mary's and
bought something. Mary herself knows."

That was the worst of being part of a family.
Everyone knew everything !

" Perhaps it wasn't for Mary," he said.

Helen sniffed. " Of course, if you don't
want to tell me," she said, " I don't care to
know."

Then he discovered the little glass bottle
with the silver stopper. It had been given him
two years ago on his birthday by a distant cousin
who happened to be staying with them at the
time. What anybody wanted to give a *boy* a
glass bottle with a stopper for Jeremy couldn't
conceive. Mary had always liked it, had picked
it up and looked at it with longing. Of course
she knew that it had been his for two years.
He looked at it, and even as Adam, years ago,
with the apple, he fell.

III

Mary's birthday came, and with it a day of burning, glowing colour. The first early autumn mists were hanging like veils of thinly-sheeted bronze before the grass wet with heavy dew, the sky of azure, the sea crystal pale. In the mist the rectory was a giant box of pearl. The air smelt of distant fires.

On such a day who would not be happy? And Mary was perhaps the happiest little girl in the kingdom. Happy as she was she lost much of her plainness, her eyes sparkling behind her glasses, her mouth smiling. Something tender and poignant in her, some distant prophecy of her maturity, one day beautifully to be fulfilled, coming forth in her, because she felt that she was beloved even though it were only for an hour. She was lucky in her presents; her mother gave her a silver watch, a little darling, quite small, with the hours marked in blue on the face, and her father gave her a silver watch chain so thin that you thought that it would break if you looked at it, and in reality so strong that not the strongest man in the world could break it. Aunt Amy gave her a muff, soft and furry, and Helen gave her a red leather blotter, and Uncle Samuel sent her a book, the very "Dynevon Terrace" that she wanted—how *did* he know? And Miss Jones

gave her a work basket with the prettiest silk
lining inside you ever saw, and a pair of gloves
from Barbara and—a glass bottle with a silver
stopper from Jeremy!

It seemed that she liked this last present best
of all. She rushed up to Jeremy and kissed him
in the wettest possible way.

"Oh, Jeremy! I *am* so glad. That's *just*
what I wanted! I've never seen such a darling.
I've never had any silver things to stand on my
table and Gladys Sampson has such a lot, and
this is prettier than any that Gladys has. Oh!
mother, *do* look! See what Jeremy's given me!
Father, see what Jeremy's given me! Isn't it
pretty, Miss Jones? You are a *dear*, Jeremy,
and I'll have it all my life!"

Jeremy stood there, his heart like lead. It
may be said with truth of him that never in his
whole existence had he felt such shame as he
did now. Mean, mean, mean! Suddenly, now
that it was too late, he hated that book upstairs
lying safely in his bottom drawer. He didn't
want ever to look at it again.

And Mary. She must *know* that this was
his old glass bottle that he had had so long.
She had seen it a hundred times. It is true
that he had rubbed it up and got the woman in
the kitchen to polish the silver, but still she must
know. He looked at her with new interest.
Was it all acting, this enthusiasm? No, it was

not. She was genuinely moved and delighted. Was she pretending to herself that she had never seen it before, forcing herself to believe that it was new? He would keep the book and give it to her at Christmas. But that would not be the same thing. The deed was done now. The shabby, miserable deed.

He did everything that he could to make her birthday a happy one. He was with her all the day. He allowed her to read to him a long piece of the story that she was then writing, a very tiresome business because she could not read her own script, and because there were so many characters that he could never keep track of any of them. He went blackberrying with her in the afternoon and gave her all the best blackberries. But nothing could raise his spirits. The beautiful day said nothing to him. He felt sick in the evening from eating too many blackberries and went to bed directly after supper.

IV

The days that followed could hardly help but be jolly because the weather was so lovely —still, breathless days, when the world seemed to be painted in purple and blue on a wall of ivory, when the sea came over the sand with a ripple of utter content, when the moon appeared early in the evening, a silver bow, and mounted gently into a sky thick with stars, when every sound, the rattle of carts, the barks of dogs, the cries of men, struck the air sharply like blows upon iron. Yet, though the world was so lovely and everyone—even Aunt Amy—was in the best and most contented tempers, something hung over him like a black, heavy cloth. His pride in himself was gone. He had done something shabbier than even the Dean's Ernest would do.

He continued to see Mary with new eyes. She was a decent kid. He looked back over the past months and saw how much more decent she had been to him than he had been to her. She had been irritating, of course, but then that was because she was a girl. All girls were irritating. Just look at Helen, for instance ! Meanwhile he never glanced at the book again. It lay there neglected in its paper.

One day Mary received in a letter a postal order for ten shillings. This was a present from a distant aunt in America who had suddenly remembered Mary's birthday. Filled with glee and self-importance, she went in to St. Mary's with Miss Jones to spend it.

That evening when Jeremy was washing his hands there was a knock on his door and Mary's voice : " May I come in ? "

" Yes," he said.

She came in, her face coloured with mysterious purpose. In her hands she held a paper parcel.

"Oh, are you washing your hands, Jeremy?" she said, her favourite opening in conversation being always a question of the obvious. The red evening sunlight flooded the room.

"What is it?" Jeremy asked rather crossly.

She looked at him pleadingly, as though begging him to save her from the difficulties of emotion and explanation that crowded in upon her.

"Oh, Jeremy, St. Mary's was lovely, and there was a man with an organ and a monkey, and I gave the monkey a penny and it took it in its hand and took off its cap. . . . Miss Jones has got a cold," she added, "and sneezed all the way home."

"She always has a cold," he said, "or something."

"And it goes straight to her face when she has a cold and makes all her teeth ache—not only one of them, but all. She isn't coming down to supper. She's gone to bed."

Still he waited, striving for politeness.

"I've got something for you," Mary suddenly said, dropping her voice in the sentimental manner that he hated. Then, as though she were ashamed of what she had done, she

took the parcel to the bed and undid the paper
with clumsy fingers.

"There," she said, "I got it for you because I thought you'd like it."

He looked at it; it was a book: it was
"Swiss Family Robinson": it was a companion to his "Robinson Crusoe." He stared
at it: he could say nothing.

"You do like it, don't you?" she asked,
gazing at him anxiously. "It's got lots and
lots of pictures. There was a funny shop at
the end of the street and I went in with Miss
Jones and the man was very nice. And I
thought it was just what you'd like. You do
like it, don't you?" she asked again.

But he could only stare at it, not coming
forward to touch it. He was buried deep, deep
in shame. There came a rattle then on the door
and Helen's voice:

"Mary, if you're in there with Jeremy,
mother says you're to come at once and have
your hair brushed because it's five minutes to
supper."

"Oh, dear, I'd forgotten." And with
one last glance of anxiety towards Jeremy she
went.

Still he did not move. Could anything
possibly have happened to prove to him
what a pig he was, what a skunk and a cur?
Mary had bought it with her own money,

five and threepence halfpenny out of ten
shillings.

He did not touch the book, but with
chin set and eyes resolved, he went down to
supper. When the meal was finished he said
to Mary :

" Come upstairs a minute. I want to speak
to you."

She followed him tremulously. He seemed
to be clothed in his domineering manner. How
often, especially of late, she had determined that
she would not be afraid of him, but would dig
up from within her the common sense, the easy
companionship, the laughter that were all there
for him, she knew, could she only be at her
ease ! She even sympathized with him in thinking her so often a fool ! She *was* a fool when
she was with him, simply because she cared for
him so much and thought him so wonderful and
so clever !

He didn't like the book ! He was going to
thank her for it in the way that he had when
he was trying to be polite, and didn't find it
easy. She followed him into the bedroom. He
carefully closed the door. She saw at once that
the book lay exactly where she had placed it
on the bed—that he had not even opened it.
He regarded her sternly.

" Sit down on that chair ! " he said. She
sat down.

"Look here, you oughtn't to have given me that book. You know that Aunt Lucy sent that money for you to spend on yourself."

"I thought you'd like it," she said, pushing at her spectacles as she always did when she was distressed.

"I do like it," he said. "It's splendid. But I've done something awful—and I've got to tell you now you've given me that."

"Oh, Jeremy! something awful! What is it?"

He set his jaw and, without looking at her, made his confession.

"That day I went in with Miss Jones to St. Mary's I was going to buy you a present. And I did buy you one. I went into that same shop you went to and I bought 'Robinson Crusoe' just like the one you bought me. When I bought it I meant it for you, of course, but when I got home I liked it so much I kept it for myself and I gave you that old bottle instead—and then I didn't like the rotten book after all and I've never looked at it since your birthday."

Mary's pleasure at being made his confidante in this way was much greater than her horror at his crime. Her bosom heaved with gratified importance.

"I've done things like that, Jeremy," she

said. " I got six handkerchiefs for Miss Jones one Christmas, and I kept three of them because I got a terrible bad cold just at the time."

" That's not so bad," he said, shaking his head, " because I gave you an old thing that I'd had for years."

" No," she interrupted; " I've wanted that bottle ever so long. I used to go up to your room and look at it sometimes when you were at school."

He went to the drawer and produced " Robinson Crusoe " and gave it to her. She accepted it gratefully, but said :

" And now I shall have to give you back the bottle."

" Oh, no, you won't."

" But I can't have two presents."

" Yes, you can. I don't want the old bottle, anyway. I never used it for anything. And now we'll each have a book, so it won't be like a present exactly."

She smiled with pleasure. " Oh, I'm so glad you're not angry."

" Angry? " he repeated after her.

" Yes," she said, getting up from the bed where she had been sitting. " I thought you were when you asked me to come up here."

He looked at her puzzled. She seemed to

him a new Mary whom he had never seen before.

"Am I often angry?" he asked.

"Not angry exactly; but I get frightened that you are going to be cross, and then I say the silliest things—not because I want to, but because I want to be clever, and then, of course, I never am."

He stood staring at her. "Am I as beastly as that?" he asked.

"Oh, you're not beastly," she reassured him. "Never—you're not," forgetting her grammar in her eagerness; "but I'm afraid of you, and I'm fonder of you than anybody— lots fonder—and I always say to myself, ' Now I'm not going to be silly *this* time,' and then I am. I don't know why," she sighed. "But I'm not nearly as silly as I seem," she ended.

No, she wasn't. He suddenly saw that, and he also suddenly saw that he had all this time been making a great mistake. Here was a possible companion, not only possible, but living, breathing, existing. She was on her own to-night, neither fearful nor silly, meeting him on his own level, superior to him, perhaps, knowing more than he did about many things, understanding his feelings. . . .

"I say, Mary, we'll do things together. I'm awfully lonely sometimes. I want some-

The Picture-Book

great time next holidays."

It was the happiest moment of Mary's life.
Too much for her altogether. She just nodded
and, clutching "Robinson Crusoe" to her,
ran.

P

CHAPTER X

UNCLE PERCY

I

THE town was ringed with fire, and out of that magic circle, like Siegfried, Uncle Percy came. The sunset flamed up the hill and wrapped the top of the monument in crocus shadows, the garden of the Coles was rose and amber.

Mary and Jeremy were hanging over the banisters watching for the arrival. The windows behind them burnt with the sun, and their bodies also burnt and their hair was in flames. In the hall there was green dusk until, at the rumble of the cab, Emily suddenly lit the gas, and the umbrellas and Landseer's " Dignity and Impudence " were magnificently revealed.

The door opened, and out of the evening sun into the hissing gas stepped Uncle Percy. The children heard him say :

" Mrs. Cole at home ? " and his voice was roaring, laughing, vibrating, resounding tumultuous. He seemed in his rough grey overcoat too huge to be human, and when this was taken from him by the smiling Emily—she always smiled, as Jeremy had long since observed, at gentlemen more than at ladies—in his bright brown tweeds he was still huge, and, with his brown hair and red face, like a solid chunk of sunset thrown into the dark house to cheer it up. He went bursting up the staircase, and the children fled—only just in time.

From the schoolroom they heard him erupt into the drawing-room, and then the bumping of his box up the stairs and the swearing of the cabman.

This was their Uncle Percy from California, South America, New Zealand, Hong Kong, and anywhere else you like; the brother of their father, the only prosperous one of that family, prosperous, according to Aunt Amy, because for twenty years he had kept away from England; according to father, because he had always had wonderful health, even as a very small boy; and to Uncle Samuel because he had never married—although that was a strange reason for Uncle Samuel to give, because he also had never married, and he could not, with the best wish in the world, be said to be prosperous.

It had been sprung upon them all with the utmost suddenness that he was coming to pay them a visit. They had but just returned from Caerlyon and the sea—in another ten days Jeremy would be off to school again—when the

telegram arrived that threw them all into such
perturbation. "Arrive eleventh. Hope you
can put me up for day or two—Percy." Percy!
Fortunately there was for them in the whole
world only one Percy or they might have been
in sad confusion, because their Percy was, they
imagined, safe in the suburbs of Auckland, New
Zealand. A letter followed confirming the
telegram. Mr. Cole had not seen his brother
for twenty years. They had received one photograph of a large fat staring man on a large
fat staring horse. Such thighs, such a back,
both of man and of horse! "Feed their animals
well in New Zealand" was Uncle Samuel's only
comment, and he, back only that minute from
painting the moors, departed at a moment's
notice for London.

"Don't you want to see Uncle Percy?"
asked Jeremy.

"I shall see him better if I study him from
a distance," said Uncle Samuel. "He's too
large to see properly close to," and he went—
voted selfish by all because he would not help
in the entertaining. "Of course I'm selfish,"
said Uncle Samuel. "No one else cares tup-
pence about me, so where should I be if I
didn't look after myself?"

In any case their Uncle Percy actually was
shut into the drawing-room, and five minutes
later the children were sent for.

It had not been intended that Hamlet should enter with them, but he had a way of suddenly appearing from nowhere and joining, unobtrusively, any company that he thought pleasant and amusing. To-day, however, he was anything but unobtrusive; at the sudden shock of that red flaming figure with legs spread wide across the centre of the carpet he drew himself together and barked like a mad thing. Nothing would quiet him, and when Jeremy dragged him into the passage and left him there he still barked and barked and barked, quivering all over, in a perfect frenzy of indignation and horror. He had then to be taken to Jeremy's bedroom on the top floor and shut in, and there, too, he barked, stopping only once and again for a howl. All this disturbed Uncle Percy's greeting of the children, but he did not seem to mind. It was obvious at once that nothing could upset him. Jeremy simply could not take his eyes off him, off his brown, almost carroty, hair that stood on end almost like an aureole, off his purple cheeks and flat red nose and thick red neck, off his flaming purple tie, his waistcoat of red and brown squares, his bulging thighs, his tartan socks. This his father's brother, the brother of his father who sat now, the dim shadow of a shade, pale and apprehensive upon the sofa. The brother of his father! Impossible! How could it be possible?

"Well, kid, what are you staring at?"
came suddenly to him. "Know your old uncle
again, hey? Think you'll recognize him if you
meet him in the Strand, ho? Know him anywhere, won't you, ha? A likely kid that of
yours, Herbert. Come and talk to your uncle,
boy—come and talk to your uncle."

Jeremy moved across the carpet slowly; he
was deeply embarrassed, conscious of the solemn
gaze of Aunt Amy, of Helen and Mary. A
great red hand fell upon his shoulder. He felt
himself suddenly caught up by the slack of his
pants, held in mid-air, then dropped, cascades
of laughter billowing meanwhile around him.

"That's a fine boy, hey? That's what we
do to boys in New Zealand to make 'em grow.
Want to grow, hey? Be a bigger man than
your father, ho? Well, that won't be difficult,
anyway. Never were much of a size, were you,
Herbert? Well, boy, go to school?"

"Yes," said Jeremy.

"Like it?"

"Yes," said Jeremy.

"Bully the boys smaller than yourself?"

"No," said Jeremy.

"Bet you do. I always did when I was at
school. Any good at games?"

"No," said Jeremy, suddenly to his own
surprise determining that he would tell his
uncle nothing.

" That's like your father. Never any good
at games, were you, Herbert? Remember when
we tossed you in a blanket and your head
bumped on the ceiling? "

Mr. Cole gave a sickly smile.

" That was a lark. I can see it as though
it were yesterday. With your legs sticking out
of your nightdress——"

Luckily at this point tea arrived, and everyone was very busy. Uncle Percy sat down and
then was suddenly aware of Helen. She was
looking her prettiest in her blue silk; she knew
better than to push herself forward. She had
waited patiently through all the examination of
Jeremy, certain that her time would come.
And it did.

" Why, there's a pretty one! " he jerked his
great body upwards. " Why, I hardly saw you
just now! And you're Helen! "

" Yes, uncle." She smiled that smile so
beautifully designed for worth-while relations.

He stared at her with all his eyes. " Why,
you're a beauty, 'pon my soul, you are! Come
and sit here beside your old uncle and tell him
how all the boys run after you. I'm sure they
do if boys are still the same as when I was
young. Come along, now, and tell me all
about it."

Helen demurely " came along," sat beside
her uncle and answered his questions with

exactly the right mixture of deference and
humour. She brought him his tea and his
cake, and was the perfect hostess—a much
better hostess, as Jeremy noticed, than her
mother; and noticing it, hated her for it.

II

Before twenty-four hours had passed Uncle
Percy had made his mark not only upon his
own family, but upon Polchester. One walk
up the High Street and everyone was asking
who was that " big, red-faced man "? But it
was not only that he was big and red-faced; he
moved with such complete assurance. He was
more like our Archdeacon Brandon (although,
of course, not nearly so handsome) than anyone
who had been to our town for years. He had
just the archdeacon's confidence; it would have
been interesting to watch the two men together.

He took charge of the Cole family in simply
no time at all. For one thing he smoked all
over the house. Uncle Samuel had been hitherto
the only smoker in the family household, and
it was understood that he smoked only in his
studio. But Uncle Percy smoked everywhere
—and cigars—and big black terribly-smelling
cigars too! He appeared on the very first
morning, just as the bell rang for breakfast,

clad only in a dressing-gown with a great deal of red chest exposed, and thus confronted Aunt Amy on the way to dining-room prayer. He arrived for breakfast an hour late and ordered fresh tea. He sat in his brother's study most of the morning, talking and smoking. He forced his way into Uncle Samuel's studio and laughed at his pictures. (Of course, Uncle Samuel was in London.)

"Call them pictures?" he cried all through luncheon. "Those daubs of paint? Why, I could do better myself if I shut my eyes and splashed coloured ink on the canvas. And I know something about painting, mind you. Wasn't a bad hand myself at it once. Gave it up because I hadn't time to waste! Call *them* pictures!"

For this Aunt Amy almost forgave him his naked chest.

"It's what I've always said," she remarked, "only no one would listen to me. Samuel's pictures are folly, folly!"

During the first day both Hamlet and Jeremy were fascinated. Hamlet recovered from his first fit of horror, smelt something in the stockings and knickerbockers in which Uncle Percy now appeared that fascinated him. He followed those stockings all round the house, his nose just a little ahead of his body, and he had to move quickly because Uncle Percy was

never still for a moment. Uncle Percy, of
course, laughed at Hamlet.

" Call that a dog ! " he cried. " I call it a
dog-fight ! " and laughed immoderately.

But Hamlet bore him no grudge ; with his
beard projecting and his eyes intent on the
pursuit, he followed the stockings. Such a
smell ! and such calves ! Both smell and calves
were new in his experience—to lick the one
and bite the other ! What a glorious ambition !

Jeremy, on his part, was at the beginning
dazzled. He had never before seen such superb
despotism ! For those twenty-four hours he
admired it all immensely—the unceasing flow
of words, the knowledge of every imaginable
quarter of the globe, the confident, unfaltering
answer to every possible question, the definite
assumption of universal superiority, the absence
of every doubt, hesitation or shyness.

Jeremy was as yet no analyser of human
nature, but, young as he was, he knew his own
shynesses, awkwardnesses and reticences, and
for twenty-four hours he did wish he were like
his Uncle Percy. He even envied his calves
and looked at his own in his bedroom looking-
glass to see how they were getting along.

It cannot, however, be denied that every
member of the Cole family went that night to
bed feeling desperately weary ; it was as though
they had spent a day with a thunder-storm or

sat for twelve hours in the very middle of Niagara Falls, or lodged for an hour or two in the west tower of the cathedral amongst the bells. They were tired. Their bedrooms seemed to them strangely, almost ominously silent.

It was as though they had passed quite suddenly into a deaf and mute world.

On the second day it might have been noticed, had there been anyone here or there especially observant, that Uncle Percy was beginning to be bored. He looked around him for some fitting entertainment and discovered his brother Herbert.

Although it was twenty years since he had seen his brother, it was remarkable with what swiftness he had slipped back into his childhood's attitude towards him. He had laughed at him then; he laughed at him now with twice his original heartiness because Herbert was a clergyman, and clergymen seemed to Uncle Percy very laughable things. Our colonies promote a directer form of contact between individuals than is our custom at home; it is a true word that there are no "frills" in the colonies. You let a man know what you think of him for good or ill without any disguise. Uncle Percy let his brother know what he thought of him at once, and he let everyone else know too—and this was, for his brother, a very painful experience.

The Rev. Herbert Cole had been brought up in seclusion. People had taken from the first trouble that his feelings should not be hurt, and when it was understood that he was "destined for the ministry," a mysterious veil had been drawn in order that for the rest of his days he never should see things as they were. No one, for twenty long years, had been rude to him. If he wanted to be angry he was angry; if things were wrong he said so; if he felt ill he said so; if he had a headache he said so; and if he felt well he didn't say so quite as often as he might have done. He believed himself to be a good honest God-fearing man, and on the whole he was so. But he did not know what he would be were anyone rude to him; he did not know until Percy came to stay with him. He had, of course, disliked Percy when they were small boys together, but that was so long ago that he had forgotten all about it; and during the first twenty-four hours he put everything down to Percy's high animal spirits and delight at being home again and pleasure at being with his relations.

It was not until luncheon on the second day that he began to realize what was happening. Over the chops he said something in his well-known definite authoritative manner about " the Church not standing it, and the sooner those infidels in Africa realized it the better."

" Bosh ! " said Uncle Percy. " Bosh ! "

" My dear Percy . . ." began Mr. Cole.

" Don't ' dear Percy ' me," came from the other end of the table. " I say it's bosh ! What do you know of Africa or of the Church for the matter of that? You've never been outside this piffling little town for twenty years and wouldn't have noticed anything if you had. That's the worst of you miserable parsons— never seeing anything of life or the world, and then laying down the law as though you were God Almighty. It fair makes me sick ! But you were always like that, Herbert. Even as a boy you'd hide behind some woman's skirts and then lay claim to someone else's actions. Don't you talk about Africa, Herbert. You know nothing about it whatever. Here, Helen, my girl, pass up the potatoes ! "

Had a large iron thunderbolt crashed through the ceiling and broken the room to pieces consternation could not have been more general. Mr. Cole at first simply did not believe the evidence of his ears, then as it slowly dawned upon him that his brother had really said these things, and before a mixed company (Emily was at that moment handing round the cabbage), a dull pink flush stole slowly over his cheeks and ended in fiery crimson at the tips of his ears.

Mrs. Cole and Amy were, of course, devas-

tated, but dreadful was the effect upon the
children. Three pairs of eyes turned instantly
towards Mr. Cole and then hurriedly withdrew.
Mary attacked once again the bone of her chop,
already sufficiently cleaned. Helen gazed at
her uncle, her eyes full of a lovely investigating
interest. Jeremy stared at the tablecloth. He
himself could not at once realize what had
occurred. He had been accustomed for so long
now to hear his father speak with authority
upon every conceivable topic and remain un-
contradicted. Even when visitors came—and
they were so often curates—his opinions were
generally confirmed with a " Quite so," or " Is
that so indeed? " or " Yes, yes; quite." His
first interest now was to see how his father
would reply to this attack. They all waited.

Mr. Cole feebly smiled.

" Tee. Tee. Violent as ever, Percy. I
dare say you're correct. Of course, I never was
in Africa."

Capitulation! Complete capitulation!
Jeremy's cheeks burnt hot with family shame.
Was nobody going to stand up to the attack?
Were they to allow it to pass like that? They
were apparently. The subject was changed.
Bread-and-butter pudding arrived. The world
went on.

Uncle Percy himself had no conception that
anything unusual had occurred. He had been

shouting people down and bullying them for
years. Something subconsciously told him that
his brother was going to be easy game; perhaps
deep down in that mighty chest of his something
chuckled; and that was all.

But for Jeremy that was not all. He went
up to his room and considered the matter.
Readers of this chronicle and the one that pre-
ceded it will be aware that his relations with
his father had not been altogether happy ones.
He had not quite understood his father, and his
father had not quite understood him, but he
had always felt awe of his father and had
cherished the belief that he must be infinitely
wise. Uncle Samuel was wise too, but in quite
another way. Uncle Samuel was closer, far
closer, and he could talk intimately to him about
every sort of thing, but people laughed at Uncle
Samuel quite openly and said he was no good,
and Uncle Samuel himself confessed this.

His father had been remote, august,
Olympian. It was true that last Christmas
he had hit his father and tried to bite him;
but that had been in a fit of rage that was madness, neither more nor less. When you were
mad you might do anything. His father had
been august—but now?

Jeremy dared not look back over the
luncheon scene, dared not face once again the
nervous flush, the silly laugh, the feeble retort.

His father was a coward and the honour of the family was at stake.

After that luncheon outburst, however, the situation moved so swiftly that it went far beyond poor Jeremy. I don't suppose that Uncle Percy was aware of anything very much save his own happiness and comfort, but to any outsider it would have seemed that he now gave up the whole of his time and energy to baiting his brother. He was not a bad man nor deliberately unkind, but he loved to have someone to tease, as the few women for whom in his life he had cared had discovered in time to save themselves from marrying him.

I say that he was unconscious of what he was doing; and so in a fashion was the Cole family unconscious. That is, Mrs. Cole and Aunt Amy and the children realized that Uncle Percy was being rude, but they did *not* realize that the work of years was, in a few days, being completely undone. So used to custom and tradition are we that in our daily life we will accept almost any figure in the condition in which we receive it and then proceed to add our own little " story " to the structure already presented to us.

Mrs. Cole did not wish, Aunt Amy even did not wish, to see their Herbert " a fool "; very much better for their daily life and happiness that he should not be one, and yet in a

short two days that was what he was, so that
Aunt Amy, without realizing it, spoke sharply
to him and Mrs. Cole disagreed with him about
the weather prospects. Of course the women
did their best to stand up for him and defend
him in his weak attempts at resistance, but,
after all, Percy was a visitor and wouldn't be
here for long, and " hadn't been home for such
a time that naturally his way of looking at
things couldn't be quite ours," and then at
Sunday supper they were forced to laugh against
their will, but " one was glad of *anything* by
Sunday evening to make things a little bright,"
at Percy's account of Herbert when he was a
boy tumbling out of the wagonette on a picnic
and nobody missing him until they got home
that night. It *was* funny as Percy told it.
Poor Herbert! running after the wagonette
and shouting and nobody noticing, and then
losing himself and not getting home until midnight. Aunt Amy was forced to laugh until
she cried, and even Mrs. Cole, regarding her
husband with tender affection, said : " So like
you, Herbert, dear, not to *ask* somebody the
way ! "

The only member of the family who did not
see something funny in all of this was Jeremy.
He was conscious only of his father. He was
aware exactly of how he was feeling. He so
thoroughly himself detested being laughed at,

especially when it was two to one—and now it was about five to one! As he watched his father's white face with the slow flushes rising and falling, the pale nervous eyes wandering in their gaze from place to place, the expression of bewilderment as Uncle Percy's loud tones surged up to him, submerged him and then slowly withdrew, Jeremy was reminded of his own first evening at Thompson's, when in the dormitory he had been suddenly delivered up to a wild troop of savages who knew neither law nor courtesy. As it had been with him then, so was it with his father now.

Uncle Percy had all the monotony of the unimaginative. One idea was enough for him, and his idea just now was to take it out of "old Herbert." I can only repeat that he did not mean it unkindly; he thought that he was being vastly amusing for the benefit of those poor dull women who never had any fun from one year's end to the other. His verdict, after he had left him and gone on somewhere else, would be: "Well, I gave those poor mugs a merry week. Hard work, but one must do one's best."

Meanwhile Jeremy watched his father.

III

Soon he saw his father hurrying off, book under his arm, umbrella in hand.

" Where are you going, father? "

" To the Greybank Schools."

" I'll walk up with you."

" Well, hurry, then. I haven't much time."

He did not reveal his surprise. It was the first time in all their lives together that Jeremy had suggested going with him anywhere. They set off together. It was a fine day of early autumn, red mist and faint blue sky, leaves thick upon the ground, the air peppermint in the mouth. Jeremy had to walk fast to keep pace with his father's long strides.

Mr. Cole suddenly said :

" I've got a headache—a bad headache. It's better out of the house than in."

In every way it was better, as Jeremy knew. During luncheon, just concluded, Uncle Percy had roared with laughter over his memories of what Herbert was like when, as a small boy, in the middle of the night he thought he heard a burglar.

" When does Uncle Percy go, father? "

" Well—I thought he was going the day after to-morrow—but now he thinks he'll stay another week."

" I don't like Uncle Percy, father," Jeremy panted a little with his efforts to keep up.

" You mustn't say that, my boy."

" It doesn't matter if I say it to you. Was he like he is now when he was young? "

" Yes; very much. But you must remember that it was a long time ago. I don't quite clearly recollect my childhood. Nor, I think— does he his." Mr. Cole coughed.

" We never had very much in common as boys," he said suddenly.

" He doesn't know much about England, does he, father? He says the most awfully silly things."

" You mustn't say that about your uncle, my boy."

" No, but he does. Why, he hasn't been *anywhere* in England—not even to Drymouth."

" No, my boy, he hasn't. You see, when people have lived in the colonies all their lives they get a little—ahem—out of touch."

" Yes, father."

Delightful to think of Uncle Percy being out of touch. Quite a savage, a barbarian. Father and son laughed a little together.

" I bet the boys at Thompson's would laugh at him," said Jeremy, " like anything."

" One has to be polite," said Mr. Cole. " After all, he is our guest. Don't forget that, my boy."

"No, father. . . . I bet he was frightened at the burglar, father; more than you were."

"Well, as a matter of fact, Jeremy, he was. I remember the incident perfectly. Percy hid in a cupboard. He's forgotten that, I've no doubt."

Father and son laughed.

"It would have to be a very large cupboard, father," said Jeremy; and then they laughed again.

Here they were at the schools, where Mr. Cole was going to teach the little girls their Catechism. They parted, and Jeremy ran all the way down the hill home.

IV

Uncle Percy loved the world and desired that, in natural return, the world should love him. It seemed to him that the world did so. Once and again the net of his jollity and fun seemed to miss some straggling fish who gaped and then swam away, but he was of that happy temperament thus described by one of the most lovable of our modern poets:

"Who bears in mind misfortunes gone,
    Must live in fear of more;
The Happy Man, whose heart is light,
    Gives no such shadows power·

He bears in mind no haunting past
    To start his week on Monday:
No graves are written on his mind
    To visit on a Sunday;
He lives his life by days, not years,
    Each day's a life complete,
Which every morning finds renewed
    With temper calm and sweet."

How could the world help but love him, jolly, amiable, sensible man that he was?

But once and again . . . once and again. . . . And so it was now. And the fish that was eluding him was young Jeremy Cole.

On the seventh or eighth day he was aware of it. At breakfast he looked across the table and saw the small square-shaped boy gravely winking at Mary. Why was he winking at his sister? It could not be, surely it could not be because of anything that he himself had said? And yet, looking behind him, so to speak, he could not remember that anyone else had been talking. This was enough to make him think, and, thinking, it occurred to him that that small boy had from the very first been aloof and reserved. Not natural for small boys to be reserved with jolly uncles. And it was not as though the boy were in general a reserved child. No, he had heard him laughing and jumping about the house enough to bring the roof down. Playing around with that dog of his. . . . Quite a normal, sporting boy. Come to think of it, the best of the family. By far the best of the family. You'd never think, to look at him, that he was Herbert's son.

Therefore after breakfast in the hall he cried in his jolly, hearty tones :

"I say, Jeremy, what do you say to taking your old uncle round the town this morning, eh? Showing him the shops and things, what? Might be something we'd like to buy. . . ."

Jeremy was half-way up the stairs. He came slowly down again. On the bottom step, looking very gravely at his uncle, he said :

"I'm very sorry, Uncle Percy, but I'm going to school to-morrow morning, and I promised mother——"

But Mrs. Cole was at this moment coming out of the dining-room. Looking up and smiling, she said :

"Never mind, Jeremy. Go with Uncle Percy this morning, dear. I can manage about the shirts. . . ."

Jeremy appeared not to have heard his mother.

"I'm sorry I can't go out this morning, Uncle Percy. There's my holiday task too. I've got to swot at it——" and then turned and slowly disappeared round the corner of the staircase.

Uncle Percy was chagrined. Really he was. He stood with his large body balanced on his large legs, hesitating, in the hall.

"It *is* his last morning, Percy," said Mrs. Cole, looking a little distressed. "He's a funny child. He's always making his own plans."

"Obstinate. That's what I call it," said Uncle Percy. "Damned obstinate." He went out that morning alone. He thought that he would buy something for the kid, something really rich and impressive. It could not be that the boy disliked him, and yet . . . All that morning he was haunted by the boy's presence. Going to school to-morrow, was he? Not much time left for making an impression. He could not find anything that morning that would precisely do. Rotten shops, the Polchester ones. He would tip the boy handsomely to-morrow morning. No boy could resist that. Really handsomely—as he had never been tipped before.

Nothing further occurred to him, and that evening he was especially funny about his brother. That story of Herbert when he was round fifteen and quite a grown boy being afraid of a dog chained up in a yard, and how he, Percy, made Herbert go and stroke it. How Herbert trembled and how his knees shook! Oh! it was funny, it was indeed. You'd have roared had you seen it. Percy roared; roared until the table shook beneath him.

But to-night, for some reason or another, Herbert did not seem to mind. He laughed gently and admitted that he was still afraid of dogs—bulldogs especially. Uncle Percy had Jeremy in his mind all that evening; he caught him once again by the slack of his breeches and swung him in the air—just to show what a jolly pleasant uncle he was.

When Mrs. Cole explained that always on Jeremy's last evening she read to him in the schoolroom after supper, he said that he would come too, and sat there in an easy chair, watching benevolently the children grouped in the firelight round their mother, while " The Chaplet of Pearls " unfolded its dramatic course. A charming picture! And the boy really looked delightful, gazing into the fire, his head against his mother's knee. Uncle Percy almost wished that he himself had married. Nice to have children, a home, somewhere to come to; and so fell asleep, and soon was snoring so loudly that Mrs. Cole had to raise her voice.

Next morning there was all the bustle of Jeremy's departure. This was not so dramatic as other departures had been, because Jeremy was now so thoroughly accustomed to schoolgoing and, indeed, could not altogether conceal from the world at large that this was footballtime, the time of his delight and pride and happiness.

He went as usual into his father's study to say good-bye, but on this occasion, for some strange reason, there was no stiffness nor awkwardness. Both were at their ease as they had never been together before. Mr. Cole put his hand on the boy's shoulder.

"Mind you get into the football team," he said.

"If I don't you won't mind, father, will you?" said Jeremy, looking very fine indeed in a new light-grey overcoat.

"I know you'll do your best, my boy," said Mr. Cole, and kissed him.

Outside in the hall, with the others, was Uncle Percy. He motioned to him mysteriously. "I say, kid, come here."

Jeremy followed him into the dining-room, where they were alone. Uncle Percy shut the door.

"Here's something for you, my boy, to take back to school. Buy something you want with it and remember your uncle isn't such a bad sort after all."

Jeremy crimsoned up to the tips of his ears. On the red palm of his uncle's big hand there were lying three golden sovereigns.

"No, thank you, uncle."

"What?"

"No, thank you, uncle. I've got—— Father gave me—— I don't want——"

" You won't take it? You won't——? "

" No, thank you, uncle."

" But what the devil——"

Jeremy turned away. His uncle caught him by the shoulder.

" Now, what's all this about? A boy of your age refuse a tip? Now, what's this mean? "

Jeremy wriggled himself free. Suddenly he said hotly : " Father's as good as you, every bit as good. Even though you have been everywhere and he hasn't. People like father awfully in Polchester, and they say his sermons are better than anybody's. Father's just as good as you are—— I——" and then suddenly burst from the room.

Uncle Percy stood there. This may be said to have been the greatest shock of his life. The boy's father? What was he talking about? The boy's father? As good as he was? The boy hated him so much that he wouldn't even take the money. Three pounds, and he wouldn't take it! Wouldn't take money from him because he hated him so! But hang it! Lord, how that dog was howling! What a horrible noise! What was he howling for? . . . Wouldn't take the money? But had anyone ever heard the like? . . . But, hang it, three pounds!

CHAPTER XI

THE RUNAWAYS

I

JEREMY, on his return to Thompson's that term, found that he had been changed to what was known as the Baby Dorm.

Hitherto he had been in a perfect barrack of a dormitory that contained at least twenty beds. The Baby Dorm was a little room with three beds, and it was a distinction to be there —a true sign that you were rising in the world. This was fully appreciated by Jeremy, and when he also discovered that his two companions were Pug Raikes and Stokesley Maj the cup of his joy was full. Raikes and Stokesley were just the companions he would have chosen, short, of course, of Riley. But Riley was away in the other wing of the house protecting, to his infinite boredom, some new kids. There was no hope of *his* company.

Raikes and Stokesley were both older than Jeremy; they had been at Thompson's a year longer than he. Pug Raikes was a fat, round boy, rather like Tommy Winchester at home. It was said that he could eat more at one go than any three boys at Thompson's put together. But with all his fat he was no mean sportsman. He was the best fives player in the school, and quite a good bat. He had an invaluable character for games; nothing disturbed him; he was imperturbable through every crisis. He had been bitten once in the hand by a ferret, and had not uttered a sound.

Stokesley was opposite from Raikes in every way except that he was a good cricketer, and perhaps it was this very attraction of their opposites that brought them together. They had been quite inseparable ever since their first suffering from tossing in the same blanket on the first night of their arrival at Thompson's, two and a half years ago. Stokesley was a very good-looking boy, thin and tall, straight and strong, with black eyes, black hair and thick eyebrows. He was known as " Eyebrows " among his friends. He was as excitable as Raikes was apparently phlegmatic. He was always up to some new " plot " or fantasy, always in hot water, always extricating himself from the same with the airs of a Spanish grandee. It was rumoured that Thompson was afraid of his father, who was a baronet. Thirty years ago baronets counted.

Jeremy would never have been admitted into their friendship had it not been for his football. They considered him " a plucky little devil," and prophesied that he would go far. They were a little condescending, of course, and the first night Stokesley addressed him thus :

"Look here, young Stocky, it's jolly lucky for you being in with us. None of your cheek, and if you snore you know what you'll get. You don't walk in your sleep, do you?"

"No, I don't," said Jeremy.

"Well, if you do, you'll have the surprise of your life. Won't he, Pug?"

"Rather," said Raikes.

"And remember you're playing footer this term for the honour of this dorm. If you play badly you'll get it like anything in here afterwards."

However, in a night or two there was very little to choose between them. Boys are extraordinarily susceptible to atmosphere. During the cricket term young Cole had been of no account at all; quite a decent kid, but no use at cricket. But before the autumn term was a week old he was spoken of as the probable scrum half that year, kid though he was. Stokesley was in the first fifteen as a forward, but his place was a little uncertain, and Pug Raikes was nowhere near the first fifteen at all and cared nothing for football.

It happened, therefore, that Jeremy was soon taken into the confidences of the two older

boys, and very exciting confidences they were.
Stokesley was never happy unless he had some
new scheme on foot. Some of them were
merely silly and commonplace, like dressing up
as ghosts and frightening the boys in the Lower
Dorm or putting white mice in the French
master's desk; but he had at times impulses of
real genius, like the Pirates' Society, of which
there is no space here to tell, or the Cribbers'
Kitchen, a rollicking affair that gave Thompson
the fits for a whole week.

Jeremy managed to keep himself out of
most of these adventures. He had the gift of
concentrating utterly on the matter in hand,
and the matter in hand this term was getting
into the first fifteen. He went in most con-
scientiously for training, running round Big
Field before First Hour, refusing various foods
that he longed to enjoy, and refusing to smoke
blotting paper on Sunday afternoon in Parker's
Wood. People jeered at him for all this
seriousness, and, had he made a public business
of his sporting conscience, he might have earned
a good deal of unpopularity. But he said very
little about it and behaved in every way like
an ordinary mortal.

Luckily for him, his school work that term
was easy. He had been for two terms in the
Lower Fourth, and now was near the top of
it, and inevitably at the end of this term would

be moved out of it. Malcolm, his form master, liked him, being himself a footballer of no mean size. It was not, therefore, until the end of the first fortnight that Jeremy discovered that something very serious was going forward between his two dormitory companions, something in which he was not asked to share. They whispered together continually, and the whispering took the form of Stokesley persuading Pug over and over again. "Oh, come on, Pug. Don't spoil sport." "You're afraid— yes, you are. You're a funk." "I can't do it without you. Of course I can't." "We'll never have a chance again."

At last Jeremy, who had more than his natural share of curiosity, could endure it no longer. He sat on the edge of his bed, kicking his naked toes, and cried:

"I say, you two, what's all this about? You might let me in."

"It's nothing to do with you, Stocky. You go to sleep."

"You'd much better tell me. You know I never sneak."

"This is too important to let a kid like you know about it."

"I'm not such a kid, if it comes to that. Perhaps I can help?"

"No, you can't. You shut your mouth and go to sleep."

Two nights later than this, however, Jeremy was told.

"I'm going to tell Stocky," said Raikes, " and see what he says."

"Oh, all right," said Stokesley, in the sulks. " I don't care what you do."

Jeremy sat up in his bed and listened. The whispering voices stole on and on, one voice supplementing the other. Soon Stokesley overbore the other and was dominant. Jeremy distrusted his ears. Beyond the window the night was lovely, a clean sweep of dark velvet sky, with two tree-tops and a single star, so quiet, not a sound anywhere; and this adventure was the most audacious conceived of by man. Neither more nor less than to run away to sea, to anywhere; but, before finally vanishing, to have a week, a fortnight, a month in London at the very finest hotels, with heaps to eat and drink and theatres every night.

" You see," explained Stokesley eagerly, warmed up now by the narration of his idea, " we're sick of this place. It's so dull. You must feel that yourself, Stocky, even with your beastly football. Nothing ever happens, and it's ages before we go to Rugby. You'd much better come too. Of course, you're a bit young, but they'll probably want a cabin-boy on the ship; and then we'll be in the South Seas,

R

where you bathe all the time, and can shy at cokernuts, and there are heaps and heaps of monkeys, and you shoot tigers, and——"

He paused for breath.

A cabin-boy! Had it not been one of his earliest dreams? His mind flew back to that day, now so long ago, when he had begged the sea captain to take him. The sea captain! His heart beat thickly. Then came the practical side of him.

"But won't you want an awful lot of money?" he asked.

"Oh, we've thought of that, of course," said Stokesley. "My father gave me five pounds to come back with, and Pug's uncle gave him two and his aunt gave him another and his cousin gave him ten and six, and I've got my gold watch and chain, which will mean a tenner at least, and Pug's got his gold pin that his dead uncle left him. Altogether, it will be about fifteen pounds anyway, and it'll cost us about a pound a day in London, and then we'll go to Southampton and go to a boat and say we want to work our way, and of course they'll let us. Pug and I are awfully strong, and you—you carry the plates and things."

London! It was the first time in all his life that that place had been brought within his reach. Of course, he had heard the grown-ups mention it, but always as something mysterious,

far-away, magical. London! He had never
conceived that he himself would one day set
foot in it. How his world was extending!
First, simply the house, then Polchester, then
Rafiel and Caerlyon, then Thompson's, then
Craxton, and now London!

Nevertheless, he was still practical.

"How will you get to the station?" he
asked.

"Oh, we've thought all about it. It will
be a Sunday—probably next Sunday. We're
allowed off all the afternoon, and there's a
train at Saroby Junction that goes to London
at four o'clock. We'll be in London by
seven."

"If they catch you," said Jeremy slowly,
"there'll be the most awful row."

"Of course," said Stokesley contemptuously.
"But they won't. How can they? We'll be
in London by call-over; and we'll move to
different hotels, and as soon as we think they're
on to us we'll be off to Southampton. There
are boats go every day."

It was plain that Raikes was caught more
and more deeply as Stokesley developed the plan.
Jeremy himself felt to the full the wonderful
adventure of it. The trouble was that now,
at once, as soon as you had heard of it, the
school looked dull and stupid. It had been all
right as he came up to bed. He had been con-

tented and happy, but now a longing for freedom surged through him, and for a moment he would like to climb through that window and run and run and run. . . .

But the football saved him. If he went on this adventure he would never be half-back for the school; he would never be half-back for any school. He would in all probability never play football again. They did not play football in the South Seas. It was too hot. What was bathing compared with football?

"I don't think I'll come," he said slowly. "I'd only be in your way."

"Of course, if you funk it——" said Stokesley hotly.

"I don't funk it. But——"

There was a knock on the door, and one of the junior masters walked in.

"That's enough talking, you kids," he said. "If there's another word, you'll hear of it."

They lay then like images.

II

We all know how adventures, aspirations, longings that seem quite reasonable and attainable in the evening light are absurdly impossible in the morning cold. Jeremy next morning, as he ran round the football ground, felt that he could not have heard Stokesley aright. It

was the kind of story that the dormitory tale-
teller retailed before people dropped off to
sleep. Stokesley was just inventing; he could
not have meant a word of it. Nevertheless,
later in the day, Raikes took him into a corner
of the playground and whispered dramatically :

" We're going to do it. It's all settled."

" Oh ! " gasped Jeremy.

" It's to be next Sunday. You're right
about not coming. You're too young."
Raikes sounded very old indeed as he said this.
" You swear you won't tell a living soul? "

" Of course I won't."

" You'll swear by God Almighty? "

" I swear by God Almighty."

" Never to breathe a word to any boy,
master or animal? "

" Never to breathe a word to any boy,
master or animal."

" You're a good sort, Stocky. Somehow
one can trust you—and one can't most of them.
They'll be on to you after we're gone, you
know ! "

" I don't care."

" They'll try to get it out of you."

" I don't care. They shan't."

" In any way they can. Perhaps they'll
stop your football."

Jeremy drew a deep breath. " I don't
care," he repeated slowly.

"We'll have a great time," Raikes said, as though addressing his reluctant half. "We'll come back ever so rich in a year or two, and then won't you wish you'd come with us!"

What Jeremy did wish was that they had told him nothing about it. Oh, how he wished it! Why had they dragged him in? Suppose they *did* stop his football? Oh, but they couldn't! It wasn't his fault that he'd heard about it.

"Look here, Raikes," he said, "don't you tell me any more. I don't want to know anything about it. . . . Then they can't come on me afterwards."

"That's sound," said Raikes. "All right; we won't."

The days, then, that intervened before Sunday could have only one motive. It seemed incredible to Jeremy that the two conspirators should appear now so ordinary; they should have had in some way a flaring mark, a scarlet letter, to set them aside from the rest of mankind. Not at all. They followed their accustomed duties, ate their meals, did their impositions, played their games just as they had always done.

Even at night, when they were left alone in the dormitory, they spoke very little about it. Jeremy was outside it now, and although they trusted him, " one never knew," and they were not going to give anything away.

The great Sunday came, a day of blazing autumnal gold, enough breeze to stir the leaves and send them like ragged scraps of brown paper lazily through the air. The Sunday bells came like challenges to guilty consciences upon the misty sky. Jeremy did not see the two of them after breakfast. Indeed, in the strange way that these terrific events have of suddenly slipping for half an hour from one's consciousness, during morning chapel he forgot about the whole affair, and stared half asleep through the long chapel window out into the purple field, wondering about a thousand little things—some lines he had to write, a pot of jam that he was going to open that night at tea for the first time, and how Hamlet was in Polchester and what, just then, he would be doing.

He went his accustomed Sunday walk with Riley, and it was only when they were hurrying back over the leaf-thickened paths towards a sun like a red orange that he suddenly remembered. Why, at this very moment they would be making for the station! He stopped in the path.

" By gum ! " he said.

" What is it ? " asked Riley. " Been stung by a bee ? "

" No ; just thought of something."

" You *do* look queer! "

" It's nothing." He moved on. It seemed impossible that the woods should stay just as they were, unmoved by this great event, hanging like old coloured tapestry with their thin dead leaves between the black poles of trees. Unmoved! No one knew. No one but himself.

The great moment came. When in chapel, looking across to the other side, he saw that their places were empty. Nothing much in that for the ordinary world—fellows were often late for chapel—but for him it meant everything. The deed was positively accomplished. They must be actually at this moment in the train, and he was the only creature in the whole school who knew where they were.

Call-over followed chapel. He heard the names called. " Stokesley! " and then, more impatiently, after a little pause, " Stokesley! " again. Then " Raikes! " and, after a moment, " Raikes! " again. Nothing, after that, happened for an hour. Then call-over once more at supper. Raikes and Stokesley again called and again absent.

Five minutes after supper the school sergeant came for him.

" Mr. Thompson to see you in his study at once! "

Jeremy went.

Thompson was walking about, and very

worried he looked. He had been talking to the
matron, and wheeled round when Jeremy came
in.

"Ah, Cole. . . . Leave us for a moment,
matron, please."

They were alone. Jeremy felt terribly
small, shrivelled to nothing at all. He shuffled
his feet and looked anywhere but at Thompson's
anxious eyes. He liked Thompson, and was
aware, with a sudden flash, that this was more
than a mere game—that it might be desperately
serious for someone.

"Come here, Cole. I want you to keep
this to yourself. Not to say a word to anyone,
do you understand?"

"Yes, sir."

"Good. It seems that Stokesley and
Raikes have run away. They were neither at
chapel nor at supper. Some of their things
are missing. Now, you're the only other boy
in their dormitory. Do you know anything at
all about this?"

"No, sir."

"Nothing?"

"No, sir."

"They said nothing at all to you about this
going?"

"No, sir."

"Gave you no idea that they were thinking
of it?"

" No, sir."

Thompson paused, looked out of the window, walked up and down the room a little, then said :

" I make it a rule always to believe what any boy tells me. I've never found you untruthful, Cole. I don't say that you're not telling the truth now, but I know what your boys' code is. You mustn't sneak about another boy whatever happens. That's a code that has something to be said for it. It happens to have nothing to be said for it just now. You're young, and I don't expect you realize what this means. It involves many people beside themselves—their fathers and mothers and everyone in this school. You may be doing a very serious thing that will affect many people's lives if you don't tell me what you know. Do you realize that? "

" Yes, sir."

" Well, then, did they say nothing at all about going away? "

" No, sir."

" Nothing at all to you? "

" No, sir."

" Very well. You may go."

Jeremy went. Outside he found the school in a ferment. Everyone knew. Stokesley and Raikes had run away. He was surrounded by a mob. They pressed in upon him from every side—big boys, little boys, old boys, young boys—everyone.

"Stocky! Where have they gone to? What did Thompson say to you? Did he whack you? Is he going to? Is it true that they've stolen a lot of the matron's money? What did they tell you? . . . Oh, rot! Of course you know? Where have they gone to, Stocky? We'll give you the most awful hiding if you don't say. Come on, Stocky, out with it! When did they go? Just before chapel? Is Thompson awfully sick?"

But Jeremy stood his ground. He knew nothing at all. Nothing at all. They had said nothing to him.

III

During the four days that followed the characters, bodies and souls of the fugitives swelled into epic proportions. Four days in such circumstances can, at a small school, resemble centuries of time. No one thought or discussed anything but this, and there was not a boy in the place, from the eldest to the youngest, but envied those two passionately and would have given a year of holiday to be with them.

On Monday Mr. Thompson went up to London. The rumours that sprang to life were marvellous. Stokesley had been seen at a theatre in London, and had been chased all the way down the Strand by an enormous crowd. Raikes had struck a policeman, and been put in a cell. They had been to Buckingham Palace, and interviewed Her Majesty. They had started on a slaver for the South Seas. They had taken up jobs as waiters in a London restaurant. . . .

To Jeremy these days were torture. In the first place he was dazzled by their splendour. Why had he been such a fool as to refuse to go with them? One might die to-morrow. Here was his great adventure offered to him, and he had rejected it.

As the tales circulated round him the atmosphere became more and more romantic. He forgot the real Stokesley and saw no longer the genuine Raikes. It no longer occurred to him that Stokesley had warts; he refused to see that so familiar picture of Raikes washing himself in the morning, trickling the cold water over his head, his two large ears, projecting, crimson. Clothed in gold and silver, they swung dazzling through the air, rosy clouds supporting them, to the haven where they would be—the haven of the South Seas, with gleaming, glittering sands, blue waters, monkeys in thousands, and pearls and diamonds for the asking.

Under these alluring visions even the football faded into grey monotony. In a practice game on Monday he played so badly that he expected to lose all chance of playing in the match at the end of the week; but, fortunately for him, everyone else played badly too. The mind of the school was in London, following the flight, the chase, the final escape—no time now for football or anything else.

The heroes that Stokesley and Raikes now were! Anyone who had an anecdote, however trivial, was listened to by admiring crowds. It was recalled how Stokesley, when a new boy, had endured the first tossing in the blanket with marvellous phlegm and indifference; how Raikes, when receiving a hamper from an affectionate aunt, had instantly distributed it round all his table, so that almost at once there was none of it remaining. How Stokesley had once conducted a money-lending establishment with extraordinary force and daring for more than a fortnight; how Raikes had fought Bates Major, a boy almost twice his size, and had lasted into the sixth round—and so on, and so on.

Jeremy, of course, was affected by all this reminiscence, and himself recalled how, in the dormitory, Stokesley had said this clever thing, and Raikes had been on that occasion strangely daring. But behind this romance there was something more.

He was strangely and, as the hours advanced, quite desperately bothered by the question of his lie. In the first immediate instance of it he had not been bothered by it at all. When he had stood in Thompson's study it had not seemed to him a lie at all; so thickly clothed was he by his school convention that it had seemed the natural, the absolutely inevitable thing to do. His duty was not to give Stokesley and Raikes away, that was all.

But afterwards Thompson's troubled face came back to him, and that serious warning that perhaps, if he kept his knowledge back, the lives of hundreds of people might be affected. It was true that by the following morning everything that he knew was known by everyone else. The station-master from the junction came up after breakfast and gave information about the boys. He had thought it strange that they should be going up to London by themselves, but they had seemed so completely self-possessed that he had not liked simply on his own authority to stop them.

But had Jeremy told all that he knew on that first Sunday evening many precious hours might have been gained and the fugitives caught at once. Alone in that little dormitory at night, the two empty beds staring at him, he had fallen into dreams, distressing, accusing nightmares. By Tuesday morning he was not

at all sure that he was not a desperate criminal,
worthy of prison and perhaps even of hanging.

He longed—how desperately he longed!—
to discuss the matter with Riley. Riley was so
full of wisdom and common sense and knew so
much more than did Jeremy about life in
general. But, having gone so far, he would
not turn back, but he moved about on that
Tuesday like Christian with his pack.

Then, on Tuesday evening, came the great
news. They had been caught—they had given
themselves up. They had spent all their
money. Thompson was bringing them back
with him on Wednesday morning.

The school waited breathlessly for the
arrival. No one saw anything; only by midday
it was whispered by everyone that they were
there. By the afternoon it was known that they
were shut away in the infirmary. No one was
to see them or to speak to them.

During that morning how swiftly the
atmosphere had changed! Only yesterday
those two had been sailing for the South Seas;
now, ostracized, waiting in horrible confine-
ment for some terrible doom; they were only
glorious, like one of Byron's heroes, in their
"damned prospects" and "fatal overthrow."
All that day Jeremy thought of them, feeling
in some unanalysed way as though he himself
were responsible for their failure. Had he not

done this, had he thought of that—and what would Thompson do?

At the end of breakfast next morning it was known. He made them a speech, speaking with a new gravity that even the smallest boy in the school (young Phipps, Junr., only about two feet high) could feel. He said that, as was by this time known to all of them, two of their number had run away, had spent several days in London, had been found, and brought back to the school. They would all understand how serious a crime this was, the unhappiness that it must have brought on the boys' parents, the harm that it might have done to the school itself. The boys were young; they had, apparently, no especial grievance with their school life, and they had done what they had from a silly, false sense of adventure rather than from any impulse of wickedness or desire for evil.

Nevertheless, they had wilfully made many people unhappy and broken laws upon whose preservation the very life of their school, that they all loved, depended. He was not sure that they had not done even more than that. He could not tell, of course, whether there were any boys in that room who had known of this before it occurred—he hoped from the bottom of his heart that no boy had told him an untruth; he knew that they had a code of their own, that whatever happened they were never to " tell " about another boy. That code had its uses, but it could be carried too far. All the misery of these four days might have been spared had some boy given information at once. He would say no more about that. The boys had been given a choice between expulsion and a public flogging. They had both, without hesitation, chosen the flogging. The whole school was to be present that evening in Big Hall before first preparation.

IV

Every seat in Big Hall was filled. The boys sat in classes, motionless, silent, not even an occasional whisper. The hissing of a furious gas-jet near the door was the only sound.

Jeremy would never forget that horrible half-hour. *He* was the criminal. He sat there, scarcely breathing, his eyes hot and dry, staring, although he did not know that he was staring, at the platform, empty save for a table and a chair, pressing his hands upon his knees, wishing that this awful thing might pass, thinking not especially of Stokesley or of Raikes, but of something that was himself and yet not himself, something that was pressed down into a dark hole and every tick of the school clock pressed him further. He saw the rows and rows

s

of heads as though they had been the pattern
of a carpet; and he was ashamed, desperately
ashamed, as though he were standing up in
front of them all naked.

The door behind the platform opened and
Thompson came in. He was white and black
and flat, like a drawing upon a sheet of paper.
The gas gave a hysterical giggle at sight of
him. Behind him came Raikes and Stokesley,
looking as they had always looked and yet quite
different—actors playing a part. Behind them
was the school sergeant, Crockett, a burly
ex-sailorman, a friend of everyone when in
a good temper. He looked sheepish now,
shuffling on his feet. He looked terrible, too,
because his coat was off and his sleeves rolled
up, showing the ship and anchor tattoo that he
showed as a favour to boys who had done their
drill well.

Thompson came forward. He said:

" I don't want to prolong this, but you are
all here because I wish you to remember this
all your lives. I wish you to remember it, not
because it is the punishment of two of your
friends—indeed, it is my special wish that, as
soon as it is over, you shall receive Stokesley
and Raikes among you again as though nothing
had occurred—but I want you all, from the
youngest to the eldest, to remember that there
must be government, there must be rules, if

men are to live in any sort of society together.
We owe something to ourselves, we owe something to those who love us, we owe something
to our country, and we owe something to our
school. We cannot lead completely selfish lives
—God does not mean us to do so. Our school
is our friend. We belong to it, and we must
be proud of it.''

He stepped back. The school sergeant came
forward and whispered something to Stokesley.
Stokesley himself undid his braces. His trousers
fell down over his ankles. He bent forward
over the table, hiding his face with his hands.
Jeremy could not look. He felt sick; he
wanted to cry. He heard the sound of the
descending birch. One, two, three, four, five,
six, seven—would it never end?—eight, nine,
ten, eleven, twelve.

He heard the whole school draw a breath.
Still he did not look. Stokesley had not made
a sound.

There was a pause. Still he did not look.
Now Raikes was there. The birch again. One,
two, three, four—— Then, as though someone were tearing the wall in two, a shrill cry:
'' Oh! Oh! '' . . . Horrible—beastly. He
was trembling from head to foot. He was
low down in that hole now, and someone was
pushing the earth in over his head. And now
with the switch of the birch there was a low,

monotonous sobbing, and then the sharp cry
again that, at this second time, seemed to come
from within Jeremy himself. Everything wa
dark. A longer pause, and the shuffling o
feet. It was all over, and the boys were filing
out. He raised his eyes to a world of crimson
and flashing lights.

v

That night they were restored to their
fellow-citizens. They were sitting on their beds
in the Baby Dorm examining their wounds.
Raikes could think of nothing but that he had
cried. Stokesley consoled him. As a last
word he said to Jeremy : "Very decent of
you, Stocky, not to give us away. We won't
forget it, will we, Pug?"

"No, we won't," said Pug, a naked,
writhing figure, because he was trying to see
his stripes.

"All the same," said Stokesley, "it was
smart of you not to come. It was rotten; all
of it. They were beastly to us at the hotel,
and just took our money. We went to a rotten
theatre; and it rained all the time, didn't it,
Pug?"

"Beastly," said Raikes.

The room was silent. So that was the end
of the adventure. Jeremy, slipping off to

sleep, suddenly loved the school, didn't want to leave it—no, never. Saw the rooms, one by one, the class-room, the dining-room, Big Hall —Thompson, the matron, Crockett. All warm and safe and cosy.

And London. Swimming in rain, chasing you, hating you, catching you up at the last with a birch.

Good old school—the end of *that* adventure. . . .

CHAPTER XII

A FINE DAY

I

IT was a fine day. Jeremy, waking and turning over in his bed, could see beyond and
above Stokesley's slumbering form a thin strip of
pale blue sky gleaming like a sudden revelation
of water behind folds of amber mist. It would
be a real thumping autumn day and he was to
play half for the first fifteen against The Rest
that afternoon. He also had three hundred
lines to do for the French master that he had
not even begun, and it must be handed up
completed at exactly 11.30 that same morning.
He had also every chance of swapping a silver
frame containing a photograph of his Aunt
Amy with Phipps minor for a silver pencil, and
he was to have half Raseley's sausage for breakfast that morning in return for mathematical
favours done for him on the preceding day. As
he thought of all these various things he rolled
round like a kitten in his bed, curling up as
it was his pleasantest habit into a ball so that
his toes nearly met his forehead and he was one

exquisite lump of warmth. Rending through
this came the harsh sound of the first bell,
murmurs from other rooms, patterings down the
passage, and then suddenly both Stokesley and
Raikes sitting up in bed simultaneously, yawn-
ing and looking like bewildered owls. In precisely five minutes the three boys were washed,
dressed and down, herding with the rest in
the long cold class-room waiting for call-over.
When they had answered their names they
slipped across the misty playground into chapel
and sat there like all their companions in a
confused state of half sleep, half wakefulness,
responding as it were in a dream, screaming out
the hymn and then all shuffling off to breakfast
again like shadows in a Japanese pageant.

It was not, in fact, until the first five minutes
at breakfast, when Raseley strongly resisted the
appeal for half his sausage, that Jeremy woke
to the full labours of the day. Raseley was
sitting almost opposite to him and he had a
very nice sausage, large and fat and properly
cracked in the middle. Jeremy's sausage was
a very small one, so that, whereas on other days
he might have passed over the whole episode,
being of a very generous nature, to-day he was
compelled to insist on his rights. "I didn't,"
protested Raseley. "I said you could have
half a sausage if you did the sums, and you
only did two and a half."

"I did them all," said Jeremy stoutly. "It wasn't my fault that that beastly fraction one was wrong. I only said I'd do them. I never said I'd do them right."

"Well, you can jolly well come and fetch it," said Raseley, pursuing in the circumstances the wisest plan, which was to eat his sausage as fast as he could.

"All right," said Jeremy indifferently. "You know what you'll get afterwards if you don't do what you said," and this was bold of Jeremy because he was smaller than Raseley, but he was learning already whom he might threaten and whom he might not, and he knew that Raseley was as terrified of physical pain as Aunt Amy was of a cow in a field. With very bad grace Raseley pushed the smaller half of the sausage across, and Jeremy felt that his day was well begun.

He did not know why, but he was sure that this would be a splendid day. There are days when you feel that you are under a special care of the gods and that they are arranging everything for you, background, incident, crisis, and sleep at the end in a most delightful, generous fashion. Nothing would go wrong to-day.

On the whole, human beings are divided into the two classes of those who realize when they may step out and challenge life, and those to whom one occasion is very much the same as another.

Jeremy, even when he was eight years old and had sat in his sister Helen's chair on his birthday morning, had always realized when to step out. He was going to step out now.

The insufferable Baltimore, who was a wonderful cricketer and therefore rose to great glories in the summer term, but was no footballer at all, and equally, therefore, was less than the dust in the autumn, came with his watery eyes and froggy complexion to ask Jeremy to lend him twopence. Jeremy had at that moment threepence, but there were a number of things that he intended to do with it. Because he detested Baltimore he lent him his twopence with the air of Queen Elizabeth accepting Sir Walter Raleigh's cloak, and got exquisite pleasure from doing so. All these little things, therefore, combined to put him in the best of spirits when, at half-past eleven, Monsieur Clemenceau (not then a name known the wide world over) requested Monsieur Cole to be kind enough to allow him to peruse the three hundred lines which should have been done several days before so admirably provided by him.

Jeremy wore the cloak of innocence, sitting in the back row of the French class with several of his dearest friends and all the class ready to support him in any direction that he might follow.

"I beg your pardon, sir," Jeremy said. "Did you say three hundred lines?"

"That is the exact amount," said M. Clemenceau, "that I require from you *immediatement.*"

"I beg your pardon," said Jeremy politely.

"I need not repeat," said M. Clemenceau. "Three hundred lines by you at once for impertinence three days previous."

"Why, sir, surely," said Jeremy, "you told me that I need not do them this term because . . ."

"No because," interrupted M. Clemenceau at the top of a rather squeaky voice. "There is no because."

"But, sir," began Jeremy; and from all sides of the class there broke out : "Why, certainly, sir, don't you remember——" and "Cole is quite right, sir; you said——" and "I think you've forgotten, sir, that——" and "It really wouldn't be fair, sir, if——" A babel arose. As the boys very well knew, M. Clemenceau had a horror of too much noise, because Thompson was holding a class in the next room, and on two occasions that very term had sent a boy in to request that if it were possible M. Clemenceau should conduct his work a little more softly. And this had been

agony for M. Clemenceau's proud French spirit.
"I will have silence," he shrieked. "This is
no one's business but mine and the young Cole.
Let no one speak until I tell them to do so.
Now, Cole, where are the three hundred lines?"

There was a complete and absolute silence.

"Vill you speak or vill you not speak?"
M. Clemenceau cried.

"Do you mean me, sir?" asked Jeremy
very innocently.

"Of course, I mean you."

"You said, sir, that no one was to speak
until you told them to."

"Well, I tell you now."

Jeremy looked very injured. "I didn't
understand," he said. "If I could explain to
you quietly."

"Well, you shall explain afterwards," said
M. Clemenceau, and Jeremy knew that he was
saved because he could deal *à deux* with M.
Clemenceau by appealing to his French heart,
his sense of honour, and a number of other
things, and might even, with good fortune,
extract an invitation to tea, when M. Clemenceau, in his very cosy room, had a large
supply of muffins and played on the flute.
"Yes," he thought to himself as they pursued
up and down the class-room, sometimes ten at
a time, sometimes only three or four, the in-
tricacies of that French grammar that has to

do with the pen of my aunt and the cat of my sister-in-law and " this is going to be a splendid day."

II

Coming out of school at half-past twelve, he found to his exquisite delight that there was a letter for him. He was, of course, far from that grown-up attitude of terror and misgiving at the sight of the daily post. Not for him yet were bills and unwelcome reminiscence, broken promises and half-veiled threats. He received from his mother one letter a week, from his father perhaps three a term, and from his sister Mary an occasional confused scribbling that, like her stories, introduced so many characters one after another that the most you obtained from them was a sense of life and of people passing and of Mary's warm and emotional heart. Once and again he had a letter from Uncle Samuel, and these were the real glories. It was natural that on this day of days there should be such a letter. The very sight of his uncle's handwriting—a thin, spidery one that was in some mysterious way charged with beauty and colour—cockled his heart and made him warm all over. He sat in a corner of the playground where he was least likely to be disturbed and read it. It was as follows. It began abruptly, as did all Uncle Samuel's letters :

Your mother has just taken your Aunt Amy to Drymouth on a shopping expedition. The house is so quiet you wouldn't know it. I am painting a very nice picture of two cows in a blue field. The cows are red. If you were here I would put you into the picture as a dog asleep under a tree. Because you aren't here, I have to take that wretched animal of yours and use him instead. He is not nearly as like a dog as you are. I had two sausages for breakfast because your Aunt Amy is going to be away for two whole days. I generally have only one sausage and now just about five o'clock this evening I shall have indigestion which will be one more thing I shall owe your Aunt Amy. The woman came in yesterday and washed the floor of the studio. It looks beastly, but I shall soon make it dirty again, and if only you were here it would get dirty quicker. There's a rumour that your Uncle Percy is coming back to stay with us again. I am training your dog to bite the sort of trousers that your Uncle Percy wears. I have a pair very like his and I draw them across the floor very slowly and make noises to your dog like a cat. The plan is very successful but to-morrow there won't be any trousers and I shall have to think of something else. Mrs. Sampson asked your mother whether she thought that I would like to paint a portrait of her little girl. I asked your mother how much money Mrs. Sampson would give me for doing so and your mother asked Mrs. Sampson. Mrs. Sampson said that if she liked it when it was done she'd hang it up in her drawing-room where everybody could see and that that would be such a good advertisement for me that there wouldn't need to be any payment, so I told your mother to tell Mrs. Sampson that I was so busy sweeping a crossing just now that I was afraid I wouldn't have time to paint her daughter. When I have done these cows, if they turn out really well, perhaps I'll send the best of them to Mrs. Sampson and tell her that that's the best portrait of her daughter I was capable of doing. Some people in Paris like my pictures very much and two of them have been hanging in an exhibition and people have to pay to go in and see them. I sold one of them for fifty pounds and therefore I enclose a little bit of paper which if you take it to the right person will help you buy enough sweets to make yourself sick for a whole week. Don't tell your mother I've done this.

Your sister Mary is breaking out into spots. She has five on her forehead. I think it's because she sucks her pencil so hard.

Your sister Barbara tumbled all the way down the stairs yesterday but didn't seem to mind. She is the best of the family and shortly I intend to invite her into the studio and let her lick my paint box.

Outside my window at this moment there is an apple tree and the hills are red, the same colour as the apples. Someone is burning leaves and the smoke turns red as it gets high enough and then comes white again when it gets near the moon, which is a new one and exactly like one of your Aunt Amy's eyelashes.

I am getting so fat that I think of living in a
barrel, as a very famous man about whom I'll tell
you one day, used to do. I think I'll have a barrel
with a lid on the top of it so that when people come
into the studio whom I don't want to see, I shall just
shut the lid and they won't know I'm there. I think
I'll have the barrel painted bright blue.

Your dog thinks there's a rat just behind my
bookcase. He lies there for hours at a time purring
like a kettle. There may be a rat but knowing life
as well as I do there never is a rat where you most
expect one. That's one of the things your father
hasn't learnt yet. He is writing his sermon in his
study. If he knew there weren't any rats he wouldn't
write so many sermons.

I've been reading a very funny book by a
man called France, and the funny thing is that he
is also a Frenchman. Isn't that a funny thing?
You shall read it one day when you're older and then
you'll understand your Uncle Samuel better than you
do now.

Well, good-bye. I hope you're enjoying yourself and haven't entirely forgotten your

UNCLE.

P.S.—I promise you that the lid shall never
be on the barrel when you're there, and if you don't
get too fat, there's room for two inside.

He read the letter through three times
before finishing with it; then, sitting forward
on the old wooden bench scarred with a
thousand penknives, he went over the delicious

details of it. How exactly Uncle Samuel
realized the things that he would want to
know! No one else in the family wrote about
anything that was exciting or intriguing.
Uncle Samuel managed in some way to make
you see things. The studio, the sky with the
little moon, the red apples, Hamlet flat on the
floor, his head rigid, his eyes fixed; Aunt
Amy shopping in Drymouth, Barbara tumbling
downstairs. That whole world came towards
him and filled the playground and blotted out
the school, so that for a moment school life
was unreal, shadowy, and did not matter. He
sighed with happy contentment. Young
though he was, he realized that great truth
that one person in the world is quite enough.
One human being who understands your
strange mixture equalizes five million who think
you are simply black, white or purple. All
you want is to be reassured about your own
suspicions of yourself. A devoted dog is almost
enough, and one friend ample. Jeremy went
in to dinner with his head in the air, trailing
after him, like Peter Pan, one shadow of the
world immediately around him, the world in
which the school sergeant was carving the
mutton at the end of the table so ferociously
that it might have been the corpse of his
dearest enemy, and the masters at the high
table were getting fried potatoes and the boys

only boiled, and Jeremy was not having even
those because he had got to play football in an
hour's time; and the other world, where there
was Aunt Amy's eyelash high in the air, and
the cathedral bells ringing, and Uncle Samuel
painting cows. Jeremy would have liked to
consider the strange way in which these two
worlds refused to mingle, to have developed
the idea of Uncle Samuel carving the mutton
instead of the sergeant, and the sergeant watching the evening sky instead of Uncle Samuel,
and why it was that these two things were so
impossible! His attention was occupied by the
fact that Plummy Smith, who was a fat boy,
was sitting in his wrong place and making a
" squash " on Jeremy's side of the table, which
led quite naturally to the game of trying to
squeeze Plummy from both ends of the table
into a purple mass, and to do it without
Thompson noticing. Little pathetic squeals
came from Plummy, who loved his food, and
saw his mutton mysteriously whisked away on
to some other plate, and knew that he would
be hungry all the afternoon in consequence.
He was one of those boys who had on the first
day of his arrival, a year earlier, unfortunately
confided to those whom he thought his friends
that he lived with two aunts, Maria and Alice.
His fate was sealed from the moment of that
unfortunate confidence. He did not know it,

T

and he had been in puzzled bewilderment ever since as to why the way of life was made so hard for him. He meant no one any harm, and could not understand why the lower half of his person should be a constant receptacle for pins of the sharpest kind. The point in this matter about Jeremy was that, as with Miss Jones years before, he could not resist pleasant fun at the expense of the foolish. He had enough of the wild animal in him to enjoy sticking pins into Plummy, to enjoy squeezing the breath out of his fat body, to enjoy seeing him without any mutton; and yet, had it been really brought home to him that Plummy was a miserable boy, sick for his aunts, dazed and puzzled, spending his days in an orgy of ink, impositions and physical pain, he would have been horrified that himself could be such a cad. He was not a cad. It was a fine day, he was in splendid health and spirits, he had had a letter from Uncle Samuel, and so he stuck pins into Plummy.

When the meal was over he walked down to the football ground with Riley, and told him about Uncle Samuel. He told Riley everything, and Riley told him everything. He never considered Riley as an individual human being, but rather as part of himself, so that if he were kicked in the leg it must hurt Riley too; and there was something in Riley's funny freckled forehead, his large mouth, and his funny, clumsy way of walking, as though he were a baby elephant, that was as necessary to Jeremy and his daily life as putting on his clothes and going to sleep. He showed Riley the piece of paper that Uncle Samuel had sent to him. " By gosh! " said Riley, " that's a pound."

" It's an awful pity," said Jeremy, " that you are not in Little Dorm. Perhaps you could come in to-night. I'm sure Stokesley and Pug wouldn't mind. We're going to have sardines and marmalade and dough-nuts."

" If I get a chance, I will," said Riley; " but I don't want to be caught out just now, because I've been in two rows already this week. Perhaps you could keep two sardines for me, and I'll have them at breakfast to-morrow."

" All right; I'll try," said Jeremy. He looked about and sniffed the air. It was an ideal day for football. It was cold, and not too cold. The hills above the football field were veiled in mist. The ground was soft, but not too soft. It ought to be a good game.

" Do you feel all right? " asked Riley.

They proceeded in the accustomed manner to test this. Jeremy hurled himself at Riley, caught him round the middle, tried to twine his legs round Riley's, and they both fell to the ground. They rolled there like two puppies.

Jeremy exerted all his strength to bring off
what he had never yet succeeded in doing,
namely, to turn Riley over and pin his elbows
to the ground. Riley wriggled like a fish.
Jeremy was very strong to-day, and managed
to get one elbow down and was in a very good
way towards the other when they heard an awful
voice above them. " And what may this be? "
They scrambled to their feet, flushed and breathless, and there was old Thompson staring at
them very gravely in that way that he had
so that you could not tell whether he were
displeased or no.

" We were only wrestling, sir," said Jeremy,
panting.

" Excellent thing for your clothes," said
Thompson. " What do you suppose the gym
is for? "

" It was only a minute, sir," said Riley.
" Cole wanted to see whether he was all right."

" And he is? " asked Thompson.

Jeremy perceived that Olympus was smiling.

" I'm a little out of breath," he said, " but
of course it's just after dinner. The ground
isn't muddy yet."

" You'd better wait until you're in football
things," Thompson said, " then you can roll
about as much as you like."

He walked away, rolling a little as he went.
The two boys looked after him and suddenly

adored him. Their feelings about him were
always undergoing lightning changes. At one
moment they adored, at another they detested,
at another they admired from a distance, and
at another they wondered.

" Wasn't that decent of him? " said Riley.

" That's because he's just had his dinner,"
said Jeremy. " It's his glass of beer. My
uncle's just the same."

" Oh, you and your uncle," said Riley.
" I'll race you to the end of the playground."

They ran like hares, and Jeremy led by a
second.

III

He was in the changing-room when
suddenly the atmosphere of the coming game
was close about him. He had that strange
mixture of fear and excitement, terror and
pleasure. He suddenly felt cold in his jersey
and shorts, and shivered a little. At the other
side of the room was Turnbull, one of the
three-quarters playing for the " Rest," a large,
bony boy with projecting knees. The mere
thought that he would have in all probability
to collar Turnbull and bring him to the ground
made Jeremy feel sick. His confidence
suddenly deserted him. He knew that he was
going to play badly. Worse than ever in his

life before. He wished that he could suddenly
develop scarlet fever and be carried off to the
infirmary. He even searched his bare legs for
spots. He had rather a headache and his throat
felt queer, and he was not at all sure that he
could see straight. One of those silly fools who
always comes and talks to you at the wrong
moment sniggered and said he felt awfully fit.
It was all right for *him;* he was one of the
forwards playing for the " Rest." It would
be perfectly easy for him to hide himself in the
scrum and pretend to be pushing when he was
not. No one ever noticed. But the isolation
of a half was an awful thing to consider, and
that desperate moment when you had to go
down to the ball, with at least five hundred
enormous boots all coming at your head at the
same moment, was horrible to contemplate.
Millett, the scrum half playing for the " Rest,"
and Jeremy's bitterest rival for the place in the
fifteen, was looking supremely self-confident
and assured. Certainly he was not as good as
Jeremy on Jeremy's day, but was this Jeremy's
day? No, most certainly it was not.

They went out to the field, and everything
was not improved by the fact that a large crowd
was gathered behind the ropes to watch them.
This was an important game. The big school
match was a fortnight from to-day, and Millett
might get his colours on to-day's game quite

easily. And then suddenly the feel of the turf under his feet, the long, sweeping distance of the good grey sky above his head, the tang of autumn in the air, brought him confidence again. He was not aware that a lady visitor who had come out with Mr. Thompson to watch the game was saying at that moment, " Why, what a tiny boy! You don't mean to say, Mr. Thompson, that he's going to play with all those big fellows? " And Thompson said, " He's the most promising footballer we have in the school. The half-back has to be small, you know."

" Oh, I do hope he won't get hurt," said the lady visitor.

" Won't do him any harm if he is," said Mr. Thompson.

The whistle went and the game began. Almost at once Jeremy was in trouble. Within the first minute the school fifteen were lining out in their own half of the field, and a moment later some of the " Rest " forwards had broken through, dribbled, tried to pass, thrown forward, and there was a scrum within Jeremy's twenty-five. This is the kind of thing to make you show your mettle. To be attacked before you have found your atmosphere, realized the conditions of the day, got your feel of yourself as part of the picture, gained your first win, to have to fight for your team's life with your own

goal looming like the gallows just behind you,
and to know that the loss of three or five points
in the first few minutes of the game is very
often a decisive factor in the issue of the battle
—all this tests anybody's greatness. Jeremy in
that first five minutes was anything but great.
He had a consciousness of his own miserable
inadequacy, a state not common to him at all.
He seemed to be one large cranium spread out
balloon-wise for the onrush of his enemies. As
he darted about at the back of the scrum waiting for the ball to be thrown in, he felt as
though he could not go down to it; and then,
of course, the worst possible thing happened.
The "Rest" forwards broke through the
scrum; he tried to fling himself on the ball,
and missed it, and there they were sliding away
past him, making straight for the goal-line.
Fortunately, the man with the ball was flung
to touch just in time, and there was a breathing
space. Jeremy, nevertheless, was tingling with
his mistake as acutely as though a try had been
scored. He knew what they were saying on
the other side of the rope. He knew that
Baltimore, for instance, was winking his bleary
eyes with pleasure, that all the friends of his
rival half were saying in chorus, "Well, young
Cole's no good; I always said so," and that
Riley was glaring fiercely about him and
challenging anyone to say a word. He knew

all this and, unfortunately, for more than a
minute had time to think of it, because one of
the cool three-quarters got away with the ball
and then kicked it to touch, and there was a
line out and a good deal of scrambling before
the inevitable scrum. This time it was for him
to throw in the ball, crying in his funny voice,
now hoarse, now squeaky, " Coming on the
right, school—shove ! " They did shove, and
carried it on with them; and then the " Rest "
half got it, threw it to one of his three-quarters,
who started racing down the field, with only
Jeremy in his way before he got to the back.
It was that very creature with the bony knees
whom Jeremy had watched in the changing-
room. The legs wobbled towards him as though
with a life of their own. He ran across, threw
himself at the knees, and missed them. He
went sprawling on to the ground, was conscious
that he had banged his nose, that somebody
near him was calling out " Butters," and that
his career as a football half was finally and for
ever concluded. After that he could do nothing
right. The ball seemed devilishly to slip away
from him whenever he approached it. He was
filled with a demon of anger, but that did not
serve him. He again went now here, now there,
and always he seemed to be doing the wrong
thing. For once that strange sure knowledge
innate in him, part of his blood and his bones,

of the right, inevitable thing to do, had left him, and he could only act on impulse and hope that it would turn out well, which it never did. The captain, who was a forward, pausing beside him for a moment, said, " Go on, Cole, you can play better than that." He knew that his worst forebodings were fulfilled.

Then just before the whistle went for half-time, just when he was at his busiest, he had a curious, distinct picture of Uncle Samuel, the red apple tree, and Hamlet lying on the floor of the studio waiting for his rat. People talk about concentration and its importance, and nobody who has ever played a game well but will agree that to let your mind wander at a very critical moment is fatal; but this was not so much the actual wandering of a mind as of a curious insistence from without of this other picture that went with the scene in which he was figuring. It was like the pouring of cold clear water upon his hot and muddled brain. It was also as though Uncle Samuel, in his thick, good-natured voice, had said to him, " Now, look here, I know nothing about this silly game that you're trying to play, but I'm here to see you go through it, and the two of us together it's impossible to beat." The whistle went before he had time to realize the effects of this little intrusion. He stood about during the interval talking to no one, wishing he were dead, but armoured in a cold resolve. After all, he would not write to Uncle Samuel and tell him that he had been left out of the school fifteen because he had not played well enough. No one as yet had scored. The teams seemed to be very evenly matched, which was a bad thing for the school. Everyone in the school team was depressed, and the men in the "Rest" were equally elated. If the whole truth were known, the play in the first half had been very ragged indeed, but, as Mr. Thompson explained to the lady visitor, "You mustn't expect anything else early in the term." She made the fatuous remark that "after all, they were such *little* boys," which made Mr. Thompson reply, with more heat than true politeness required, that his boys, even though they were all under fourteen, could on their day show as good a game as any public school, to which the lady visitor replied that she was sure that they could—she thought they played wonderfully for such little boys.

The whistle sounded, and the game tumbled about, up and down, in and out. Jeremy knew now that all was well. His "game sense" had suddenly come back to him, and the ball seemed to know its master, to tumble to him just when he wanted it, to stick in his hands when he touched it, and even to smile at him when it was quite a long way away, as though it were

saying to him, " I'm yours now, and you can
do what you like with me." He brought off a
neat piece of collaring, then a little later passed
the ball back to his three-quarters, who got,
for the first time that day, a clear run, leading
to a try in the far corner of the field. Then
there came a moment when all the " Rest "
forwards were dribbling the ball, the school forwards at their heels, but not fast enough to
stop their opponents; and he was down on the
ball, had it packed tight under his arm, lying
flat upon it, and the whole world of boots, legs,
knees, bodies seemed to charge over him. A
queer sensation that was, everything falling
upon him as though the ceiling of the world
had suddenly collapsed. Then the sensation of
being buried deep in the ground, bodies
wriggling and heaving on top of him, his nose,
chin, eyes deep in earth, some huge leg with
a gigantic boot at the end of it hovering like a
wild animal just above his head; and then the
whistle and the sudden clearing of the ground
away from him; his impulse to move, and his
discovery that his right leg hurt like a piercing
sword. He tried to rise, and could not. He
was quite alone now, the sky and the wind, the
field and the distant hills encircling him, with
nobody else in the world. The game stopped,
people came back to him. They felt his leg,
and it hurt desperately, but not, he knew at

once, so desperately that he never would be able to use it again. They rubbed his calf and jerked his knee. He heard somebody say, " Only a kick—no bones broken," and he set his teeth and stumbled to his feet and stood for a moment feeling exquisite pain. Then, like an old man of ninety, tottered along. At this there was universal applause from behind the ropes. There were cries of " Well stopped, Stocky! Good old Stocky!" and he would not have exchanged that moment for all the prizes in the bookshop or all the tuckshops in Europe. " Are you all right?" his captain shouted across to him. He nodded his head because he certainly would have burst into tears if he had spoken, and he was biting his lower lip until his teeth seemed to go through to his gums. But, in that marvellous fashion that all footballers know, his leg became with every movement easier, and although there was a dull, grinding pain there, he found he could move about quite easily and soon was in the thick of it once more. He was only a " limper " to the end of that game, but he did one or two things quite nicely, and had the happiness of seeing the school score another two tries, which put the issue of the game beyond doubt. At the end, after cheers had been given and returned, the pain in his leg reasserted itself once more, and he could only limp very feebly

off the field, but he had the delirious happiness
of the captain—who was going to Rugby next
year, and was therefore very nearly a man—
putting his hand on his shoulder and saying,
" That was a plucky game of yours, Cole.
Hope your leg isn't bad."

" Oh, it isn't bad at all, thank you," he
said very politely. " I almost don't feel it,"
which was a terrific lie. He had done well.
He knew that from the comments on every
side of him. The crowd had forgotten his
earlier failure, which, if he had only known it,
should have taught him that word of wisdom
invaluable to artists and sportsmen alike:
" Don't be discouraged by a bad beginning.
It's the last five minutes that count." Finally
there was Riley. " You didn't play badly," he
said. " You were better than Millett."

IV

Later he was sitting with Riley, squashed
into a corner of Magg's, eating dough-nuts.
The crowd in there was terrific and the atmosphere like a slab of chocolate. Riley and he
were pressed close together, with boys on every
side of them. The noise was deafening. It
was the last ten minutes before Magg's closed.
It was Saturday evening, and everyone had
pocket-money. The two boys did not speak

to one another. Jeremy's leg was hurting him horribly, but he was as happy as "Five kings and a policeman," which was one of Uncle Samuel's ridiculous, meaningless phrases. His arm was round Riley's neck, more for support than for sentiment, but he did *like* Riley and he did *like* Magg's. He was, perhaps, at that moment as completely alive as he was ever to be. He was so small that he was almost entirely hidden, but somebody caught sight of his hair, which would never lie down flat, and cried across the room, "Three cheers for Stocky, the football hero!" The cheers were hearty if a little absent-minded, the main business of the moment being food, and not football. Jeremy, of course, was pleased, and in his pleasure overbalanced from the edge of the table where he was sitting, slipped forward, and disappeared from men. His leg hurt him too much, and he was too comfortable on the floor and too generally sleepy to bother to get up again, so he stayed there, his arm round Riley's leg, swallowing his last dough-nut as slowly as possible, feeling that he would like to give dough-nuts in general to all the world.

Yes, it had been a *fine* day, a splendid day, and there would be days and days and days. . . .

Magg's was closing. He limped to his feet, and, with their arms round one another's necks, Riley and he vanished into the dark.

PRINTED BY
CASSELL & COMPANY, LIMITED,
LA BELLE SAUVAGE, LONDON, E.C.4.
F85.823